GHOST

DEVIL'S DISCIPLES BOOK 3

SCOTT HILDRETH

DEDICATION

To the late Jerry Hicks.
Thanks for the rock. It helped me until I could find a way to come to
believe.

AUTHOR'S NOTE

This book contains scenes of criminal acts, some that are typical of gangs and motorcycle clubs, and some that aren't. The fictitious club name, Devil's Disciples, is in no way tied to the real-life club, Devils Diciples. Different spelling, different club. The acts and actions depicted in the book are fictitious, as are the characters.
Every sexual partner in the book is over the age of 18. Please, if you intend to read further than this comment, be over the age of 18 to enjoy this novel.

Cover design by Jessica www.jessicahildrethdesigns.com

Cover photo by Golden www.onefuriousfotog.com

Follow me on Facebook at: www.facebook.com/sd.hildreth

Like me on Facebook at: www.facebook.com/ScottDHildreth

Follow me on Twitter at: @ScottDHildreth

PROLOGUE

In the grand scheme of things, the loss of human life goes unnoticed. Not surprising, as one hundred and five people die with each revolution of the clock's second hand. Loss after regretful loss, the world, however, continues to turn.

Nonetheless, on *that* day the planet's balance was askew.

The straps from the lowering device steadied the casket over the grave, giving it an appearance as if it were hovering over the darkened opening that lied beneath it. The beautiful Rosetan velvet interior was concealed from view, as was the body that had encapsulated the gracious soul for more than three decades.

A man and a woman stood hand in hand beside the casket. The man's jaw was clenched tight, a product of his inability to accept the untimely death of the deceased. *I would have given my own life to spare this one*, he thought.

The woman, wearing a black dress and matching coat, rocked back and forth on the balls of her feet. Beneath San Diego's midday sun, she filled with regret for her choice in attire. She nonchalantly raised her left hand to her cheek and wiped a tear, hoping the action would go unnoticed. Nothing made sense to her. *How much grief*, she thought, *should one person endure in a lifetime?*

The grieving added to the profound pain that whittled away at her heart.

In the distance, the drone of five approaching motorcycles gave hint that the deceased's parents would not lament alone. As the men grew closer, startled birds flew from a row of Weeping Acacias that decorated the roadside.

The motorcycles parked side by side beneath the blanket of shade the trees provided. One by one, the men, clad in jeans, black tee shirts, and black leather boots, dismounted their motorized steeds and turned toward the gravesite.

After glancing at the flock of birds, one of the men reached into his right pants pocket, feigned surprise, and paused. "I need to grab something," he said, directing his remark toward no one. "I'll be there in a minute."

He turned toward his motorcycle and lowered his head slightly. A tear rolled along the bridge of his nose, and then lingered at the edge of his nostril before it trickled onto his upper lip. Unlike the mother, he didn't brush it away.

He'd promised not to.

As he prayed for a breeze that never came, he peered toward the distant horizon. Their last days together came to mind, and with them came slivers of peace. With some hesitation, he turned around and swallowed the lump of compassion that had risen in his throat.

He then took the first step of many that he knew he'd be taking without the deceased at his side.

ABBY

I threw the brick at the window as hard as I could. Much to my surprise, it bounced off the glass and shot at me like a rectangular brown rocket. Before I could dodge the projectile, it slammed into my knee so violently I feared I may be crippled for life.

In the brick-filled bed of an unknown man's pickup truck, I stumbled to keep my footing. I glanced at my throbbing knee. Blood trickled down my leg. Fueled by equal parts anger and compassion, I grabbed another brick from the selection piled at my feet.

I had to act quickly. At least one life was at stake. I raised my hand and took aim at the truck's back window.

"Abby!" a familiar voice shouted from behind me. "What in the hell are you doing?"

Brick in hand, I glanced over my right shoulder. "Saving a life," I declared.

George was the owner of the *Devil Dog Diner*, a restaurant I ate in no less than ten times a week. He was looking at me the same way he did the first time I ordered a cheese sandwich with apple slices on it.

He'd retired from the Marines after serving thirty years. Even though he was in his mid-fifties, he still resembled his barrel-chested brethren that spent their current days traipsing through battlefields in distant countries. His massive biceps and permanent scowl made him an intimidating figure to those who didn't know him. To me, he was nothing but a big teddy bear.

Unless he was angry. And, from what I could see, he was angry.

"Get down from there before someone starts filming this," he said, glancing over each shoulder as he spoke. "The last thing you need is to be on the six o' clock news with a brick in your hand and blood gushing out of your leg."

I acted as though I didn't hear him. Using the brick, I gestured toward the sidewalk. "Watch out," I warned. "Glass is going to go everywhere."

I hurled the brick with every ounce of energy I could harness. I watched in horror as the event played before my eyes like a slow-motion scene from a low-budget black comedy movie.

The brick hit the center of the truck's back window. The glass flexed but didn't break. The brick changed directions, seeming to gain speed as it did so. Then, it plowed into the shin of my good leg.

I stumbled backward, almost toppling over the tailgate and into the street. "Son-of-a-bitch," I shrieked, reaching for what was left of my mangled shin. "That hurt like hell."

After steadying myself against the edge of the truck's bed, I glanced at George and tried not to burst into tears.

"You know how I hate repeating myself, but I'll ask again." He opened the truck's tailgate. "What in the hell are you doing?"

He was frustrated with me. I could clearly see – and hear – it. I swallowed heavily, and then took a deep breath.

"There's a puppy locked inside he was bouncing around and looking out the window when I came in for lunch when I came out I noticed the truck was still here the windows are rolled up tight he's on the floor and looks like he's dying I need to save him," I said in one breathless sentence.

He extended his arms toward me. "Let's get you out of there."

"He's going to die," I pleaded, my voice cracking from emotion. "I need to get him out of there."

He hopped into the back of the truck with ease and then lifted me from my feet. After lowering me gently onto the street he gestured toward his restaurant. "Go stand on the sidewalk."

Before I hobbled to the edge of the curb, I heard the glass shatter. While the shrill sound of the truck's alarm filled the air, George disappeared through the broken window and into the cab of the truck. I limped to the passenger door and pulled against the handle frantically. After three or four yanks, the door lock clicked.

The door flew open.

The brown and white bull dog puppy George cradled in his arms looked to be exhausted. He was alive, and that was all that mattered.

"Thank God he's not dead," I said.

"Hey, shithead!" someone shouted. "What the fuck are you doing in my truck?"

George handed me the puppy as he climbed out of the truck's cab. With the shivering pup held tightly in my arms, I turned toward the angry voice.

A lanky young man stood between us and the restaurant. He was dressed in khaki work pants, canvas boots, and a black sweat-stained tee shirt. He raked his sun-bleached hair from his face and shot me a sunken-eyed glare. "Gimme my dog."

I had all the patience in the world unless stupid people were involved. He'd proven his stupidity when he parked the truck beneath San Diego's summer sun and rolled up the windows.

"Go to hell," I snarled. "You locked this dog in that truck with the windows up and left him there for two hours, you dumb jerk. He's not yours any longer. You're too stupid to take care of an animal."

After my tirade, his cheeks went red with anger. "Gimme the dog."

"F-you," I hissed.

I wouldn't give him the dog if he held a gun to my head. While I made plans to knee him in the balls and make a run for it, George stepped between us.

"If you take one step in our direction, I'll pull off your arms and beat you with the bloody stubs," George growled, puffing his massive chest as he spoke. "You've got two options. Hop in your truck and leave or get those skinny little arms of yours pulled off. I'll let you pick which one."

The man studied George, but not for long. Upon realizing it was a fight he simply couldn't win, his shoulders slumped.

"That dog's a dipshit anyway," he muttered.

He stepped into the street and stomped toward his truck. As we walked past, George eyed the man over his shoulder. The thought of such a foolish person having control of an animal's welfare had my blood boiling. I followed George toward the diner, glaring at the animal abuser the entire way.

As he got in his truck, he gave his parting comment under his breath.

"Asshole," he murmured.

I flipped him the middle finger over my left shoulder while clutching the pup to my chest.

George glanced at the puppy and then at me. He brushed his palm along the edge of his freshly buzzed scalp and shook his head lightly before looking away.

"What?" I asked.

"You throw bricks like a girl."

"Learn to throw a brick like a Boss," I said with a laugh. "I'll add that to my list."

"The ever-growing list," he said, flashing a slight smile.

"I'll check one off today I never thought I'd get to," I said.

"Which one is that?"

"Saving a life," I said. "That only leaves six."

"What are you going to do when you reach the end?" he asked.

It was a good question. At one point in time, my to-do list had over two hundred items on it. Somehow, I'd managed to accomplish all but six. Out of what remained, five would require nothing more than a little ingenuity and a sprinkle of effort on my part.

The sixth?

It was highly unlikely I'd ever achieve it.

"After the last one?" I cradled the pup in my arms. "You'll probably never see me again."

"What?" he gasped. "Why's that?"

"Because," I said. "I want to let that one consume me."

2

GHOST

Holding my arms outstretched and parallel to the floor, I traipsed the length of the room with the grace of a two-hundred-and-thirty-pound ballerina. A week earlier, standing was difficult. Proud of my accomplishment, I looked at the sun-spotted face of the seventy-year-old doctor and hoped for a little recognition.

A golf clap.

A simple nod.

Other than blinking twice, his face remained expressionless.

I gave him a *what the fuck's wrong with you* glare.

After a moment, he lifted his chin ever so slightly. "In the last week, there's been remarkable improvements in your coordination and balance. It doesn't relieve the fact that the magnetic resonance imaging scan revealed a tumor eleven by eight by thirty-three millimeters in size. If you're hoping for a clean bill of health you're not going to get it, Mister Reeves."

I don't know what I wanted. Reassurance that I could live a normal life until it was time for me to check in with my maker, I suppose.

Something.

After falling at the gym, I woke up the next morning with a pounding headache. Incapable of rising to my feet, I eventually admitted defeat and called an ambulance. An MRI gave news that many people secretly feared, but that I knew was inevitable.

Mister Reeves, we've determined that you have a brain tumor.

I grew up in a single parent home of sorts, being raised by my mother and grandparents. My mother acted as mothers do. She comforted me, supported me, and was sensitive to my childhood needs.

My grandfather died from skin cancer when I was very young, and what memories I had of him were mostly manufactured. I used them to satisfy me that my home wasn't fatherless. After his death, my grandmother stepped into the role as my fatherly figure.

She was stern and opinionated. My friends and I knew we had to toe the line with her, or else. We respected her. In turn, she treated us with respect. She died of breast cancer when I was thirteen. After losing her, I stumbled through high school full of rage and depressed. I eventually turned to weight training as an avenue to rid myself of the anger and stress that followed her death.

It worked well, providing an outlet I couldn't seem to find anywhere else. Then, mid-way through my senior year in high school, my mother developed lung cancer. She didn't live long enough to see me graduate.

After I buried my mother, I shut down. My seventeen-year-old heart was broken. I became numb to life and all things in it. I was convinced I didn't have the ability to let another human being into life, much less my heart.

There were four people left on earth I that cared about. We'd been friends since kindergarten. We were inseparable hooligans who had managed to stay one step ahead of the law as juveniles. As soon as we turned eighteen, the five of us moved – as a group – away from Great Falls, Montana, and far from the memories of what cancer had taken from me. We settled in San Diego, California.

Certain that I was destined to one day die from the same dreaded disease, I spent every day as if it were my last.

Intimidation had always worked for me in the past, so I loomed over the desk and flexed on the old man. "No treatment. Period. End. Of. Story."

"Considering your background, I can understand your reservation," he said dryly. "But there's no shame in receiving treatment for cancer. Men do it every day. Men just like you. Big men. Tough men."

Apparently, his hearing was as bad as his comb over. I locked eyes with him and crossed my arms. "I don't have *reservations*. The answer's *no*."

Unfazed by my tactics, he leaned against the back of his chair and cocked his head to the side. "Why are you here, Mister Reeves?"

"I need that prescription refilled so I can live with these headaches."

"Very well," he said, his voice monotone. "Be forewarned, the pressure against your skull will increase as the tumor grows. Your vision will likely blur. Eventually, you'll lose many of your cognitive skills. You'll be reduced to using a wheelchair, and you'll certainly die. All of this may be able to be prevented. The first step is a biopsy."

"Not. Going. To. Happen," I said though clenched teeth.

Truthfully, I was no different than anyone else. I didn't want to die. Yet. My time had come, and there was nothing I could do to change it. Accepting it was a different story altogether. I expected my remaining days on earth would be spent angry and alone.

His jaw tightened. He studied me for a moment. His gaze fell to his desk. He scribbled something down on a pad of paper and then tore off the sheet.

"Here," he said.

"Thank you."

I glanced at the scribbled note. It wasn't a prescription. It was an address and a phone number. I looked at him and arched an aggravated eyebrow.

"It's a meeting you'll need to attend," he said. "An oncology social worker runs it, and she'll be able to help you with coping. I'll reserve hope that your attendance will open your mind to proceeding with treatment."

I tossed the note in his direction. It fluttered onto his desk like a leaf that had fallen from one of the thirty-foot-tall oak trees along the river of my home town.

He picked up the sheet of paper and stretched his arm over the top of his desk. "The meeting, Mister Reeves, is mandatory."

My eyes thinned. The only mandatory meetings I planned to attend were with the motorcycle club. Sitting in a room filled with strangers and discussing my life wasn't something I was willing to do.

"It's required by your insurance carrier," he explained. "It's considered mental health treatment. If you don't attend, your insurance company will not pay your bills. Treatment, or no treatment, the bills will likely exceed half a million dollars."

I took the note from his grasp and gave it a second look.

He nodded toward my hand. "All you must do to comply with your insurance carrier's requirement is attend. I'll ask that you do so with an open mind."

"I'll attend," I said. "But you're not drilling a hole in my head. Not now, or ever. There's no one in your little meeting that'll change my mind about that, either."

ABBY

Because of their ferocious nature during the Battle of Belleau Wood, the Marines were called *Dogs from Hell* by the German soldiers who fought against them. The Marines proudly embraced the moniker. Soon, *Devil Dog* became a nickname for all Marines.

Upon retiring from the Marine Corps, George opened the *Devil Dog Diner*. His entire staff was an assembly of veterans who had chosen to serve meals after retiring from serving their country.

I initially favored the restaurant because they bought fresh local produce and used organic meats, fruits, and vegetables in making their meals. Knowingly introducing chemicals into my body wasn't something I would ever do.

I later grew to admire George, his staff, and his way of conducting business. He wasn't getting rich running the deli, but he gave back to the community, nonetheless. On the last Sunday of every month, he held *The Flapjack Flashback*, an all-day pancake extravaganza and fundraiser.

Pancakes, eggs, and a side of meat were all that was available during the fundraiser, and they were sold until the restaurant closed at ten o' clock at night. For that day, breakfast was priced at a dollar and fifty cents per plate. Most of the customers left huge tips, but George didn't expect it. He said he wanted to turn back the clock to a time when breakfast was affordable.

His revenue for the day went to charity. On that same day, his employees – at their own insistence – refused to be paid. State law didn't allow them to work for free, so they simply donated their wages right along with George's revenue to the chosen charity for the month.

In support of him, his workers, and the restaurant's way of conducting business, I ate at his establishment more than I ate at home. In many respects, the diner *was* my home.

I sucked a cream cheese remnant from the tip of my finger. I would have never guessed anything could have made a grilled chicken sandwich taste better, but the cream cheese, grilled jalapenos, and peach jam sure did a good job of it. I pushed my plate to the far side of the table and grinned a toothy grin. "That was awesome."

George's eyebrows raised. "How awesome?"

"There aren't levels of awesome," I explained. "Acceptance of foodstuffs is explained using the following expressions: okay, good, great, fantastic, and awesome. Awesome is the pinnacle of goodness."

While searching my face for an answer, he reached for my empty plate. "Out of every sandwich you've eaten here, how does it rate?"

"For someone who hates repeating himself, you sure don't mind asking others to do it, do you?" I asked jokingly. "I said it was awesome. So, for me, it's the number one sandwich."

"Good." He flashed a quick smile. "We'll call it *The Abby*."

Having the sandwich named after me would be as awesome as the sandwich itself. "Get outta here," I shouted excitedly. "Seriously?"

"If it's your number one, that's what we're going to call it."

"As soon as it's on the menu, I'll promote it to everyone I know," I blurted.

He let out a laugh as he topped off my iced tea. "This place is far too small to have all of San Diego County in here trying to order the same sandwich. Maybe just tell the people in your meeting. How's that?"

"Right now, there's only six people in it. That's if everyone comes, and they don't all come at once," I said.

"I know you've come to enjoy it, but that's one meeting I wished was empty."

The meeting he spoke of was a cancer support group. As much as I enjoyed doing what I could to help others cope with the emotions that came with being diagnosed – and with surviving – I wished the same thing. Despite that wish, I'd seen many faces come and go over the years.

"Are you walking, riding, running, or driving?" he asked.

"Riding," I said.

He nodded toward the clock. "You better get to peddling."

I glanced over my shoulder. It was fifteen before one, and the meeting started at one. Shocked at how much time had passed, I reached into my purse and fumbled to find my wallet. "I really need to start wearing a watch," I murmured.

"Get to your meeting," he said with a dismissive wave of his hand. "The sandwich isn't on the menu yet. I can't charge you for it."

"Thank you," I blurted. I took off in a dead run for the door. As I yanked it open, I shouted over my shoulder. "Love you, George."

"Love you, too, Abby," he said.

Love. It was the one thing that was missing from my life. I loved many people and I made it a point to tell them so. There was an equal amount of people who loved me in return.

But. I wasn't *in love.*

For love to be reciprocal, I needed to feel it was genuine. I was convinced finding sincerity was impossible. It seemed everyone who had any interest in me was either after notoriety or money. It was the price I had to pay, I suppose, for being successful.

A price I wasn't always convinced was worth the reward.

GHOST

I'd never feared anything in my life, dying included. Yet, I stood in front of the door and dreaded pushing it open. According to the doctor, my means of accepting death was on the other side.

Filled with nervous apprehension, I pushed it open and peered inside.

An oil painting centered on the opposite wall captured my attention. It was a simple rendering – a lone cedar tree positioned at the base of a grassy hill. I wondered if the piece of artwork was chosen for a reason, or if someone simply selected it randomly. After a moment, I decided it was intentional.

The tree stood as a reminder that when my clock stopped ticking, I would be alone. Frustrated upon realizing the painting's symbolism, I dropped my gaze to the floor and let out a silent sigh.

I chose the seat closest to me and sat down. A quick glance around the room revealed that it was decorated with various pieces of furniture, no differently than if it were a living room in a conventional home. Four complete strangers were seated across from me. Despite having never met, I knew we had one thing in common. We were either dying at an accelerated rate, or we'd somehow managed to cheat death.

Across the room to my right, two women who I guessed to be in their mid-sixties were sitting side by side in a loveseat, smiling and laughing quietly. Their resemblance caused me to wonder if they were twins. I studied them long enough that the one closest to me noticed. Our eyes locked. She smiled.

I forced a crooked grin.

In a rust-colored chair on the left side of the room, a man chewed his fingernails. His knee bounced up and down anxiously. His pale cheeks were gaunt. The width of his shoulders told me he was once much larger. Dressed in a powder blue suit and a white button-down shirt, he looked the part of an insurance salesman or a financial advisor. The cap he wore was in complete contrast to his outfit and didn't completely conceal his bare scalp.

In the matching chair next to him, a beautiful young woman was seated. Her pale legs were crossed and the floral print dress she wore was wadded between her athletic thighs. On her feet was a worn pair of dingy white Converse sneakers.

Her attention danced around the room, pausing at each object of significance for just long enough to snap a mental picture. Her straight brown hair cascaded down her shoulders, coming to a stop just above her perky little tits.

Energy radiated from her like sunshine.

I studied her for a moment, wondering if the insurance company would deny my coverage if I got caught fucking one of the patients in the broom closet. In mere seconds, I was lost in a daydream about her pouty lips being wrapped around my stiff cock.

Halfway through an imaginary blowjob, the pain from my erection caused me to snap out of my dreamlike state. Aroused beyond comprehension – but fearing the elderly twins might notice the mile of dick that had risen to attention – I laid my hands in my lap and faked boredom.

I glanced in the sneaker-wearing beauty's direction. Her eyes darted past me, and then quickly returned, meeting mine before I could look away. One side of her mouth sprouted upward.

I smiled. I couldn't help it.

With her eyes still locked on mine, she draped her shoulder-length hair over her left ear. She playfully wagged her index finger toward the empty seat beside me and raised her eyebrows. I glanced to my side. Upon realizing I was seated in one half of a two-person loveseat, I looked at her and mentally objected.

Despite my desire to hike her dress over her hips and shove her full of dick, sitting next to a stranger would make an already awkward situation much worse.

Before I could blurt out my rejection, she rose from her seat. As she sauntered toward me, I filled with regret for failing to verbally oppose her offer to sit with me. I shifted my eyes to the elderly twins and wondered why I didn't say *something*. Sarcastic one-liners were my specialty and being rude was second nature. When she sat down at my left side I was staring off in the distance and planning my departure.

"Hi, I'm Abby," she said. "This must be your first meeting."

I gazed out the far window, into the courtyard. After deciding I would simply tell her I preferred to be alone, I glanced over my left shoulder. The regret that had built within me for allowing her to sit down promptly vanished.

She had the most amazing eyes.

They weren't *one* color. A combination of blues and grays and silver, all merged together as if they'd been painted by an extremely creative artist. The color seemed to change as I studied them. No matter where I looked, however, they provided reassurance.

A fog of innocence surrounded her. Normally, I would have wanted to pin her hands behind her back, bury her face deep into the cushions of the loveseat, and shove her full of three pounds of dick. Instead, I wanted to pin her against the wall and kiss her until she became putty in my arms.

I hadn't made out with anyone since I was in high school but kissing her became the only thing that seemed to matter. The pressure on my brain was obviously creating far more problems than headaches. The tumor was reducing me to a hopeless romantic.

Hoping to disguise my desires, I pursed my lips and offered my hand. "Ghost. Porter," I stammered. "Porter."

She squinted. "Did you say Ghost Porter-Porter?"

"Ghost's a nickname," I said dismissively. "Call me Porter."

She set her purse between us. "That's a pretty awesome nickname."

Being in the presence of strangers troubled me. Apart from the men in the motorcycle club, I trusted very few people. I felt uneasy sitting next to her, but for different reasons. I wanted to touch her.

Everywhere.

I wanted to taste her. To run my fingers the length of her naked body, pausing at the dimples I was sure that existed just above the small of her back. To run my fingers through her hair while I pressed my naked chest to hers.

I shook my head, hoping to clear it of the odd thoughts that were quickly filling it. She wasn't the type of woman I typically associated with. As a means of self-preservation, I preferred one-night stands, strippers, and women who idolized bikers. She looked like an actress from a Covergirl commercial and smelled like a spring rain shower.

I swallowed heavily. "What did you say your name was?"

"Abby. Like the Beatles album, *Abby Road*." She reached into her purse and pulled out a small weathered notepad. "Is this your first meeting?"

"It is," I admitted.

"It's weird," she said, flipping through the pages as she spoke. "Before you come through that door, you feel helpless and alone. You push it open and walk in, hoping for answers. To find someone that you can hold accountable. Then, you find out all that's available is a roomful of compassion, a little experience, and a lot of understanding. You know what, though?"

"What's that?" I asked.

"It's all we need." She handed me the notepad. "Look at number thirty-two."

I smiled again, even though I told myself not to. Her energy was undeniable. I glanced at the small sheet of paper. Eight hand-written items were on the page, seven of which had been crossed out. The one that remained, *take a ride on a motorcycle with a real biker*, was number thirty-two.

She extended her arm, holding her open hand over my lap. I glanced down, and in doing so, checked the status of my stiff dick. Relieved that I wasn't going to embarrass myself, I gave her the notepad.

"What is it?" I asked. "A bucket list?"

"It's a to-do list," she said in a matter-of-fact tone. "I've hand it since I was thirteen. I've added things to it over the years."

I tilted my head toward the notebook. "How many things are in there?"

She folded it closed and then dropped it into her purse. "Hundreds."

I was fascinated. I wanted to know things about her. Everything. Why her skin was so pale. If her lips were natural, or if she'd had them injected with collagen. Why she wore sneakers with a dress. Why she had two four-inch squares of gauze taped to her legs. What the other one hundred and ninety-nine items on her list were.

"How many have you completed?"

She beamed with pride. "All but six."

I wondered if I took the time to make such a list what it may include. The thought of it satisfied and scared me at the same time.

She leaned close enough to kiss, and then looked me in the eyes. "Are you a real biker?"

Her outspoken nature would normally cause me tremendous grief. For some reason, however, I found it intriguing. The problem with my dick slowly began to resurface.

"Who says I'm a biker?"

"I heard one pull up earlier. I know the sisters didn't ride it, and I'm pretty sure Larry didn't, either. That leaves you and me. The bike I rode had pedals and didn't have an exhaust so loud it shook the windows."

"Yes," I said, quickly going back to thoughts of her dress being hiked over her hips. "I'm a real biker."

She leaned against the arm of the loveseat, crossed her legs, and then looked me up and down. When she did, her hair fell into her face. "So, Ghost Porter-Porter." She swept her hair behind her ear. "When do you want to go for that ride?"

I chuckled. "Are you always so blunt?"

Her eyebrows raised. "I haven't got time to be anything but blunt. I've got a busy schedule and beating around the bush is dumb."

Taking women for rides on my motorcycle wasn't on *my* to-do list, and it never had been. Considering the circumstances, I decided to make a minor adjustment to my standard policy.

"How about after the meeting?" I asked.

"Sounds great," she said with a smile. "If you want to ride to Borrego Springs, we can cross another thing off my list."

If things like going to Borrego Springs were on her list, it made taking a ride with a real biker seem like not that big of a deal. Suddenly, I felt unimportant and easily replaced.

"A trip to Borrego Springs? *That* is on your list?"

"Not Borrego Springs, *specifically*," she said. "But holding a live rattlesnake is, and that's the closest desert."

I chuckled at the thought of her hunting rattlesnakes in sneakers and a dress that came to mid-thigh. "You're going to hunt rattlesnakes bare-legged?" I asked, stifling a laugh. "That's a good way to get bitten."

"We're all going to die sooner or later," she said. "I'd rather it happened while I was having fun than when I was asleep."

One week earlier, I was at a strip joint in Oceanside without a care in the world. Now, I was mentally planning my death and preparing to go rattlesnake hunting with a fearless Covergirl makeup model.

I'd always wondered what life would be like if I could truly throw caution to the wind.

Without warning, she lifted my hand and looked at my watch.

"Crap," she said as she released my wrist. "I've got to get this meeting started."

She stood and brushed the wrinkles from her dress. "Hi, I'm Abby, and I'm a survivor."

"Hi, Abby," everyone chimed.

Everyone but me.

I wondered what being a survivor meant.

If the doctor's diagnosis was accurate, I'd have twelve months to find out.

5

ABBY

I had two major concerns if I chose to exclude hunting for a live rattlesnake from the equation.

My first worry was the motorcycle ride.

Riding on the back of Porter's motorcycle was eye-opening. The trip to Borrego Springs was not at all what I expected. I anticipated being thrilled, scared, and excited. Those feelings were present during the two-hour journey but summarizing the experience could only be done with one word.

Liberating.

I had no idea I lived with constraints until I felt the freedom riding offered. We'd been parked for thirty minutes, and I yearned to get back on and go somewhere.

Anywhere.

It was going to be an issue of epic proportion if he wouldn't give me a ride at least once a week. My mind was reeling with the notion of finding another real-life biker – in the event Porter chose to tell me to get lost after the rattlesnake hunting adventure.

The thought of Porter permanently ridding himself of me brought me face-to-face with concern number two.

Porter.

I was thirty years old and didn't look a day over twenty-four. By my own admission, I was attractive. According to the masses, I was drop-dead gorgeous. I sided more with my belief that I was simply good-looking, choosing to dismiss the social media outbursts from frat boys with a hard-on for anyone with pouty lips and blood pumping through her veins. Nonetheless, my self-esteem cup was half-full, and it allowed me to see myself as mildly attractive.

I'd been single since I was *really* twenty-four. It wasn't a conscious decision I made. It was a direct result of my inability to find someone that was attracted to me for all the right reasons.

My lack of interest in men could have been a result of the volume of dick pictures that filled my inbox daily. If that was not enough of an eye roll moment, the chiseled ab pictures (that generally followed the dick pictures) caused me to skate through life attached to the belief that my righteously-minded male counterpart simply didn't exist.

Dicks were ugly and only served one purpose as far as I was concerned. Using them as a greeting card was a surefire way for the sender to end up stacked in the ever-growing pile of men I graciously labeled as *pigs*.

I told myself when the day arrived that I truly found interest in someone, I'd open my eyes, close my mouth, and pay attention.

Without announcement, warning, or my permission, that day may have arrived. And, it brought an intriguing two-hundred-pound hunk of motorcycle riding man with it as proof.

The man of interest was standing at my side with his eyes locked on the base of a Crucifixion Thorn because he *saw something*. His left hand dangled loosely at his side and his right held a three-foot-long stick he'd picked up from the desert floor.

Porter walked – strutted was more like it – as if San Diego County owed him something and he was on a mission to get it. I was convinced if I sliced open his wrist that blood would not drip from his veins.

Confidence would.

He smelled like leather that had been sprinkled with a spritz of cologne twenty-four hours prior to his arrival. There was enough of a hint of the unidentifiable scent to do more than pique my interest. In fact, I wanted to inhale his aroma and somehow memorize it, recalling it at will any time I felt a desire to be aroused beyond comprehension.

His scent, manliness, and sheer presence had me an uncomfortable mess. Despite the dry desert's one-hundred-and-eight-degree temperature, I was uncomfortably *wet*.

I was sure that most would find Porter intimidating. His muscular structure and massive size. The chiseled facial features. His high cheekbones, angular jaw, and the light scruff peppering his cheeks topped off his imposing presence.

I found him intoxicating.

His hazel eyes weren't piercing or menacing. They were quite the opposite. If anything, they revealed all too much about him. When I peered into them, something unmistakable stared back at me.

Fear.

Seeing it let me know he was vulnerable. In my self-written guide to all things men, vulnerability was right up there with having a sense of humor, honesty, chiseled abdominal muscles, and a big ugly dick. Hot men who were vulnerable were exponentially hotter.

Therefore, Ghost Porter-Porter was *en fuego*.

"How'd you get the nickname Ghost?" I asked.

With his eyes fixed on the base of the bush, he slowly raised his left hand to chest height. He then balled it into a ham-sized fist.

The universal sign for *shut up, Abby*.

I looked at him – not hoping for a response – but expecting an explanation for why I needed to be quiet. Instead of speaking, he bent at the knees – slowly – until the leather-clad shoulders of his six-foot-plus frame were even with mine.

My eyes darted back and forth between him and the thorny bush that had become his object of desire. I saw nothing fascinating about it, only a few red berries and countless intimidating four-inch long thorns.

He remained statue-still, pointing the stick at the ground beneath the seemingly brittle branches. I searched the surrounding area and saw nothing more than sand, rocks, and an occasional twig. Convinced he'd become delirious from a combination of the brutal heat and blinding sun, I stood quietly and waited for him to collapse from heat exhaustion.

If he did crumble into a pile of dehydrated flesh, moving him would be out of the question. Unless he had water in saddlebags of his motorcycle, he'd die a slow, miserable death. The closest place to get a drink was miles away, and I'd be forced to walk through the blistering heat in search of relief. By the time I returned, the vultures would have every ounce of his two-hundred-plus-pound frame picked free of flesh.

I envisioned ripping a splined leaf from an agave cactus and squeezing the nectar onto his swollen tongue. After accepting a few drops of the bitter juice, he'd come back to life and look me in the eyes.

His sun-cracked lips would part, and he'd mouth the words *thank you, Abby*. Later he'd confide in me how he owed me his life. In true biker tradition, he'd show up at my home every Christmas with a fruit cake and a cheesy card, telling whoever happened to be visiting at the time about the day my problem-solving skills saved him from what was sure to be an untimely death.

While in my trance-like state, his right hand shot forward like a bolt of lightning. Startled, I jumped to the side. The rattling sound that followed gave hint as to what he'd been staring at while I became drunk with his scent and enamored by his looks.

"Holy crap!" I gasped. "Did you find one?"

"He's under the stick," he said, pointing toward the ground with his free hand. "Grab him behind the head."

Holding a live rattlesnake sounded like a courageous idea. A brave stunt. Something I'd talk about for many years in the future. Heck, I'd planned on telling my grandchildren about it.

Frozen in place, I was hypnotized by the shaking tail of the venomous serpent. I stared at its angry body as it coiled around the stick like a speckled brown spring of scaled flesh, wondering all the while if I'd simply have to abandon item number fifty-six and admit defeat.

He glanced over his shoulder. "Well, are you going to grab him, or not?"

I glanced at the ball of fuming mad muscle that was wadded around the end of the forked stick and then looked at Porter.

"Or not," I said.

It came out more like a question than a statement. I desperately wanted to strike item fifty-six from my list, and the opportunity had fallen in my lap. To do so, however, I had to risk my life. Even if the snake wasn't poisonous, getting bitten by it seemed like a bad idea.

A very bad idea.

I assessed the situation.

Porter was an experienced snake hunter, that much was clear. Along with that experience, I expected he'd be versed in first aid techniques. I mulled over each step that would take place if I attempted to grab the venomous viper.

After I was bitten, I'd be flailing around like a beached shark. He would lie me flat on the ground at his feet, comfort me, and attempt to calm me. Using his massive hand, he'd brush the hair away from my face, peer into my eyes, and check the dilation of my pupils.

He'd whisper into my ear that a tourniquet would need to be applied, to prevent the venom from rushing to my heart. The tourniquet would be torn from the most delicate piece of fabric available, which was my dress.

Then, he'd need to tie the tourniquet between the bite mark and my heart. My upper thigh would be the most logical spot. Being the observant soul that he was, while securing said tourniquet, Porter would undoubtedly make note of two things:

One, that I was wearing a pair of red lace boy short panties. And two, that they – and my pussy – were dripping wet messes.

So, in summary, Porter would look me in the eyes, whisper in my ear, rip my dress to shreds, and then see soaked pussy. All while he was saving my life.

It sounded like a fool proof plan. With my eyes locked on the snake, I took the first step in starting the process.

"Where'd you say to grab him?" I asked.

"Right behind the head," he said. "It's the only safe place to hold them."

I took a step in the snake's direction. "Have you done this before?"

"I spent my childhood hunting snakes in Montana. Why?"

With my eyes glued to the snake, I gave a crisp nod. "Just wondering."

"Slide your hand along the stick until you get to the snake," he explained. "Grab it right where I've got it pinned down. Hold it firmly, but not like you're trying to strangle it."

The snake's head was pressed hard against the densely-packed sand beneath it. Furious for being torn away from a day of basking in the sun, its body was coiled tightly around the stick, attempting to constrict it to death.

My heart pounded against my ribs. What little moisture was in my mouth evaporated, leaving a big ball of unswallowable cotton-like yack in its place. Fearful of what the immediate future might hold, I took a step toward the snake, reached under the tree, and paused.

I looked at Porter. Not for direction or reassurance – I simply wanted to see him one last time before things went awry.

He was strangely calm. The half-assed smirk he wore told me he was at least mildly entertained. I snapped a mental picture of his strikingly masculine jawline, turned to face the snake, and did just as he'd instructed.

I expected slimy and slippery. Instead, I got rough and warm to the touch. I gripped the two-inch diameter piece of muscle between my thumb and forefinger and then gave Porter a blind nod.

"I think I've got him," I exclaimed.

"You better know," he said with a laugh.

I increased pressure on the deadly reptile's neck. "I've got him."

He lifted the stick. In turn, I lifted the snake.

Its body began coiling upward toward my hand.

"Shake it up and down," he said.

Fearing that it was going to wrap around my arm and constrict me into submission before it sank its fangs into my sunscreen slathered flesh, I promptly filled with regret for having picked it up in the first place.

"Shake it up and down?" I asked, frantic that his only instruction made zero sense. "What does that even mean?"

"Like you're jacking off your boyfriend," he said, moving his fist up and down like he was stroking a two-foot-long dick.

Just before the snake wrapped around my wrist, I did what he said. Miraculously, the snake's body straightened. A second or two later, he began to coil upward. I shook him again, and down he went. The third time he coiled, he seemed less interested in completing the task. I shook him lightly, and he straightened.

Now dangling loosely from my grasp, the snake simply hung there.

"Holy Moses!" I shouted. "I tamed a live rattlesnake."

"How's it feel?" he asked.

"Empowering," I responded.

My eyes scanned the ground for my purse. Upon seeing it, I nodded my head toward the ground where it laid.

"Will you grab my phone? Please?" I asked. "I want to take a picture of this."

He did as I asked. Standing ten feet in front of me with my phone in one hand and the stick in the other, he looked at me. The pain in his eyes was gone. "Do you want me to take a picture?" he asked, pointing the phone at me.

"Yes, silly," I responded, alternating glances between my outstretched arm and the badass biker who took me rattlesnake hunting. "But I want you to be in it. Come over here."

He stepped to my side and swept his thumb across the screen of my phone. "It's locked."

"Zero-nine-two-seven," I said.

He pressed the buttons with his thumb, fumbled to find the icon, and eventually got the camera rotated to take a selfie.

"Take off that jacket," I said. "Who wears a leather jacket in this heat, anyway?"

He chuckled a dry laugh as he peeled off the coat. "Someone who doesn't want to be bitten by a snake."

After tossing the coat on the ground beside my purse, he pressed the side of his chest against my shoulder and extended his arm. With the snake dangling from my shaking hand, I tilted my head toward his, looked at the screen, and grinned.

"Take several," I said.

A puff of dry desert air wafted his scent into my nose.

The excitement of holding the lethal reptile, the heat from the mid-day sun, and the soul-stirring scent of his manliness proved to be too much. My head spun and my knees went weak. In response, I rested my head against his chest.

At that same instance, he snapped what would be the first picture of many.

"What do I do with this guy?" I asked, nodding toward the snake.

He took the snake from my grasp and handed me the phone. After releasing it fifty feet away from where I stood, he returned just in time to find me posting the photo of my head on his shoulder to my Instagram account.

"Let me see that one," he said.

I held the phone between us, trying not to smile a cheesy grin at the disgustingly cute picture of me, him, and an exhausted three-foot long rattlesnake.

"I like it," he said. "Can you send it to me?"

"You can go to my Instagram and get it," I said.

He choked on his laugh. "I don't know anything about that shit."

"Instagram?" I asked, quite relieved by his apparent disgust.

"Facebook, Instagram, Twitter, Bumbler, Fumbler, Yourspace, Myspace, any of it," he said.

My eyebrows raised much higher than I wanted them to. "You're not social media savvy?"

"I'm not social media *interested*," he said. "I'm computer savvy. I don't think my business is anyone else's business. I don't subscribe to any of that shit."

He had no idea who I was or what I did for a living, that much I was sure of. Thrilled that he was blind to me and my social media following, I contemplated telling him the truth.

"I don't see why people feel the need to blast their personal business all over the internet," he said, reaching for his jacket. "It's fucking ridiculous."

Okay. Maybe telling him wasn't such a good idea. At least not yet. There'd be plenty of time to tell him if I felt the need. Hopefully I'd be seeing much more of him at the meetings. If nothing else, I could get his phone number.

"Do you text?" I asked.

"If I have to," he said.

"But you know how it works?"

He laughed a genuine laugh. "Yeah. I'm not a complete idiot."

After getting his number, I texted him a copy of the picture. Proof of our successes in accomplishing number fifty-six on my to-do list. I drew a line through two tasks we'd completed and tossed the pad into my purse.

There were four to go, three of which I could tackle with little effort. I doubted the man strapping on his helmet could help me with the fourth, which was number two on my list.

He secured the latch of his saddlebag. Now wearing nothing more than a tee shirt, jeans, and boots, his muscles bulged as he was straddled the motorcycle seat.

Number two.

An unconscious sigh escaped me.

It never hurt to dream.

6

GHOST

I was slumped against the arm of the sofa in the MC's clubhouse. Lost somewhere between my childhood and my funeral, I was mentally vacant as the men discussed the club's fall cross-country trip.

"Brother Ghost," I heard someone say.

It sounded like a distant whisper. Not something I needed to respond to. I wondered for a moment if it was imagined or real.

"Brother Ghost!" Baker howled.

I stumbled through my mind's fog and blinked until my vision was clear. Baker's head was cocked to the side and he was looking at me with wide, waiting eyes.

"What?" I asked.

"What's your vote?" he asked.

"On what?"

He glanced at the rest of the men and then shifted his eyes to meet mine. "Are you okay, Brother?"

"I think I faded off for a minute," I said.

"Hard day at the gym?" he asked.

I shrugged one shoulder. "Didn't go."

"That's a first." He straightened his posture, stroking his beard as he sat up in his seat. "Connecticut or Rhode Island?"

"Connecticut," I said, not really giving half a fuck what he was talking about or where we'd be going.

I knew the discussion was about our fall motorcycle trip, or at least it was when I slipped into a semiconscious slumber. Hell, I didn't know if I'd even be around when fall arrived. If I was, I doubted I'd be in any shape to ride.

"Great," he said sarcastically. "Now we've got a three to three tie."

"Rhode Island," I said, my tone indifferent.

"Seriously?" Cash whined. "Rhode fucking Island?"

"I'm guessing you were team Connecticut?" I grinned and clapped my hands. "Decision's made. We're going to Rhode Island."

Cash flipped me his middle finger. "You weren't even paying attention."

"Doesn't matter." I shrugged. "Vote was whether we wanted to go to Rhode Island or Connecticut. Club voted. Rhode Island it is."

Cash's face distorted. "Asshole. If you don't give a fuck, you should side with me, not Reno, Bake and Tito the turd."

"If I sided with you, it'd be a tie. Then, we'd be voting on two new places. We did that three years ago and ended up in fucking Florida. Not interested in going to that shit-hole again."

"Ghost needs to take a fucking nap," Cash complained, turning to face Baker. "We can re-vote this next week."

"Vote's complete," Baker said. "We're going to Rhode Island."

"Fuck that shit," Cash snapped. "I want to see the leaves turning color in Connecticut. Rhode Island's nothing but rocks and water."

Seeing the fall leaves sounded like a great idea. I'd never been through Connecticut in the fall. If I were to make a list like Abby's, going to Connecticut in the fall would certainly be on it.

"Connecticut." I raised my index finger. "I'm changing my vote."

"If I allow the vote change, we're in a tie," Baker said. "If we're in a tie, you know the rules."

"I don't give a shit," I said, turning to face Cash. "You want to ride to Connecticut this fall?"

"Hell yeah," Cash said.

"Fuck it," I said openly. "Cash and I are going to Connecticut."

"You're all over the place," Baker said. "What the hell's wrong with you, Ghost?"

Normally, I was decisive. Even if I happened to thrust myself into a situation that I later regretted, I never changed my mind. I was the poster boy for stubborn behavior, and the men knew it.

"I'm exhausted," I said, which was partially true. "Went to Borrego Springs earlier today. Caught a fucking rattlesnake. It was hotter than ten kinds of fuck, too."

"Borrego Springs?" Goose asked. "Why the fuck did you go to Borrego Springs?"

"Rattlesnake?" Tito asked. "Was it a Western, Diamondback, Panamint, Sidewinder, Mojave, or Red Diamond?"

Tito was a walking information vault, and often expected others to be as intelligent as he was. It was never the case. "How the fuck would I know?" I spouted. "It had a rattle on one end, and a pissed off head on the other."

"Was just wondering," Tito said. "California has six species."

I pulled out my phone, opened the picture Abby had sent me, and handed the phone to Tito. "You tell me what that angry fucker is."

He looked at the photo. After his eyes shot wide, I decided whatever it was must have been what he was hoping for. He glanced at me, back at the phone, and then looked at Baker. His jaw was all but in his lap.

"What?" Baker asked.

Tito turned the phone to face Baker. Baker squinted in response. "Big snake. Don't know what it is. Chick's cute, though. Who is it?"

"Uptown Abby," Tito said.

My eyes narrowed. "You know her?"

Goose coughed out a wad of surprise and then snatched the phone from Tito's hand. "You went to Borrego Springs with Uptown Abby?"

"No shit?" Reno asked. "She's hot as fuck."

I looked at each of them as if they were on fire. "Who the fuck's *Uptown Abby*?"

Tito grabbed the phone from Goose, fumbled with it for a moment, and then handed it to me. "This one's funny. Just press *play*."

A YouTube video was loaded on the screen of my phone. I pressed *play*. After a five second video about the new BMW SUV, a woman appeared. Her hair was in a bun, and she was wearing glasses, but it was undoubtedly Abby. A much younger Abby, but it was her.

Finding a man in San Diego that's suitable for dating isn't an easy task. Personally, I prefer a big man. A tall man. A man who makes me feel small and protected. So, I ventured to the gym in search of my perfect mate. What did I find?

Well, I'm still single.

I did come up with an idea, though.

The personality gym.

I think it's a great concept. Instead of going in, lifting weights, and leaving with shredded abs, bulging biceps, and a missing neck, you would go in, get an awesome cup of Italian roast coffee and a bran muffin.

While munching the muffin and sipping the coffee, you'd talk to a personality counselor. After six weeks, you'd graduate with manners, the ability to communicate with others, and a reasonable sense of self-worth.

Why is it that most men who spend their idle time in the gym are referred to as meatheads?

Because their heads are nothing more than a slab of meat, that's why.

The screen flashed to a sidewalk scene, where Abby was interviewing a man in front of a gym. He was wearing remnants of a tee shirt, spandex shorts, and carried a half-full protein shaker in one hand.

Who was president when you were a senior in high school? Abby asked.

The man took a drink from his plastic bottle and then gave her a confused look. *Of what?*

The United States, she replied.

After giving the question some serious thought, the man responded. *Donald Trump.*

How many ounces are in two pounds of coffee? she asked.

I don't drink coffee how would I know? Next question.

Who shot John F. Kennedy? she asked.

I'm twenty-two. He took another gulp from his shaker, making sure to flex his bicep as he took the drink. *That was before my time.*

Is it the Pacific or Atlantic Ocean that touches the coastline here?

I'm not big into American history, he responded. *Ask me something about proteins or carb loading--*

Does a man's sperm have protein in it? she asked.

He grinned. *It's got tons of it.*

How much? she asked. *Per serving?*

He shrugged. *Couple of grams.*

Gone with the Wind or Gone in Sixty Seconds? she asked.

He drank the remained of his protein shake. *Gone in Sixty Seconds.*

She motioned toward his protein shaker. *How much of that stuff do you drink in a day?*

He raised the plastic cup. *Three of these.*

How long does it take you to finish one set of curls? she asked.

Twenty-two minutes, he responded proudly.

That's all I've got, she said with a smile.

The screen switched to a split screen. On the left, the man's body was visible, but his head had been swapped with a large wad of hamburger. On the right, Abby held the microphone.

Does a man's sperm have protein in it? she asked

A makeshift mouth opened in the hamburger-shaped head. *It's got tons of it.*

How much of that stuff do you drink in a day?

The hamburger-headed gym rat lifted the plastic cup. *Three of these.*

How long does it take you to finish one? she asked.

He raised the cup to his hamburger head half a dozen times, and then lowered it. *Gone in sixty seconds, gone in sixty seconds, gone in sixty seconds...*

The screen switched back to the original one, with Abby sitting in front of the camera. Her eyebrows raised slowly, until they were at maximum height. After blinking repeatedly, she smiled.

No male sperm was consumed in the making of this video, no douchebags were harmed, and, with the exception of mine, no 'thank you's' were spoken. I'll see you next week, when we'll discuss rush hour traffic on the five, the rising price of cauliflower rice, and the migration of the Monarchs.

She brushed her hair behind her ear, and then scratched the bottom of her nose with her index finger. She pointed at the screen. *I'm uptown, I'm Abby, and I'm unfiltered.*

The screen faded to black.

I turned off the phone, uncertain if I liked what I'd seen. I wondered why most of the men seemed overjoyed with the fact that I'd met the girl in the ridiculous video. I further wondered why all of them knew who she was.

"That's her," I said, searching each of the men's faces as I spoke. "What's the big deal?"

"She's got twenty million followers," Tito said.

I stared at him in disbelief. "Twenty *million*?"

He nodded. "Million. She makes about ten million a year off advertisements alone."

My eyes went wide. "Dollars? Ten million dollars?"

"I can't believe you don't know who she is," he said. "She's been on Jimmy Kimmel, The View, The Tonight Show...Hell, I think she's even met the president. How'd you meet her?"

I had no intention of telling the men about my diagnosis, at least not yet. "I had no idea who she was." I pushed my phone into my pocked. "She just randomly asked me if I'd give her a ride on my motorcycle. We ended up in Borrego Springs hunting rattlesnakes."

"Was rattlesnake hunting on her list?" Goose asked.

I looked at him in disbelief. "You know about her list?"

"She talks about it all the time," he said.

"Yeah," I said. "It was on there."

Over the next few minutes, the men hit me with a barrage of questions, wondering if I was going to see her again and whether I fucked her before or after our trip to the desert.

The day I left the doctor's office, I had plans on going to one meeting, and one meeting only. After meeting Abby, I considered going to another just to see her again. I now felt I *had* to attend a meeting.

Not because I needed therapy, or because thoughts of her caused me to smile.

I needed to prove that some gym rats *do* have a personality.

7

ABBY

I ate my pancakes with the grace of a starving dog. The three oversized flapjacks reduced my desire for carbohydrates but did nothing to curb my appetite to see Porter again.

Incapable of deciding whether I should send him a text message or order one more pancake, I stared blankly through the diner's window. With a far more casual stride than normal, Lawson ambled into my line of sight.

"Can I get another pancake?" I asked as his image walked past.

He paused. "Just one?"

I narrowed my blank stare and shifted my eyes to him. Two pancakes would fill the stomach of most of the Marine men who regularly ate at the diner. I'd already eaten three, but I had the metabolism of a greyhound, especially when something was bothering me.

"Make it two," I said, raising two fingers. "I might go for another run when I'm done."

He nodded and turned away.

When I couldn't decide what to do about one of life's obstacles, I either ran or overate. At the end of my run, or by the time I wiped the corners of my mouth, I always had the answer. When I ran *and* overate,

I was generally stuck – centered between what I wanted and what I truly needed – incapable of grasping either.

Leaning one way or the other was the answer, and I couldn't decide what direction was in my best interest.

"What's on your mind?" George asked from behind me.

Seated at the end of a row of booths with my back facing the wall, I peered over my shoulder, toward the kitchen. "Nothing, really."

His square jaw tightened. He narrowed his eyes playfully and gave me a stare. "Lawson just came in the kitchen. The last time you ate six pancakes was the evening before you broke up with Kevin."

"Kelvin. His name was Kelvin, with an 'L'," I said. "And, I'm only having five."

He leaned over the back of the booth and looked me in the eyes. "I'll ask again. What's on your mind?"

Immediately after meeting George, he stepped into my life as a father of sorts. Protecting me from Southern California's undesirables seemed to be his calling. Upon hiring his male employees, he advised them of his hands-off policy when it came to me. If a patron acted overly friendly, George was at my table in an instant, squashing their advancements completely. Luckily, his clientele were regulars. Therefore, everyone knew his position on all things Abby related.

I gestured to the empty seat across from me. "Sit down. It makes me nervous when you loom over me like that."

He sat across from me, resting his massive forearms on the edge of the table. He cocked an eyebrow. "Did you run this morning?"

I nodded. "Five miles."

His mouth twisted into a smirk. "So, we've got a big problem."

"You know me all too well." My gaze fell to the table top. "There was this guy at the meeting. He was really nice. We went to Borrego and I caught a rattlesnake."

I looked up, hoping I'd satisfied his curiosity.

In complete contrast of my optimistic view, he coughed out a laugh. "Were you planning on stopping there, or are you going to continue with the rest of the story?"

"That's pretty much it," I lied. "We rode out there, caught a rattlesnake, and then we rode back to the meeting. After that, I came home."

"I know you didn't ride your bicycle to the desert." He cocked an eyebrow. "Motorcycle?"

I nodded.

"Number thirty-whatever?" he asked.

"Two," I said. "It was number thirty-two."

"A biker. You're contemplating a *real* biker?" He crossed his arms and peered down his nose at me. "What makes him special?"

"I don't know."

It was true. I didn't know. He possessed the external qualities I liked in men, but beyond that I knew very little about him. I feared, however, that it was what I *didn't* know that drew me to him. I wanted to find out what the root of his fear was. In time, I wanted to fix it.

"What's his…" He twisted his mouth to the side, seeming uncertain of how to continue. "Condition?"

"I'm not sure," I said. "He didn't want to talk about it. We were discussing faith in the higher power, and he didn't want to talk about that, either. But, he was really nice. I mean, we rode to Borrego Springs and back, and he never hit on me. Not once. And, he had no idea who I was, so that's a plus."

His eyes widened a little. "Are you sure?"

"Positive," I assured him. "He doesn't believe in social media. He thinks it's dumb."

"So, what's your plan?" he asked.

I scrunched my nose and shrugged one shoulder. "Eat two more pancakes and see what I think?"

"Bring him in here," he said.

It sounded like more of a demand than a recommendation. Mentally, my head shook vigorously. Outwardly, I tried to remain calm and seem unaffected by his request.

"I don't think that's necessary," I said, using caution to keep my tone emotionless. "Not yet."

"Bring him in here." He slid out of the booth and stood. "I want to meet him."

I had my doubts Porter would show up to the next meeting. He lacked interest in sharing with the group. I suspected his attendance was mandated by his insurance company, and not driven by his desire.

"Let me see if he even shows up to the next meeting." I offered a smile. "We'll go from there."

"Bring him in here." He folded his arms over his chest. He did it when he was frustrated, and by my count, had already done it twice since sitting down. "That's three times, if you're keeping count."

I gave him an innocent look. "Three times?"

"I said *bring him in here* three times." He unfolded his arms and tugged against his apron. "Four, including this one."

I mouthed the words *I'm sorry*. "If he comes back, I'll see what I can do."

"A fucking biker," he murmured as he walked away.

The instant George was gone, Lawson set my plate in front of me. After George's interrogation I expected to be drawn to the steaming hot plate of goodness like a great white shark to a bleeding surfer. Instead, I looked at the Frisbee-sized discs of fried batter with disgust in my eyes. According to my lack of appetite, I wasn't stuck in the middle any longer. My decision was made.

Without so much as a moment's thought I pulled my phone from my purse. I scrolled through my contacts and found Porter's name. When I started to type him a text message, I noticed I had received one that I wasn't aware of. It was an hour and a half old, and it was from Porter.

I opened it.

Ghost Porter-Porter: Have time to talk?

I was instantly overcome with the same giddy excitement that filled me when Trent Rothchild asked me to senior prom. I fidgeted in my seat to thoughts of riding on Porter's motorcycle, and of wrapping my arms around his muscular torso. I closed my eyes and tried to resurrect his scent but fell short, relying solely on a mental image of his handsome face and muscular physique as fuel to make me squirm.

I wondered if he had questions about the meeting, about cancer, or if his interests were more along a personal level. Hoping his concerns were minimal and his interest in me was vast, I opened my eyes and typed a quick response.

I'm eating a late breakfast. Other than that, I'm free all day. What did you have in mind?

Instantaneously, my phone beeped. I glanced at the illuminated screen.

Ghost Porter-Porter: Want to meet for lunch?

My heart stammered. Short of a day dream, I'd shared no intimate moments with Porter. Nonetheless, I felt I was battling a premature teen crush.

I searched the diner and found George standing fifty feet away, talking to a young couple I didn't recognize. There'd be plenty of opportunities for him to meet Porter whenever I felt it was necessary. To do so now would have been awkward. When he looked up I flashed him a quick grin, feeling slightly guilty for not wanting to bring Porter to the diner.

With my phone hidden in my lap, I typed my response.

I'd love to. How does sushi sound?

Upon reading his *sounds great* response, an involuntary squeal shot from my lungs. Embarrassed, I pushed the plate of cold pancakes to the far side of the table and dropped my phone in my purse, hoping I was the only one who heard the audible outcry.

Instead of waiting for my bill, I tossed an ample amount of cash on the table and jumped from my seat.

"Love you, George," I shouted openly.

"Love you, too, Abby," he responded. "See you in a few hours."

"I won't be in for lunch." I lengthened my stride, all but scurrying toward the door. "I've got some things to do."

"Bringing him in?" he asked.

He knew me all too well. With my eyes fixed on the exit, I raised my hand in the air and gave a playful wave. "Bye, George."

"Bringing him in?!" he shouted from behind me.

I pushed the door open and paused. "Love you, George."

"Fucking biker," he muttered.

8

GHOST

The waitress set a slender plate of rice-wrapped raw fish in front of me. I'd seen sushi before, but I'd never planned on eating it. Now that I didn't have a choice, I wasn't sure how in the fuck I was going to pick it up.

I nonchalantly searched the table for utensils and found none. In unrolling my napkin, two ornately painted white sticks fell onto the table and bounced a few times before they came to a rest between Abby and me. I stared at them as if they were the cause of a ten-car collision on the five.

Unless I planned to use them as miniature spears, I was going to go hungry. My chopstick skills were equal to my ability to walk a tightrope.

"Aren't you hungry?" Abby asked as I fumbled to pick up the sticks. "I'm famished."

I grinned in acknowledgement and then shifted my eyes to my food. I had my doubts I'd be able to pick up anything, short of a few stares and a laugh or two. I searched the restaurant. Two dozen adults and half a dozen children used their chopsticks as an extension of their fingers, eating their food with ease. For them, it seemed like a simple task.

In my attempt to hold the slippery sticks, I looked like a drunken carnival clown trying to juggle pencils. If I continued, I was going to make an utter fool of myself. Aggravated, I scanned the table one last time for a useable utensil. A fucking butter knife would have been better than what I had.

"I never use those things," Abby said. "Eat it with your hands, it's more fun. That's how they do it in Japan."

Relieved, I slid the cherry blossom adorned sticks to the side and looked up. Abby held a piece of sushi between her fingers, no differently than if she were eating a French fry.

"You can eat this stuff with your hands?" I asked. "I thought it'd be an etiquette thing. I'm not looking to have some pissed off Japanese guy over here yelling at me."

"A good rule of thumb is if it has rice attached to it you can eat it with your fingers," she explained. "If it's sashimi – raw fish – it needs to be eaten with chopsticks."

I glanced at my food. "What if it's both?"

She chuckled and nodded toward my plate. "It's surrounded by rice, so it's finger food."

"That's a good thing," I said. "If I would have had to use those chopsticks, there would have been more of this stuff on the floor than in my mouth."

"How do you normally eat it?"

"This is my first time," I confessed.

Her face contorted. "I asked you if you liked sushi. You said yes."

"You said *how does sushi sound.* I said it *sounded great.*" I studied the piece I held. "I've never tried it, though."

"I hope you like it." She brushed her hair away from her face, eventually draping it over her ear. After rubbing the bottom of her nose with her index finger, she grinned. "Try it and see what you think."

I poked the piece into my mouth. Surprisingly, it tasted good. Excited by the complexity of flavors, I looked at Abby with wide eyes. "I ordered the spicy tuna roll because I like tuna and I like spicy things. Looks like I made a good choice. This is pretty tasty."

"I love sushi," she said. "I could eat it every day. It's not fun to eat it alone, though."

I ate everything alone and didn't see the complication. "What's a good *alone* food?"

She brushed her hair behind her ear again and cocked her head to the side. After some consideration, her gaze met mine. "Salads. Scrambled eggs. Soup. Sandwiches. Those types of things."

I reached for another piece of sushi. "Things that start with an 'S'?"

She laughed. "No. Things that are boring. Boring things are okay to eat alone. Things that are fun should be shared with someone."

I ate the piece of sushi and then wiped my mouth with my napkin. "What's fun?"

She shrugged. "Pizza. Sushi. Spaghetti. Any Italian food, really. Tacos. Ice cream. Pie. Those are all fun, and they shouldn't be eaten alone."

I looked her up and down. Her arms were the size of my wrists. I couldn't see her legs, but I didn't need to. I'd seen them plenty when we were in the desert. They were lean and muscular, like that of a conditioned runner. By my guess, pie wasn't a staple in her diet.

"You don't look like you eat much pie," I said.

"I can eat an entire pie." She leaned forward and raised her brows. "All by myself."

I spat disbelief on the table between us. "Bullshit."

"I'm dead serious," she said, beaming with pride. "I love pie."

"What's your favorite?"

She smiled. "Pecan."

"A pecan pie has five thousand calories in it." I argued. "There's no way on earth you could eat one of those."

"I have the metabolism of a cheetah."

I chuckled at the thought of her attempting to eat an entire pie. "I'd pay money to see you eat a whole pecan pie."

Her eyes widened a little. "How much?"

I shrugged. "Fifty bucks."

She looked me over. "Make it a hundred."

If Tito's claim was correct, she made ten million dollars a year. She sure didn't act like it. I decided he was misinformed and challenged her on her pie eating abilities.

"I'm not talking about a six-inch pie or some dumb shit like that," I said. "A standard sized pie."

"I'll eat a nine-incher for a hundred," she said with a smile.

I choked on a laugh. "If I offered to pay you a hundred to eat a nine-incher, wouldn't that make you a prostitute?"

"If you offered to pay me a hundred to eat a nine-incher, you better have a nine-incher for me to eat. If not, it'd make you a liar. I don't like liars." she said, straight-faced.

Upon hearing the remark, half my blood shot to my face and the other half rushed to my cock. Now sporting a full-fledged hard on and sure I was blushing, I slid to the edge of the booth and tried to act suave.

With my manhood available for view, I looked right at her and raised both eyebrows. "I don't lie."

She peered over the edge of the table. Upon seeing my denim-encased wonder, her eyes went wide. "I'd uhhm. Wow," she stammered. "An honest man is an attractive man."

Her eyes remained glued to my crotch.

"So, what's it going to be?" I asked. "Pie, or *that*?"

She lifted her gaze to meet mine and then shook her head, as if to clear it of impure thoughts. "I think I'm going to have to stick with the pie."

"What?" I snapped back.

She flashed a guiltless smile. "My mouth gets me into trouble sometimes."

"I want your mouth to get you in trouble," I said. "Nine inches of trouble."

"Men's minds always go to sex." She giggled. "I was offering to eat a pie."

I slid into the booth. "You started this with your little sexual innuendo."

"Like I said. It's my mouth," she said, feigning innocence with a half-assed shrug. "It often says what I don't want it to."

"My guess is that it says what you're thinking," I said with a flick of my hand. "And you're too embarrassed to admit it."

She picked up a piece of sushi but didn't eat it. It appeared she was in deep thought. Deep thought about sucking my dick, I hoped. I decided a little encouragement wouldn't hurt.

"Are you going to tell me that you don't think about sex?" I asked. "Ever?"

"Never." She tried not to laugh but did anyway. After recovering from the laugh, she continued. "The thought of sex never crosses my mind."

I laughed. "You don't fart, either, do you?"

"I've never farted," she said, stone-faced. "I have no idea what it feels like to pass gas."

"Well, I do fart, *and* I often think about sex," I said with a laugh. "Not at the same time, though."

She tilted her head to the side and gave me a curious look. "Have you ever thought about sex with me?"

"Are we being truthful?" I asked.

She grinned. "Let's try it for a while."

"The day we met?" I locked eyes with her and leaned forward. "I thought about bending you over the couch and hiking that little dress of yours over your waist."

She covered her face with her hands and slumped into the booth until she all but disappeared. "What else?"

I grinned at the sight of her. My honesty was either embarrassing her or torturing her. It was exactly what she deserved. "You sure you want to hear it?"

She spread her fingers apart and peeked at me through the space between them. "Uh huh."

I grinned a sly smirk. "Poking my dick in your pretty little mouth."

"Oh God," she moaned. "It's the lips, isn't it?"

"It's everything about you, really." I lifted my chin slightly. "Hell, I'm thinking about fucking you right now.

She swallowed heavily and then lowered her hands. Her face was glowing red from embarrassment. "Are you like this with every girl you meet?"

I shook my head. "Nope."

"What. What uhhm. What…" she stammered. "What makes *me* different?"

"Everything," I said flatly.

"Like what?"

"At first, I liked your outfits. The sneakers with a dress look pretty sexy in my book. You were eager enough to come sit with me. I liked that. I thought you were bold. The to-do list let me know you were goal-oriented A driven woman is attractive as fuck. Then, the entire rattlesnake thing? Yeah, you're different. And, you're pretty as fuck."

In what I was sure was a subconscious gesture, she swept her hair behind her ear and scratched the bottom of her nose with her index finger.

"You do that thing with your hair quite a bit," I said. "I like it. It's cute."

"It's a habit." She said, still glowing red. "I do it all the time when I'm nervous. Or when I'm in deep thought about something. I don't even realize it."

I rested my chin in my hand and looked at her admiringly. "What were you thinking about when you did it at the meeting?"

"I do it and I don't even realize it, so I don't really know when you're talking about. It's funny. George can tell when I'm thinking about something because of it. He always says, 'what's on your mind, Abby?'"

A tinge of jealousy washed over me. I'd never felt jealous in my life, and it took me by complete surprise.

"Who's George?" I asked, my tone slightly bitter.

"He's a retired Marine who owns a deli. He's like my second dad," she replied. "I eat there all the time."

A rush of relief came from hearing her response, and it troubled me. I hadn't had a girlfriend since I was in high school, and I had no desire to change – or at least that's what I thought. For whatever reason, I felt attracted to Abby beyond simply admiring her looks. It seemed my swollen brain was changing my manner of thinking. I wasn't sure I liked it. Nonetheless, I forged on.

"You were sitting across from me. You did that thing with your hair, and then you pointed to the seat beside me." I pointed to the empty booth space beside her. "So, what were you thinking? When you pointed?"

One side of her mouth curled up. "I thought you were handsome."

I wasn't a bad looking guy, but I was far from handsome. I cocked an eyebrow. "Handsome?"

Clearly embarrassed, her gaze fell to the table. "Uh huh."

She did the hair thing again, and then scratched her nose with her finger.

"What's on your mind, Abby?" I asked, citing the question she said George asked, word for word.

She looked up. A guilty grin was plastered on her face. "Nothing."

"You were doing that hair thing," I said. "So, you were thinking about something."

"Are we being truthful?" she asked mockingly.

I shrugged. "Let's try it for a while."

Her mouth twisted into a smirk. "I was thinking about what you said earlier."

I raised my brows in interest. "Which part?"

"About the pie," she deadpanned. "I think I'm ready to give it a try."

It wasn't what I was hoping for. Seeing her devour a pie would be entertaining. Watching her writhe in sexual bliss while I shoved her full of cock would be better. I reached for my wallet, hoping the blood would drain from my stiff dick before I stood.

"Fine," I whined. "Pie it is."

She gave a coy smile and turned to the side. "I was thinking about the sex, silly."

Now, instead of me torturing her, she was tormenting me. "What about it?" I asked, shoving the heel of my palm against my stiff dick.

"It's been a long time for me," she admitted. "Thinking about it is nice."

Thinking about it was nice. Doing it would be better. Much better. I wondered if she was as deep in thought as I was.

"Is your pussy wet?" I asked.

Her face blushed instantly. She choked on her attempt to respond. After taking a drink of water, she recovered enough to speak.

"What?" she asked.

"You heard me." I gestured to her lap with a nod of my head. "Your pussy. Is. It. Wet?"

She swallowed heavily. Her head nodded ever so slightly.

"I'll take that as a *yes*." I slid to the edge of the booth, so she could see my lap. With my eyes locked on her, I nodded toward my stiff dick. "I could hammer nails with this thing."

Without argument or hesitation, she took a lingering look.

"So, I'll ask again," I said. "What's it going to be? Pie or *this*?"

"*That* is tempting." She shifted her eyes from my cock to my face. "But I'm going to have to stick with the pie. At least for now."

I couldn't believe it. I was trying to coerce a died-in-the-wool prick tease to give me some pussy. "We're both adults," I fumed. "You've got a wet pussy, and I'm rocking some serious wood. Explain to me why you want to eat fucking pie."

"I just want to get to know you a little more before we take it to the next level," she said. "So, for now, it's going to have to be pie."

"Fine," I huffed. I pulled out my wallet and flipped through the bills. "You want to follow me to my place?"

"Do you have a pecan pie?"

Being turned down for sex would normally be my signal to pay the bill and leave. With Abby, however, I had no intention of walking away. My cock wanted to fuck her, but my brain wasn't opposed to getting to know her better. I decided to merge the two and agree to watch her eat a pie, but only after she rode on the back of my bike. Nothing stimulated sexual desire more than a ride on a Harley.

"No, but you're going to ride on the back of my bike to get the pie. You've got your rules, and I've got mine. You can leave your car at my place."

"You can follow me to my place," she said. "I'll gladly park my car and get on that bike again."

Her tone let me know I was headed in the right direction. I tossed a hundred-dollar bill on the table and stood, hoping her pie-eating efforts fell within the *getting to know me* slot.

If not, the agony associated with my brain tumor wasn't going to be limited to headaches.

9

ABBY

I was in desperate need of some dick, and had been for a long, long time. I wanted Porter to be the guy to take me out of my sexless slump, but I needed to make sure I was stepping out of the single life for all the right reasons. Sexually frustrated to the point of a meltdown, I exercised restraint and settled for devouring a pecan pie.

It seemed like a responsible decision.

We decided to ride to Julian, California. My first ride with Porter was an awakening, of sorts. The ride to *Julian Pie Company* was different. After the sexual innuendos, blowjob banter, and the glimpse of Porter's massive manhood, I was a horny mess.

When I got on the motorcycle, I was already soaking wet. One hour into the ride, the motorcycle's vibration had me on the verge of an orgasm. I spent the next thirty minutes with my eyes cinched closed, my mind adrift, and my soaking wet pussy at the mercy of an eight-hundred-pound vibrator. During that half-hour ride, my sexual tension increased to an all-time high.

In my daydream, Porter's face was buried between my legs. He ate me while I ate slice after slice of pie. I was truly in heaven – both in my dream, and in reality.

The last fifteen minutes of the trip were in stop and go traffic, during which time I couldn't find my happy place. Frustrated, I opened my eyes and tried to regain my composure.

Much to my surprise, we'd arrived in the small town. I fidgeted in my seat. Nothing seemed to relieve the tension that had built within me. I was soaking wet and my pussy was begging for attention.

"What the fuck are you doing back there?" Porter snarled.

"Trying to get comfortable," I whined.

"With you thrashing around like that, it's not easy to keep this son-of-a-bitch on the road," he growled. "We'll be there in five minutes. Sit. Still."

I lifted my weight from the seat, stuffed my dress under my thighs, and sat down. "Sorry," I huffed.

For the first time since we'd exited the highway, I surveyed my surroundings. Short of the cars that lined the narrow streets, the town looked like something from the turn of the nineteenth century.

Wooden buildings with porches that hung over the entrance, homes that had been converted to craft shops, and residences that doubled as restaurants lined the streets. We came to rest at a pie shop that looked like a century old New England cottage. He turned off the engine and lowered the kickstand.

I was excited to get to know Porter, but I was mentally exhausted. I'd been daydreaming about him eating my pussy for the entire two-hour ride. Sexually frustrated and still soaking wet, I climbed off the motorcycle and brushed the wrinkles from my dress.

He hung his helmet on the handlebars, looked at the pie shop's small covered patio, and then at me. "You ready?"

Before I could answer, his eyes darted to the motorcycle seat. "What the fuck is *that*?"

He reached toward the seat.

I shifted my gaze to the area in question. Upon seeing it, embarrassment balled up in my throat. The leather was slathered in what appeared to be proof of my joyous ride. He dragged his finger across the slippery surface, wiping a clean path through the six-inch wide wet spot I'd left there.

A prickly feeling crept up my neck. My face flashed hot. With his focus on his finger, and mine on him, I held my breath as he moved his hand toward his mouth.

Oh. My God. Please. Lick it. I'm begging you.

With my mouth agape and my mind in the gutter, I followed the movement of his hand as it moved closer and closer to his face. He straightened his finger. His lips parted. The instant the tip of his tongue touched the juice covered digit, my legs went weak.

His eyes thinned. He licked it again and then looked at me. "Enjoy the ride?"

I nodded. A full-on blush enveloped me. Instead of playing the embarrassed innocent, I decided to simply own it.

"I had a good time," I said, cocking my hip as I spoke. "Is that a crime?"

"I'll tell you what the crime is." He wiped the palm of his hand over the remnants of my sexual daydream-infused ride. "Letting this go to waste."

Just when I thought my degree of sexual agony couldn't worsen, it did. In an overly dramatic fashion, he licked his hand clean. As if it were a daily occurrence, he then turned toward the sidewalk that led to the pie shop.

"You ready to eat that pie?" he asked.

"I'm ready for you to eat *my* pie," I responded, saying what was on my mind before I could get my brain to stop my mouth from spewing out the words.

"You tortured me by making me agree to do this," he said. "I don't give a single solitary fuck how horny you got on the ride up here. It's my turn to torture you. We're eating fucking pie."

He took a few long strides toward the entrance. "C'mon."

Eating an entire pie sounded like a great idea when we talked about it in the sushi restaurant. Now it seemed a complete waste of an afternoon. Nonetheless, I followed Porter up the sidewalk, second-guessing my denial of his offer to have sex the entire way. My dripping wet pussy agreed.

Once inside the nostalgic establishment, I was met by an old-school glass pie display case that was filled with various pies. My mouth watered at the sight of the flaky crust and the aroma of the fresh pies. As I ogled the pies, Porter stepped to the counter.

"I'd like one slice of the boysenberry apple crumb, and an entire pecan pie, please," Porter said.

"A slice of boysenberry apple, and a whole pecan pie?" the lady asked.

"Yes, ma'am."

"Any toppings?" she asked, pointing to a sign that was suspended over her head.

I glanced at the sign. There were two ice cream options – vanilla and cinnamon, caramel sauce, cinnamon sauce, whipped cream, and cheddar cheese.

"Cinnamon ice cream on top of the boysenberry, please," Porter responded without looking at the sign. He glanced over his shoulder. "Do you want anything on your pie?"

Still struggling to rid myself of lingering sexual thoughts, I simply shook my head. "No, thank you."

"You don't want the pecan pie boxed?" the lady asked.

Porter smiled. "No, ma'am. She's going to eat it."

Her eyes went wide. "She can't eat an entire pecan pie. That's impossible."

"According to her, she can eat it," Porter assured her. "We've got a bet."

She was a middle-aged woman that looked like she belonged in a nineteen sixties television sitcom. Her short graying hair was fixed in a series of close curls, and she wore an apron that was dusted with flour. Halfway up the bridge of her nose, a pair of glasses rested.

She peered over the tops of the lenses and fixed her eyes on me. "Sweetheart, you're going to get sick if you eat an entire pie."

"I'll be okay," I said.

"Have you done this before?" she asked.

"I ate seven hotdogs once," I admitted. "Not on a bet. Just because."

"That's a far cry from eating one of our pecan pies. I wish you the best of luck." She offered a reassuring smile. "Anything to drink?"

I stepped to Porter's side. "Milk, please."

He draped his arm over my back and squeezed my shoulder, pulling me into him as he did so. It was a simple gesture and I doubted he meant anything by it. My heart – and my slowly recovering lady bits – seemed to think otherwise.

I looked at him with the intention of asking – playfully – what the hell he was doing. Instead, a face-splitting smile formed. He squeezed my shoulder with his massive hand and grinned in return.

Lost in blissful thoughts of the moment we shared, I walked at Porter's side as he carried the pies, admiring him along the way. Once outside, he gestured toward an empty table with a nod. "How's that one?"

Patrons of various ages were scattered about the seating area. I was going to become a spectacle while I ate the pie, and there was nothing I could do about it. Even so, I agreed to sit in the seat he recommended.

"It's fine," I said.

Porter seemed, at least during our pie-eating adventure, to be kind, playful, and extremely polite. Those qualities, when combined with his intimidating looks and massive size, garnered my interest. All of it.

I wanted to get back on the orgasm machine. Or go order another pie and have him put his arm around me. We could ride around the countryside, stopping every fifteen miles or so for him to lick the seat free of my juices.

I could simply bring up the topic of sex and see if it aroused him as much as it did in the sushi restaurant, stealing glances under the table at his crotch as we talked. I had no interest, however, in the pie that sat between us.

"I'm pretty full." I pushed myself away from the table and looked at the pie with disgust. "That sushi is swelling in my belly."

Acting disinterested in the comment I'd made, Porter cut the tip from his pie. He lifted it to his mouth and paused.

"You said you wanted to get to know me." He nodded toward the pecan pie. "While we're eating we can get started on getting to know one another. What do you detest? What aggravates you?"

"Surprises," I responded without much thought. "I hate surprises."

He seemed surprised. "Really?"

"Yep. Can't stand them," I said through gritted teeth. "They make me itch. I'm itching right now just talking about it. What about you? What do you detest?"

"Liars," he responded. "Just tell me the truth, no matter what you think I want to hear. If someone out and out lies to me, it's over."

"I can't stand them, either," I admitted. "Liars suck."

He studied me for a moment, cut off a piece of pie, and then paused. "I want to know three things. One, what's your all-time favorite song, and why. Two, I want to know if you were required to put one saying on your headstone what it would be. And, three, what's the item on your little list that likely going to be the last one you achieve."

I loved question-answer games. By asking those three simple questions, Ghost Porter-Porter inched a little closer to my heart. Two of the questions were going to be easy to answer. The third, not so much.

"My favorite song is from a movie," I said. "At least that's where I heard it first. *Solsbury Hill*, by Peter Gabriel. I like it because it's perfect. It's written in imperfect time – a seven-four beat – which makes it feel like it's missing a beat in every measure. It sounds like the song is struggling to continue. It was his first song as a solo artist, and I wonder if he was struggling to continue at that time as well. I find it to be a spiritual song, but it doesn't feel like he's shoving spirituality down your throat when you listen to it. I love it. It's uplifting."

"I don't think I've ever heard that song." He sliced the tine of his fork through the ice cream-pie mixture. "I'm not a spiritual person, maybe that's why."

"The song has spiritual meaning, but it's not a spiritual song. I'll play it for you sometime," I said. "It's awesome."

"Keep going." He rolled his hand in a circle as if he were bored. "There's two more."

His admittance of not being spiritual troubled me. I wondered how he'd ever make it through cancer treatment without having a good relationship with God. I couldn't comprehend what it would be like, and the more I thought about it, the more bothered about it I became. I decided I'd ask about it later.

At least for the time being, I felt I needed to stick with the questions he'd asked of me. The next one was easy to answer. I'd given it considerable thought, long before meeting Porter. As far as I was concerned, it was the perfect epitaph. "If I had to put a saying on my headstone, it'd say, *it's not that bad.*"

"It's not that bad?" He laughed. "What's not that bad?"

"Everything," I said. "Life. Cancer. Whatever troubles you. Death. *It's not that bad.* I thought the saying would make people wonder as they looked at my headstone, especially about death. When I was diagnosed, I came to peace with death quickly. I wasn't afraid to die, and I don't think other people should be, either. It's not that bad."

"I like it. It covers a lot of ground," he said. "I might paint that shit on the fender of my bike."

I smiled. "Do it."

He set his fork down on the side of his plate. After studying me, he drew a slow breath and then looked away. A moment of awkward silence followed. Then, he met my gaze.

"What's your status?" he asked. "Now? With cancer?"

"It's gone," I replied. "I had an odd blood cancer. They cured it with treatment."

He gave me a look of disbelief. "Why do you go to the meetings?"

"It's important for survivors to go," I explained. "It's the equivalent of a sober man going to an AA meeting. It gives those just stepping in a ray of hope. My experiences help others."

He nodded. "I see."

"Can I ask what your diagnosis is?" I asked.

"I've got a brain tumor," he said as if it were no big deal. "Still don't know much."

"Treatment is a wonderful thing," I said.

The look on his face changed from acknowledgement to indifference. His cheeks lost their color.

I reached for his hand. "Remember, *it's not that bad.*"

He forced a crooked smile. "Number three?"

He'd eaten half his pie, and I hadn't so much as touched mine. I gestured toward his plate with a nod. "Let me get caught up, and then I'll answer."

With little effort, I gobbled down two pieces of pie. I'd eaten plenty of pecan pie in the past, none of which came close to the quality of what I was eating. I reached for another piece. "How did you find out about this place."

He pulled the fork past his tightened lips, wiping it clean as he removed it from his mouth. "We ride up here all the time."

"We?"

"I ride in a motorcycle club. We come up here as a group." He chuckled. "A couple of the guys really like pie."

"Are you one of them?" I asked. "The pie lovers?"

"Pies are a lot like women," he said. "A man can live the rest of his life without one as long as he's never reminded of their existence. However, once one is placed in front of him there's not much else that matters."

His response was cute and sad at the same time. I swallowed my pie and gave him my best sultry look. "What if there's a woman *and* a pie in front of you?"

He opened his arms wide. "All of what surrounds him vanishes." He gestured to the table. "Then, all that's left is her and the five and a half pieces of pie she needs to eat."

"Until she gets up and walks away. Right?"

His eyes narrowed. "What do you mean?"

"You said a man can live the rest of his life without a woman as long as she's not in front of him. Per your theory, when she walks away he's left needing nothing."

"That's not what I said. I said a man could live the rest of his life without a woman in it as long as he wasn't reminded of their existence. A smell, a sound, my wandering mind, the rear seat on my bike being empty. All those things could remind me of your existence. That reminder makes it impossible to live without you."

I liked the thought of him not being able to live without me but didn't particularly care for his analogy.

"You've got five and a half pieces of pie and one question to go," he said. "You better get busy, or we'll be stuck in rush hour traffic."

I could have told him anything for the answer to question number three, and he'd never know the difference. Telling him the truth would leave me feeling incompetent and weak. I was sure of it. I hated admitting that there was something everyone else on earth seemed to acquire without much effort, and for some reason, I wasn't allowed to have it.

"The task on my to-do list that's likely to be accomplished last, if at all, is number two." I poked the remaining piece of pie into my mouth and spoke over my mouth full of food.

"Fawn lub," I muttered.

He scrunched his nose and gave me a funny look. "What?"

"Fawn lub."

"If I spoke with my mouth full my grandmother would have smacked my ass," he said. "Swallow your pie, Abby."

I washed my pie down with a drink of milk and reached for another piece. "Sorry. Fall in love."

"Falling in love is on your to-do list?" he asked.

I sloved half the piece into my mouth and nodded. "Yeth."

"That's cute," he said.

I swallowed the wad of pie. "You think it's cute?"

He nodded. "I do."

"I think you're cute," I responded.

There went my mouth again, saying what my mind was thinking without giving me time to stop it. It was a common problem.

"Thank you," he said. "But, I'm far from cute."

"The grandmother comment made you cute," I explained. "I can imagine her slapping your shoulder with the back of her hand."

He laughed as if recalling a distant memory. "That's exactly what she did, too."

"Can I ask you three questions?" I asked.

He rocked his chair onto the rear legs. After looking me up and down, he grinned. "Sure."

I hadn't given it much thought, but I really didn't need to. My ability to think on my feet had been honed to perfection from years of interviewing people for my weekly YouTube show. While I considered my questions, I devoured the remaining portion of scrumptious pie I held, and then reached for piece number four.

I peered beyond the piece of pie and looked him over. His arms were crossed over his chest. Veins stood out in his massive forearms, both of which were decorated with various tattoos. His muscular shoulders rose into his thick neck. A day of stubble peppered his angular jaw. He looked rugged, unapproachable, and handsome all at the same time. Beneath that hard exterior, he was kind. With each moment we spent together, it became clearer.

Porter was a walking contradiction.

I brought the pie close enough that I could smell it, and hesitated. "Okay. One, do you believe in God? If not, please explain. Two, what living person do you admire the most? Then, the last one. Have you ever been in love?"

His gaze went skyward, and then drifted around the small patio, not stopping on any one thing for very long. Eventually, he lowered the chair onto all four legs and looked right at me.

"I'm not convinced God exists. I won't swear he doesn't, but I'm not convinced he does, either. For now, I'm sticking with this: God is a good thing for weak-minded people to attach themselves to. It allows them to find something to believe in when they are incapable of believing in themselves. Religion is one huge farce."

I wanted to go on a rant about his *weak-minded people* comment but knew not to. If a person of belief went on a tirade toward a skeptic or nonbeliever, it never ended well. I swallowed my desire and lowered my piece of half-eaten pie.

"I'm not religious," I said. "I'm spiritual."

A confused look washed over him. "What, exactly, does that mean?"

"I don't go to church. I believe everything a church going Christian believes, but I don't think I need to go to church to profess my beliefs. That's the only real difference. Spirituality is religion void of church service."

He nodded. "Always wondered what that meant."

"Is there a reason you don't believe in God?" I asked.

"Of all the shit we could be talking about, you had to pick this," he muttered under his breath.

He looked away. It seemed he was considering giving a response. I reached for my pie, hoping my lack of prying would encourage him to explain. After eyeing the entire patio, he met my gaze.

"I didn't know my father," he said. "My mother and I lived on my grandparent's ranch, in Montana. My grandfather acted as my father when I was young. He died of cancer when I was four. So, my grandmother stepped in as my father. She died of cancer when I was thirteen. My mother and I continued living on their ranch, with me taking care of all the livestock while she tried to keep the place picked up and presentable. She died of cancer when I was seventeen. So, there I stood. A man in a boy's body, in charge of one hundred and sixty acres that did nothing but remind him that everything he once loved was lost. All to cancer."

"I'm so sorry," I whispered, almost choking on the words.

"Explain to me what kind of God would do that to a little boy? Take everyone he's ever loved, and leave him alone?" He rocked the chair onto the rear legs and folded his arms over his chest. "A heartless one?"

He was remarkably calm. I, on the other hand, was an emotional wreck. Hearing of his losses made me want to leap over the table and take him in my arms. Instead, I summoned my inner strength and suppressed my emotion.

"I can't make you believe in God," I said. "So, I'm not going to try. I'll just hope that someday something will happen that might give you reason to believe."

He cocked an eyebrow of disbelief. "What might that be? What would be so significant that I'd forget about all the death?"

"I don't know. I do know how hard it will be for you to get through what you're going through alone. Are your friends in the motorcycle club a good support system?"

"Brothers," he said. "They're brothers, not friends."

"Your brothers. Do they provide support?"

He looked away. "They don't know."

My heart sank. He was going through cancer treatments alone. I couldn't imagine how helpless he was feeling. In my mind, there was a reason for everything. At that instant, I believed at least one of the reasons Porter was in my life was to receive my unconditional support.

"I'm here for you throughout this entire ordeal," I said. "I mean it. We'll get through this together."

"I'm pretty good at grieving alone," he said. "I'm experienced at it."

If we didn't change the subject, I was going to start crying. "What about the other two questions?" I asked.

He cocked his head to the side. "What were they?"

"What living person do you admire the most, and have you ever been in love?"

He lowered his gaze to beneath the table and stared for a moment. "Right now," he said, looking up as he spoke. "I think I admire you the most. And, no. I've never been in love."

I was flattered, confused, and, once again, filled with more emotion than I could handle. I mentally stammered to make sense of what he'd said.

"Me?" I coughed. "I don't deserve that kind of admiration."

"Beyond sitting in a meeting, hunting a rattlesnake, and eating together today, you don't know me. But, you offered to help me through this. You earned my admiration with that offer."

"Thank you." I smiled. "I'll try not to disappoint you."

His eyebrows raised slightly. "I'll try not to let you."

His lack of faith in God – and in mankind – was painfully obvious. I wanted to ask a question but feared the answer would do nothing but strengthen my belief that he had no faith in anything the world had to offer him. Eventually, my curiosity got the best of me.

"Why haven't you ever found love?" I asked.

"I've never looked for it. In fact, I've done a pretty good job of avoiding it. I figured if I ever allowed myself to fall in love, she'd just be taken from me. We don't get to choose our family, but we can choose who we let in our lives. If I don't let anyone in, I don't have to worry about getting hurt." Wearing a long face, he gestured toward the pie, half of which was now gone. "Don't worry about finishing that. You did better than I could have. We should probably look at riding back."

Our perfect day had been transformed into one that was filled with sorrow. Despite the clear sky, a cloud of sadness hovered over me. I wanted to fix him but feared I couldn't. Disappointed and depressed, I accepted defeat.

"Okay," I murmured, reaching for one last piece of pie as I stood. "I'll eat this on the way to the motorcycle."

He reached for the pie and pulled a piece from the tin. "I'll have one, too."

He rose from his seat and tossed the pie tin in the trash. For Porter, it was just another day. For me, it was a day that would always be earmarked with sadness. Shoulders slumped, I shuffled around the edge of the table and to his side.

I wanted to touch him. To hold him. To explain that although I had no idea why he had been exposed to so much loss, I believed that everything happened for a reason. At that moment, however, I couldn't fathom any reason that would call for him to lose so much.

We turned toward the street. Porter took a bite of pie. After swallowing it, he looked at me. His face was plastered with surprise. "This is good fucking pie."

I was too busy wallowing in my sadness to carry on a meaningful conversation. My gaze dropped to the sidewalk. "It's okay."

He pushed against my shoulder, forcing me to turn and face him. "What's wrong?"

"I'm sad." I bit off half the piece of pie in one bite. "Sad affuck."

"Why?" he asked. "It's been a good day."

I swallowed the mouthful of pie. "Not for me," I said without looking up. "I don't like it that you're so uncomfortable with life that you won't let people in it."

The index finger of his free hand came into view. He raised it to my chin, lifting it until our eyes met. Instead of continuing the conversation, which was what I expected, he leaned closer. In my sad state of being, I thought for an instant that he was going to kiss me.

And then. He did.

His tongue parted my lips. The sweet taste of syrup, pecans, and buttery pie crust tickled my taste buds. I closed my eyes. Starting at my feet, a tingling sensation ran through me, working its way up my body until I was completely encompassed by a sensation of euphoria.

I followed his every lead, kissing him in return. With a half-eaten piece of pie held loosely in my left hand, I pressed my right palm against the taut muscles of his upper back. Our chests collided. My heart faltered.

Sparks flew.

I wanted the kiss to last forever. We continued our embrace for an amount of time I couldn't accurately describe. When our lips parted, it seemed that we'd been kissing for a lifetime. I drifted back to earth. A kiss had never transformed me into mindless ball of emotion, but that one did.

Elated, I looked at him admiringly.

My mouth opened slightly, but my mind was incapable of sending a signal to my tongue. While I tried to remember how to turn thoughts into discernable dialogue, he broke the beautiful silence.

"I just let you in. All I ask is this." He swept my hair over my ear with a gentle finger. "Don't hurt me."

Gracious that he trusted me enough to allow me to cradle his damaged heart in my hands, I swallowed heavily, hoping to speak without revealing the mindless state he'd left me in.

"I won't hurt you," I breathed. "I promise."

As we walked to the motorcycle, with him so close I could taste the sweetness of his pecan pie laced breath, I hoped like hell I was right.

10

GHOST

I'd walked into the kitchen hoping to find a piece of pizza in the refrigerator. While I rummaged through the leftovers, my mother sat down at the kitchen table.

"What are you looking for?" she asked.

"Pizza."

"I threw it out," she said.

I spun around. "Why?"

"Because it was from Monday night." She gestured to the chair across from her. "You don't need to get sick."

I noticed a plate of cookies on the table that weren't there when I left for school. My mother often baked, and cookies were her specialty. I meandered to the table, lowered my backpack to the floor, and sat across from her.

"They're oatmeal and raisin," she said.

I searched my mind for what I might have done to warrant an after school sit down discussion. I'd been difficult to deal with since my grandmother's passing, but not so much that a face-to-face with my mother was necessary.

I looked her over, hoping to find a hint on her face as to what the conversation was going to be about. Short of her long dark hair and natural beauty, I found nothing.

She was a tall woman, standing five feet and ten inches without shoes. Lean and as muscular as most farm workers, she seemed much younger than her age of thirty-seven years. Her youthful appearance and hourglass figure earned her MILF – Mom I'd Like to Fuck – status from most of the kids at school.

They said it in my absence. I needed to kick off my boots to count the amount of kids who got their asses whipped for saying they wanted to fuck my mother. Nonetheless, I'd often overhear a conversation where someone wanted to *fuck Ghost's mother*. It never ended well for the person making the claim.

She reached for a cookie. "I just baked them."

It didn't take much coercing to get me to eat an oatmeal cookie. As my mother was aware, they were my favorite. Somewhat hesitant, I reached for the plate, still wondering what I did wrong.

I bent the cookie until it broke in two, and then met her hard-to-read gaze. "What did I do?"

She pinched a thumbprint-sized bite from the cookie and paused. "Nothing. I just wanted to have a talk with you."

It was never that simple. My mother rarely stuck her nose in my business. When she did, there was always a reason for it.

"About what?" I asked.

"You're sixteen," she began. "We probably should have had this talk long ago."

The sex talk.

She was going to have the sex talk with me over a plate of oatmeal cookies. I couldn't tell her that Amy Betterman had given me a hand job in her dad's truck, or that Shelly Pickert had sucked my dick at the end of sophomore year, just before summer break. I damned sure wasn't going to let her find out that I'd shared half a bottle of Goose's dad's whisky with Patty Wilson, and that she let me fuck her in her back yard while we were half drunk.

The hand job sparked interest in having girls do what I'd already spent twelve months trying to perfect. I learned that it was much more satisfying to watch a girl stroke my dick than do it myself.

Shelly's blowjob opened the door for me to try and stick my dick in every willing mouth in Great Falls, Montana. That love for blowjobs got my dick into Patty's very willing – and capable – mouth.

I found her insistence to swallow my spunk grotesque at first but was fascinated by it later. That fascination lured me to return day after day, while her mother was at work. Her willingness to suck my dick on any given day made her the perfect candidate for experimental sex.

The whiskey was more to boost my courage than to lower Patty's resistance. She was willing from the start. When the deed was done, I left Patty in the wet summer grass with her panties around one ankle and an empty bottle of whisky at her side. Filled with guilt, I couldn't run home fast enough to escape the cloud of shame that seemed to loom over me.

Her foul-smelling pussy left me wondering if sex was worth it. I spent a half hour in the shower trying to scrub the rotten residue off my dick, only to find out later that she had some sort of an infection.

Sitting across from my mother, I seriously doubted I'd ever have sex again. Blowjobs, on the other hand, were as commonplace as going to the movie theater, and I went to the movies quite often.

I situated my backpack but didn't look up. "Is this about sex?"

"Should it be?" she asked.

Not wanting to make eye contact with her, I fidgeted with the bag. "No."

"There's nothing down there that needs your attention, Porter. Look at me when I'm talking to you," she said.

I looked up. "Yes, ma'am."

"You're sixteen," she said. "We need to have this talk."

"I know about sex, ma." As if it would save me from continuing, I poked both halves of the cookie into my mouth.

"Have you had sex?" she asked.

I chewed the mouthful of cookie, wondering if I should tell her about Patty. I wanted my first sexual encounter to be memorable. Something

I'd talk about with my four half-brothers while we smoked cigarettes and drank warm beers. Instead, it was something I'd chosen to forget. It had only been seven months. It seemed like a lifetime had passed.

If I couldn't recall the details surrounding that night, I wondered if I could convince myself it didn't happen. A drunken dream. A sexual tale conjured up by a half-drunk teenage boy with a hard on and a mind filled with sexual desire. But the memories wouldn't go away. The underwear and jeans I threw away stood as a reminder each time I searched for a pair of jeans to wear to school.

Lying to my mother wasn't something that I'd ever done, and Patty Wilson's stinky pussy wasn't going to get me to start. I drew a long breath, reached for another cookie, and braced myself for her reaction.

"Yes," I murmured.

"Porter Quentin Reeves," she screeched. "You're sixteen!"

I slumped into my chair. "I'm sorry."

It was true. I was sorry. Not for the hand jobs or the blow jobs, but for the sex. I wished I could take it back, primarily because of the putrid stench that caused me to throw away my clothes.

She forced a sigh. "So am I. I shouldn't have yelled." She reached for another cookie. "Who was she? Will you tell me?"

I didn't want to. I doubted she'd be happy with my choice. Patty's mother was a barfly, and was talked about more than religion, politics, or the weather in our town. She wasn't married, and never had been. If the stories about her were true, she paid her rent with money she made from having sex with the ranch hands that flocked to town seeking seasonal work.

I looked away. "Patty Wilson."

"Dear God," my mother gasped. "We need to get you to the doctor."

My heart shot into my throat. "Why?"

She pushed herself away from the table. "If she's like her mother, she's liable to have a plethora of diseases. Did you wear a condom? Please tell me you wore a condom."

I didn't. I wondered if the foul odor was a hint of the many diseases she carried. "I uhhm." I offered an apologetic shrug. "I forgot."

Her eyes widened to the point I feared they'd fall from the sockets and roll across the table. "You forgot?" she bellowed. "Forgot? Porter, you don't *forget* the condom. That's like forgetting to get dressed before you step out into a blizzard."

"Yes, ma'am."

Her face distorted into a look that could only be described as disgust. "We'll get you to the doctor on Monday."

I reached for another cookie only because I didn't know what else to do. "Am I going to be okay?"

The look on her face faded, but not completely. She looked like she did the night she tried oysters for the first – and last – time. It was as if she could taste what I'd spent two weeks smelling.

She swallowed hard, and then forced a cracked smile. "I'm sure you'll be fine."

With a cookie in my left hand, I reached for my backpack with my right. I wanted to go to the upstairs shower and scrub my dick until I knew it was clean of everything Patty Wilson left on it.

"Is that all?" I asked.

"No," she said in a stern voice. "That's not all,"

I broke the cookie in two and waited for the wrath of my mother to come down upon me. Instead of attacking, she pinched a small piece of cookie between her fingers and gingerly placed it in her mouth.

After swallowing it, she sighed. "There will be girls that you'll want to have sex with for the sake of satisfying your urges," she explained. "It's sad, but that's what boys do."

"Then, one day, you'll meet someone you fall in love with. When you find that woman, you'll know who she is. She'll be different than the rest." She broke off another piece of cookie but didn't eat it. "Until you find her, you'll have meaningless sex. You need to be truthful – *before* you have sex – about what your intentions are. It's the right thing to do. The women are either a one-night-stand, or they're not. Do you know what a one-night-stand is, Porter?"

"Yes, ma'am," I responded. "I do."

"Don't you dare leave a woman wondering which category she

falls into. Ever. If she knows upfront what your intentions are, it'll save you – and her – a lot of emotional problems down the road."

"Yes, ma'am."

"Saying nothing leaves a woman to believe she's special. In her mind, the two of you are sharing something sacred. She'll believe, unless you tell her otherwise, that she's in a relationship with you. If you tell her upfront that you're only wanting sex, it gives her an opportunity to decide if she wants to simply satisfy her urges. You owe it to every woman to let her know where she stands. *Before* you have sex."

I nodded but didn't respond.

"One more thing," she said. "Don't you dare tell a woman she's special just to get in her pants. If I find out you've done such a thing, I'll hit you in the head with your grandmother's cast iron skillet."

"Yes, ma'am."

She cocked an eyebrow. "Porter?"

"Yes?"

She held my gaze. "Promise me."

"I promise."

"Now, and forever," she said.

"Yes, ma'am," I said. "I promise."

She studied the piece of cookie she held. "There's nothing that'll break a woman's heart quicker than believing she's special, only to find out later that she's been used for sex."

"I promised, ma. It won't happen."

I assumed she was speaking of my father but didn't ask. He was a subject we didn't discuss. I'd always suspected he was one of the ranch hands that came and went, and that she never really knew him. I now wondered if he had misled her into believing she was special, only to leave her with every indication that she was nothing more than a one-night-stand.

"Ma," I said, hoping to take her attention away from the cookie.

She looked up. I no longer questioned if she was speaking of the man who fathered me. Her wet eyes gave all the answers I needed.

"Yes?"

"I'll be honest with them, I promise." I glanced at my cookie and then met her teary-eyed gaze. "When can we go to the doctor?"

She chuckled as she wiped her eyes. "We'll go on Monday."

That Monday I found out I had Chlamydia. A dose of antibiotics cured it but left me forever fearful of having unprotected sex. From that day forward, I never had sex without using protection – or without first explaining to the woman that all we were doing was fucking.

My mother passed away the following year, but her words of wisdom were the fabric that held me together.

I blamed kissing Abby on my altered state of mind. The tumor had undoubtedly caused pressure to build on whatever portion of my brain produced logic. Consequently, it appeared I'd lost my ability to reason.

I was now forced to categorize her. She didn't fit in the one-night-stand slot, but I struggled to admit it. Nonetheless, she didn't belong there. That only left one place for her.

Placing her there scared the absolute shit out of me.

ABBY

Much to my satisfaction, we got stuck in rush hour traffic. By the time we reached San Diego three hours later, I had my doubts that the tingling sensation in my clit would ever subside.

Porter proved me wrong.

He was seated across from me. On the floor in front of him were his boots. His eyes were glued to them. He'd been frozen in that exact position since we walked into the room ten minutes earlier. The magical moment we shared at the pie shop was being dwarfed by the awkward silence.

"Is everything okay?" I asked.

Glassey-eyed, he continued to stare.

I waited for what seemed like an eternity. I cleared my throat. Snapped my fingers. Hummed. Sang softly. Turned on some music. Drummed my fingers on the end table. Sang louder.

Nothing.

After twenty minutes, I'd reached the breaking point.

"Porter!" I shouted.

He looked up. It wasn't like I'd startled him. He simply shifted his gaze upward until it met mine. Upon seeing me, his face distorted.

Confused, he rubbed his eyes and glanced around the room as if he didn't remember walking in.

"Are you okay?" I asked.

"Sorry," he said. "I was just thinking."

"About?"

"My mother," he said. "Something she told me when I was a kid."

In the amount of time it took to snap one's fingers, I went from being angry with him to hoping I could do something to comfort him. I tried to imagine losing my entire family to cancer. I couldn't comprehend it. I doubted anyone could. I wanted to hold him in my arms and tell him everything was going to be alright, but I didn't know if it was going to be.

"Do you want to talk?" I asked.

He wrung his hands together nervously. "We probably need to."

What I thought was confusion now appeared to be concern. He laced his fingers together, but it didn't last. He began to rub his hands along his thighs, and must have found comfort in it, because it was then that he began to speak.

"My mother once explained that there's two places you can categorize women when it comes to sex. A one-night-stand, or a relationship. I don't want to have a one-night-stand with you, Abby." He shifted his eyes to meet mine. "That only leaves one place for you to be."

His words bounced around in my head until I understood them. Incapable of speaking – at least for that moment – I took every inch of him into view. He was muscular from head to toe. He had a keen sense of humor. He had manners. He was a real biker. He had a big dick. He knew how to kiss a woman. And, he didn't want to use me for sex.

He was an anomaly.

A glitch in the male population.

"I don't want to have a one-night-stand with you, either," I said.

It wasn't the complete truth. Immediately following that kiss, I would have tossed my belief system aside, have let him screw me bow-legged and be on his way. Now that I knew he had other intentions, I wanted more. I wanted what every woman wants.

I wanted a relationship.

My mind began to assemble the pieces of Porter's puzzle. In doing so, I got confused. He said he'd never been in love. He'd never allowed himself to be. I couldn't help but wonder...

"You're not a uhhm," I stammered. "You've had sex before, right?"

He spit out a laugh. "A couple of times, yeah."

"Okay." I wiped my brow. "Me, too."

"I just. I've never," he muttered. "I've never done this."

I leaned forward. "*This* being *what*?"

"I've never been in a relationship," he admitted.

I studied him as I formulated my response. His look morphed to one of innocence. At that instant it came to me. Porter's hard exterior was his protection. The pursed lips. The muscles. His glare. Since we met, he'd been peeling away his outer layers and setting them aside. During his twenty minutes of silence, he'd removed his last layer of defense. I realized beyond the muscles and tattoos Porter was no different than anyone else. He was vulnerable.

Exposed and unprotected, he waited for me to respond. He may have been thirty years old on the inside, but the person seated across from me was seventeen and without a family.

Seventeen and scared.

"I've been in a relationship before," I said. "But I've been single for six years."

His eyebrows raised. "Six years?"

I nodded. "Uh huh."

"Holy shit," he gasped. "Why so long?"

I met Kelvin in college. We began having sex because having sex was fun. The sex changed from fun to freaky. Four years later, I realized all he and I shared was sex. He wanted nothing from me but to screw me at will, and I granted his wish.

Realizing it left me feeling foolish. It was my own fault. A relationship that begins for all the wrong reasons never becomes right. So, I left him, vowing to never place myself in the same position again.

I swallowed six years of frustration and let out a long, exhaustive breath. "At first because I was angry about how my last boyfriend treated me. To him, I was someone to screw and nothing more. When the anger faded, I realized no one put me in that relationship but me. I decided the next time I committed myself to someone, it was going to be because I wanted to be in a *relationship* with them, not because I simply wanted sex. Hopefully, knowing that lets you make some sense of my choice to eat pie instead of jumping in bed."

"It does," he said with a nod. "Thanks for explaining it."

Thirty minutes earlier, my plans were to christen each room in my home, stopping only when we'd completed the task. After verbally admitting what caused the failure of my previous relationship, I now felt a need to remind myself that it wasn't simply sex that drew me to Porter.

It wasn't going to be easy, but I needed to exercise sexual restraint for at least one night. Looking at the big picture, I knew it wouldn't make a difference. In my manner of reasoning, however, it would prove to me that I was in it for all the right reasons.

It a was necessary step in securing my relationship's future. Ridiculous, but necessary.

"I'm exhausted." I stretched and did my best to fake a yawn. "I want to take a shower and unwind."

He reached for his boots. "Okay."

"You don't have to leave." I waved my hands toward the bathroom. "You can take a shower with me, or after me, I don't care."

I couldn't believe the words that were spewing from my mouth.

I swallowed heavily. "We're uhhm. We're not having sex, though."

He returned a blank stare.

I managed a slight smile. "I can cook something light to eat afterward if you like."

He tossed his boots aside and stood. "This is crazy."

"What's that?"

"Not having sex," he said.

I studied him, trying to imagine what he'd look like soaking wet. "Does it bother you? Being here and not having sex?"

It bothered me, but I wasn't about to admit it. I regretted telling him he could take a shower with me. I knew if he chose to accept my offer that it would take every ounce of my willpower not to ride him like a pogo stick.

"It's just not what I'm accustomed to," he said. "I guess if I want things to be different, I have to do different things."

"So, you're going to stay?" I asked, trying to hide my excitement.

"I'll go downstairs and grab a change of clothes off my bike while you're in the bathroom." He turned toward the door. "I'll shower after you're done."

I guessed he felt the same way I did regarding showering together. It was a good thing, because I planned on relieving myself of some serious tension when I was in there.

"Your loss," I teased. "It's probably for the best, though. I doubt you'd be able to keep your hands off me. I'm irresistible when I'm wet."

"That sounds like a challenge." He turned around and looked me over. "I've never been one to back down from a dare."

"Wait. What?" I stammered.

"Hold on just a minute while I grab my clothes." His mouth formed a smug little smile. "I'll go ahead and shower with you."

Being in the shower with Porter would be a true test.

One I was sure to flunk.

12

PORTER

A lthough I fantasized about having sex with Abby, I didn't feel the need to act on those desires. The absence of sex left me at a loss for what I should be doing with our time. In the past, if I spent more than an hour with a girl it was because we were having sex. Consequently, the time I spent with women taught me very little about what to do with a woman if we weren't having sex.

I had zero experience at being romantic but wanted to act in a manner that she found pleasing. More than anything, I wanted whatever Abby and I shared to be in complete contrast to the one-night-stands that defined the sexual experiences of my past.

The trip to Julian drew me even closer to Abby. A ray of hope now shined from her being. A hint that cancer didn't always consume its victims. Some people beat deadly disease, and she stood as proof. I doubted I could defeat a brain tumor without medical attention, but I could always hope.

Filled with that hope, I began to inch my way into her life.

While Abby poured two glasses of wine, she confirmed my decision was a good one. "Truthfully, I'm glad you decided to let me shower alone."

"I know me well enough to know I would have made achieving your goal difficult."

She corked the bottle of wine and handed me a glass. "What goal?"

I lifted my wine glass. "Why's this stuff pink?"

"It's pink Moscato." She sipped the wine. "What goal?"

I tasted the wine. The sweetness was such that I almost spit it out. I gave a taut smile and looked at the glass in disbelief. "Holy shit. This stuff's sweet."

"What. Goal?" she asked, her tone demanding.

"Not having sex."

"Oh." She gestured toward the living room. "That."

Her home was along Mission Beach Boulevard on a corner lot that faced the ocean. I had no idea what it cost, but I knew it wasn't cheap. If Tito's opinion of her income was correct, I doubted she had any problems paying for it.

The floors were constructed of wide slats of gray hardwood. There weren't many interior walls, but what was there was painted white. A winding staircase manufactured of steel and contrasting wood planks led to an upstairs loft, and the kitchen was filled with state-of-the-art stainless-steel appliances.

Decorated in a colorful array of yellows, blues, reds, and greens, it looked like what I expected a beachfront condo to look like. Her furniture was a combination of leather and fabrics, all of which were contemporary in design. Personally, I felt most of it would be more suitable in an art studio than a home.

I meandered to one end of a pea green fabric sofa. It looked as uncomfortable as a concrete park bench. When I took a seat, I was surprised by the comfort. "Damn." I pressed my palm against the cushion. "This thing's comfortable."

She took a seat at the left end of the same piece of furniture. "I think everything in here is comfortable."

"That weird-looking chair I sat in earlier was," I admitted.

She looked at the chair. "It's not weird-looking, it's ergonomic."

While her attention was elsewhere, I admired her. Dressed in a pair of cut-off sweat shorts and a tattered white tee shirt that said *mermaid* on the front and *off-duty* on the back, she looked adorable. While she took a drink of her wine, I noticed her nipples were as hard as rocks.

Normally attracted to girls with curvy asses and huge boobs, it seemed strange to be so physically drawn to Abby. She was petite, short, and had boobs that may not have filled a "B" cup bra. Nonetheless, her looks alone sucked me in like a vortex.

Noticing her hard nipples started me on a rapid downslide. Knowing I'd be trying to hide a hard on if I continued to look at her, I shifted my eyes to the white leather chair. It was low in the front, high at the knees, low in the seat, and then curved upward again.

"It's shaped like a backward 'S'," I said. "It's weird-looking."

"That's what makes it comfortable."

I studied the chair. Upon a closer inspection, it seemed to be designed for fucking. The high spot intended for one's knees would be perfect for her hips, forcing her ass high in the air. I glanced at her, and then at the chair. In seconds, I was mentally fucking her while she was face-down on the surface of the *ergonomic* piece of furniture.

I took a shallow drink of my wine. In being reminded of the sweetness, I opted to raise the bottom of the glass and down the contents. With the empty glass dangling loosely from my hand, I shifted my eyes from the chair to Abby.

My cock twitched.

I rested my left arm over my lap and tried to hide my rapidly growing appreciation of Abby's beauty. Knowing if I didn't immediately divert my train of thought that she'd soon notice my level of excitement, I decided to change the subject to something that would kill the mood.

"I showed the fellas that picture you sent me," I said.

Her eyes narrowed. "Which one?"

I pressed my forearm against my cock. "How many pictures have you sent me?"

She tugged against the hem of her shorts and then crossed her athletic legs. "Only one that I can remember."

Her toned legs all but tossed me off the edge of the celibacy cliff. I pressed my forearm firm against my rigid cock.

I winced in pain. "That'd be the one. You, me, and a rattlesnake."

"What did they say?"

"They said *what were you doing rattlesnake hunting with Uptown Abby?*"

The color drained from her face. "They recognized me?"

It wasn't easy to have a conversation while my cock was standing at attention. I repositioned myself in the seat and pushed against it with my elbow. It pushed back with greater force. The pain made me feel that I might just fucking faint.

She gave me a funny look. "Are you okay?"

"I'm fine," I lied. "Why?"

She swiveled her upper body to face me, giving me a full view of nipples that were trying to cut their way through the worn fabric of her tee shirt. I tore my eyes away from them and focused on the wall behind her.

"You look like you're uncomfortable," she said.

I was uncomfortable. I had a raging hard on and wanted to fuck her so bad I was dizzy. Light-headed and feeling half sick from a lack of sex and overindulgence in pink wine, I gazed beyond her, toward the kitchen. "I think I drank that wine too fast."

"Do you want a glass of water?" she asked.

I didn't. I wanted her face down in the ergonomic chair with her bare ass in the air and her wet hair balled in my clenched fist. But now wasn't the time. I needed to honor her desire to be sex-free for one night. I had no idea how an evening of sexual agony was going to solve any problems, but it was what she wanted. Therefore, I intended to give it to her.

In support of her wishes, I pressed my forearm against the head of my rising dick. When I did, the pain caused my back to arch.

"Are you sure you're okay?" she asked.

I arched my back even more. "Back spasm."

"From being on the bike all day?"

"Probably from the gym," I lied. "Might have pulled a muscle."

"Want me to rub your back?" She set her glass of wine on the end table. "It might make you feel better."

She raised her hands and fanned her fingers as if preparing to rub my shoulders. If she touched me, there was no doubt the problem would escalate. I needed to make some space between us. Standing was out of the question. I inched my way to the arm of the sofa, gaining six inches of distance and nothing more.

Pinned against the pea green burlap fabric, my throbbing cock reminded me of each heartbeat. I looked at her with fear in my eyes.

"What?" she asked. "You don't like being touched?"

The thought of her touching me excited the absolute fuck out of me. Moving my arm away from my cock would lead her to believe I was exactly what she didn't want me to be. There was no way I could hide my state of arousal if she was giving me a back rub.

"No." I shook my head. "I like being touched."

She moved closer. "Let me rub your shoulders."

If she touched me, I'd probably come in my pants. Before I could blurt out an objection, she came even closer. Her milky smooth thigh brushed against mine.

The contact, albeit small, pushed me over the edge of the cliff.

Enough was enough. I was thirty-one years old, my days on earth were limited, and I was in the presence of the most attractive woman I'd ever seen. My arousal was natural. Whether I acted on my desires or not, there was no sense trying to hide it any longer.

"Look," I said, lifting my forearm. "I'm sorry, but I can't stop thinking about what it would be like to fuck you on that stupid chair. I'm not saying I want to do it, I'm just saying I can't stop thinking about it."

Her gaze dropped to my bulge. Upon seeing it, her eyes shot wide. "This is dumb," she said. "Let's do it."

"Do what?"

"Let's screw." She motioned toward the chair. "On that."

"You said you needed to--"

"You're wearing jeans and a wife beater," she said. "This is torture. I can't take it anymore. My nipples are so hard they ache. I'm so wet it's uncomfortable. I'm attracted to you because I'm attracted to you. What am I trying to prove?"

"So, you're okay with--"

She nodded. "I am."

"You want to--"

She tugged against the hem of her shorts. "I do."

"I don't want to force you to--"

"Come here," she said.

I shook my head. "I can't stand up."

She lifted the oversized leg of her shorts and nodded toward the opening she'd created. "Stick your hand in there."

I wasn't about to argue with her. With my eyes locked on hers, I slid my hand along the inside of her thigh, from her knee to her pussy.

She began to giggle like a teen.

"Sorry," she said, her face blushing as she spoke. "It's been a while."

I smiled in return and continued. As the knuckle of my index finger bumped against her clit, she flinched and let out a moan. Her pussy was just as she said it would be. Soaking wet. It was also, much to my surprise, surrounded by hair.

I grabbed her shorts by the waistband and pulled them away from her stomach. With the curiosity of a cat, I peered inside. A two-inch long vertical strip of hair as wide as my index finger was just above her otherwise perfectly pretty little pussy.

"What the fuck is that?" I gasped.

Her eyes shot wide. "What?"

I nodded toward the trail of pubes. "That. It looks like a caterpillar is crawling out of your twat."

"It's a landing strip," she said matter-of-factly. "They're popular again."

I took one last look for conversations sake, and then released the elastic waistband of her shorts. I had news for her. That shit was never popular in my eyes. It needed to be shaved off and shaved off quickly.

Before I puked.

I laughed until I vomited in my mouth. After swallowing a

mouthful of pink wine and bile, I shook my head in disagreement. "You need to shave that shit off." I chuckled. "Really."

"They're coming back. They really are," she said with a laugh. "By the end of the year, everyone will have one."

I burst into laughter, again. I couldn't help it. When I finally caught my breath, I shook my head. "Everyone but you."

She crossed her arms over her chest. "I shouldn't have believed that article, huh?"

"What article?"

She looked away. "In Cosmo. It said they were the new thing. The new *old* thing. It was like a jungle down there when we met. After reading that article, I trimmed it into that. I thought you'd like it."

"So, you've been planning this?"

"Hoping." She laughed. "I was hoping."

"Well," I said. "I'm hoping you'll shave that strip of nastiness off."

She looked at me. "Now?"

"That's my recommendation," I said. "I'm not interested in getting hair stuck in my teeth."

"Oh, yeah. This thing's coming off." She leaped from the couch. "Right F-ing now."

After five agonizing minutes, the sound of her clearing her throat caused me to look up.

"How's this?" she asked.

She was standing in the opening of the corridor that led to the bathroom. Wearing nothing but a grin, she pressed her hands to her hips.

Awestruck by her naked beauty, I stared.

"Well?" she asked.

Her hair was disheveled and partially obscured her face, hiding one of her insanely sexy blue eyes. The other one looked right at me. Her breasts were small and perky. Upon seeing them, I decided everything about her was exactly the way I wanted it to be.

My eyes dropped to her waist. Her pretty little pussy was as bald as the palm of my hand.

"You look good enough to eat," I said.

She cocked her hip. "Are you hungry?"

My first sexual experience with Abby was going to be a selfless act. I'd never had sex with the intention of satisfying anyone other than myself. I was eager to have Abby be my first.

Certain there were going to be many firsts with Abby, I grinned and nodded. "I sure am."

13

ABBY

Although I hadn't tried it out yet, I'd purchased the chair in question with the sole intention of using it for sex. Eager to feel Porter's skin against mine, I nervously walked the length of the living room.

He rubbed the light scruff that had developed on his jawline over the last few days. When I stopped in front of him, he let out a long breath. "Jesus."

"What?"

Starting at the floor, he took every inch of me in, slowly. When his gaze met mine, he smiled. "You're perfect."

I worked hard to keep myself in shape, but there was nothing I could do about my teenage breasts. I'd been self-conscious about them since high school.

I felt like covering them, but I didn't. "I'm far from perfect."

"Turn around," he breathed.

I faced the bathroom.

"No," he said. "Turn in a circle. I want to see every inch of you."

I did a low-speed pirouette with my hands over my head, feeling self-conscious as my front side came into his view. I wished I had boobs, but not so much that I was ever going to alter my body. Porter needed to find a way to accept me as his flat-chested girlfriend.

"You are…you're fucking gorgeous." He looked me up and down, taking his time to do so. "Come here."

I took a few hesitant steps.

He slipped one hand behind my waist and pulled me into him. After spinning me in a semi-circle, he planted his lips against mine.

Once again, the kiss transported my mind to another place. An existence not of this earth. As if I wasn't already prepared to give myself to Porter, the kiss confirmed that something between us was special.

The chemistry we shared during a kiss could not be denied, and I loved being reminded of it.

He broke our embrace, placed his hands on either side of my face, and looked me in the eyes. "Beautiful."

An almost indiscernible *thank you* puffed from my lips.

He looked me over. A worried look washed over him. "Are you sure you want to do this?"

I couldn't believe he was second-guessing our decision to have sex. Prepared to fight for the dick that was rightfully mine, I lowered my hands and cocked my hip. "I haven't had sex in six years," I coughed. "You can either give it to me, or I'm going to take it."

"Not that. The relationship thing. With me. It's just…you're more beautiful than…" He took a long look at me. It appeared he was on the verge of tears. "You're more beautiful than anything I've ever seen in my life. You could be with any man on this planet. Are you sure you want to be with me?"

The thought of sex excited me. But. I also wanted Porter. He was kind, had a dry sense of humor, and seemed to mesh well with my inability to retain my thoughts. If there was any doubt in my mind that he was the right man, it vanished after his confession of my beauty. I fought against the lump that was rising in my throat and nodded my head.

"Take off your pants," I said, my voice cracking from emotion. "I'll show you how much I want to be with you."

Obviously as eager as I was to get started, he fumbled with his belt. In a moment, he carefully pushed his jeans past his rigid member. When the denim cleared the tip, the fleshy monster sprung free.

I gasped. Not because it was oddly shaped. Or because it was shocking. It was shocking, but that wasn't why I gasped. I gasped because I was in cock-heaven.

His dick was so big it needed its own postal code.

Unlike many women, I'm a true believer that bigger is always better when it comes to sticking things in my pussy. I've never been one to hope that my hips get dislocated from a sexual encounter, but I want to be as close to a dislodging a hip as I can possibly be, that much I know.

Not knocking a hip out of socket with the schlong Porter was packing was going to take some precautionary measures. With my eyes glued to his rigid thickness, I rubbed my hands together feverishly. "Holy mother of all things dick related."

"You think it's going to be alright?" he asked. "You're like, tiny."

His stiff cock bounced when he talked. I wanted him to tell me a three-thousand-word story, so I could watch it, but there was no way I could wait that long. I needed that dick, and I needed it desperately.

"Babies come out of these things," I said excitedly. "We can make it fit, I know we can."

I had my doubts that it would *fit*, but I knew if we forced it long enough, it would eventually either slide in or rip me apart. I was beyond eager to feel it inside me, and I didn't care what happened through the course of getting there. Porter would find out in time that I was kind of a weirdo when it came to sex, anyway.

He tossed his wife beater into the pile of clothes that was gathering beside the white ergonomic chair. Now standing in front of me wearing nothing but a massive dick and a pair of socks, I got my first glimpse of Porter without a shirt on.

Drool pooled against the inside of my lower lip.

I was already horny. Blindingly so. After seeing his washboard abs and the two slabs of meat that made up his chest, I was horny and mesmerized by *Porter's* beauty. I needed to say something. Not in an effort to be a copycat, or because of my sarcastic nature.

His body was just…perfect.

I pointed at him and wagged my finger up and down. "*That* is beauty. Dear God, you look divine."

He blushed. "Thank you."

I made Ghost Porter-Porter blush.

He *was* human.

Naked and horny, I could feel my heart beating between my legs. I was done with the small talk and ready to get down to business. Sexual business.

"Where do you want me?" I asked.

He gestured toward the chair. "Face down, on that weird chair."

I all but dove head-first onto the odd-shaped chair, hiking my ass high in the air. I had no idea how or where he wanted me, but something about the chair's shape screamed face down-ass up, so that's what I did.

As I situated myself onto the soft leather, I felt Porter's hands against my inner thighs. In response, I spread my legs wide enough to drive a truck through them. While I juggled the possibilities of fingers, dick, or a combination of both being poked into my willing cavities, I felt something soft and wet part my lower lips.

I drew an uneven ecstatic breath as he forced his tongue deep into me.

"Oh, God yes. Fuck me with your tongue," I moaned.

I was a natural dirty talker, saying what came to mind before I had a chance to stop myself from speaking. I hoped Porter was okay with my sexual banter, because stopping it was impossible.

In an instant, he let me know by doing just as I asked.

A jolt of electricity ran through me – from my clit to my painfully hard nipples. I flinched in ecstasy while his talented tongue traveled in and out of my wetness, teasing my deprived – and freshly shaved – pussy.

In a matter of seconds my body shuddered, expelling its first orgasm. Porter sensed it, burying his tongue even deeper into my cavern of desire. Having him feed off my sexual bliss was a huge turn-on and made the peak of that orgasm wilder than anything I'd previously experienced.

I collapsed from the climactic release, catching myself before I face-planted onto the chair.

"Holy shit," I gasped. "You've got a talented tongue."

"Your little pussy was made for licking," he said.

I felt his weight shift and glanced over my shoulder just in time to see him unrolling an oversized condom onto his rigid shaft. Giddy with excitement, I turned away, hoping to have his penetration be a complete surprise.

He didn't let me down. Not really, anyway.

I felt his weight against the chair. Immediately following, the tip of his massive dick pressed against my opening. My mouth opened wide as he pushed his size X dick against my size Y pussy.

Then, the pressure went away.

"What are you doing?" I whined.

He sighed. "You're too tight."

It was the craziest excuse I'd ever heard. "Don't be a pussy," I fumed. "Force it in there."

"Did you just call me a pussy?" he asked.

He didn't sound *overly* angry, so I pushed a little more.

"I did," I admitted. "Because you were being one. I might be little, but I'm a big girl. Fuck me like one."

It was all the encouragement he needed. After positioning the head of his throbbing cock against my dripping wet slit, he did just as I asked. Five seconds later, I was ready to grab his wife beater from the floor and wave it high in the air in surrender. And then…

Pop!

His entire length, or so I thought, shot into me. When it did, all the air shot from my lungs. I gasped in delight and partially collapsed tits-first onto what was supposed to be the back of the chair.

"You're freaking huge," I exclaimed.

He chuckled a sinister laugh. "That's half of it."

I closed my eyes. *Thank you, Jesus.*

I clenched my jaw. "Give it to me."

Slowly, he began to push his weight against me. Inch by satisfying inch, he entered me until there was no more space. the tip of his dick was bottoming out against inner flesh I had no idea existed.

I caught my breath. "Is that all of it?"

"That's it."

Relieved, I let out a breath in preparation of what was to come. "That's good," I said. "Because you just ran out of real estate."

He withdrew himself slowly, and then pushed the entire length back in. When he was halfway in, I felt myself contract. I couldn't help it. Having him inside of me felt magical.

"Are you having another--"

"You're going to have to be quiet I'm having an incredible orgasm right now and I don't want to talk about it," I blurted. "I'm sorry, this is so perfectly oh my God..."

I lifted my head and smiled into the living room's abyss. When the tip of his dick pressed against the bottom of what I always felt was a bottomless pussy, I sucked a breath.

"Don't move," I groaned.

Micro-orgasms shot through me like miniature shock waves, one after the other. After being pleasured by no less than a dozen, the mother of all orgasms began to build within me. I had no idea if a man could sense when he was preparing to climax – because I'd never asked – but I could sense when mine were coming.

And the one that was en route would tilt the seismograph at a nine-plus on the Richter scale.

His massive chest pressed against my back. feeling his weight against me was oddly comforting. I allowed myself to collapse against his weight, feeling small and powerless, which was a place I loved to be when having sex.

He kissed my neck. There were a few things that drove me bat shit crazy, and kissing my neck was on the top of the list. I moaned to let him know where I stood on neck kissing. Hearing that expressed satisfaction drove him to kiss and chew against my sensitive flesh from my shoulders to my earlobes.

In a sexually-induced frenzy, and on the verge of a serious meltdown, my body tensed and released repeatedly.

I felt his cock twitch. Then, I felt it swell.

That little bit of movement was all it took. My pussy clenched him like a vise. He gave two quick full-length thrusts. His breathing began to sound labored. He gave two more thrusts.

I arched my back and bellowed out my satisfaction for a job well done while the orgasm took control of my soul. My muscles seized. I pushed my weight against his, lifting the two of us from the surface of the chair I was quickly developing a loving relationship with.

Then, he gave one last savage thrust.

Amidst the smell of musky cologne, the climax came to a head, blasting my mind into outer space.

Porter let out a blood curdling howl.

When the screaming ended, I crumbled into a pile of very happy flesh. Porter came to rest at my side. Side-by-side we remained, silently admiring each other's sweaty bodies.

In the past, sex had been more of a mechanical act than anything. Insert dick and fuck hard – while taking time to pull hair, slap an open palm against my ass, bite me anywhere, or dig your nails into my flesh.

When the sex ended, I always regretted the extremes I allowed myself to experience – all in hope of achieving an orgasm that was better than the last.

Sex with Porter was the opposite. There was feeling involved. I felt *the act* on the outside. I felt constant bliss on the inside. The difference between what we shared and what I'd experienced in the past was vast.

I had my doubts that I could ever go back to having someone simply fuck me. After thinking about it, I decided there was no freaking way.

"If you leave me, ever, I'll find you," I said with a laugh. "I just want you to know that. I'll be that crazy bitch that's lurking outside your window with a butcher knife and a big rock."

He looked at me like I'd kicked his dog. "Where the hell did that come from?"

"You ruined me." I chuckled "I love how it feels to have you inside of me. I mean it. I F-ing love it. I was joking about the rock, though. Not the knife."

He grinned. "Really?"

"No."

He shook his head, and then smiled. "That was phenomenal. For me, anyway."

"More than anything," I said. "More phenomenal than anything."

"More than pecan pie?"

"Any. Thing," I clarified. "I have no idea how I'll ever make it through life without that dick, or the guy that's attached to it."

"That was some good pie," he said. "I can't believe I topped it."

I slapped my hand against his bare ass, and then wished I hadn't. It was harder than I wanted it to be.

"Stop it, or you're going to get it," he said.

I didn't know what *getting it* meant, but I knew I wanted whatever Porter had to offer. So, I slapped his ass again, only harder.

He rolled me onto my back and kissed me deeply. The kiss took my mind where sex simply couldn't. It was a place where nothing else existed but the two of us. A place where passion thrived. Where hearts faltered. Where a magical sense of belonging to something bigger than life took control of a person's very being.

It was there that I realized Porter was special.

So special, that I could never let him go.

GHOST

It had been eight days since Abby and I made love for the first time. In that time, I'd all but abandoned my brothers in the MC, only seeing them during our mandatory Wednesday meeting. Abby had become the most important element in my life. From what I could see, I'd become an equally important part of hers.

I was fascinated with my unquenchable desire to spend time with her. My mother had explained that when I found the love of my life I would know it. Although I hadn't fallen in love with Abby yet, I had my suspicions that she was that woman.

I opened the diner door and held it open. No less than fifty eyes ratcheted toward me. After Abby walked past, I released the door and sized up each of the men who seemed to be more interested in us than their food. Eventually, they all went back to eating their meals.

"Does this place only serve Marines?" I whispered.

"No," she responded. "But a lot of them come in here."

We took a seat at an empty booth. A matter of seconds after were seated, a middle-aged man approached our table. He wore a buzz-cut, was built like Rambo, and possessed the ability to burn holes through solid objects with his glare. After warming my skin with his stare for a few long seconds, he shifted his eyes to Abby.

"Has he been feeding you?" He looked her over. "You look like you've lost weight."

"*He* has a name," she said in a snide tone. "It's Porter."

I felt as though she was introducing me to a member of her family. One who was angry about her decision to bring me into his diner for lunch. Nonetheless, I put on a smile, stood, and extended my hand.

"Porter Reeves," I said. "Pleasure to meet you, Sir."

"I was an enlisted Marine," he barked. "I'm not a *Sir*."

"Geeeoooorge," Abby said. "Be nice."

He looked me over as if we were preparing to fight. He cocked his head to the side. "This is as nice as I'm going to get," he responded, directing his comment to Abby, but keeping his eyes locked on me.

"Sorry," I said in an apologetic tone. "*Ma'am* and *Sir*. It's habit."

"The military, a Boys Ranch, or upbringing instill such habits." He looked me dead in the eyes and shook my hand firmly. "Which is it?"

Through that handshake, he let me know what Abby meant to him. Any mistreatment of her would be dealt with harshly. As a reassurance that he had nothing to worry about, I held his gaze and returned his firm grip.

"Upbringing," I said. "I was raised in Montana by two women. My mother and my grandmother. If I wasn't polite, I got my ear twisted in a knot."

He released my hand. "Damned fine country, Montana. Been fishing there a few times."

I grinned. "I grew up on a hundred and sixty acres. We had four ponds and a stream that ran through it. I've pulled many meals out of those ponds."

He pursed his lips and shook his head lightly. "A fresh stream trout on the grill is about as good as it gets."

I nodded. "I'll agree to that."

George sat across from Abby and gestured toward the seat next to her. As directed, I took a seat at her side.

He lowered his chin and looked Abby over. "You look tired."

"I am. We were up all night," she said. "Talking."

His eyes shot to me. One eyebrow raised. "Talking?"

"We talked," I said with a nod.

It was true. We had talked. While we were having sex.

His brows knitted together. That look of disbelief remained locked on me for a moment, and then he shifted his gaze to Abby. "Talking?"

Abby rested her forearms on the table's edge and returned George's glare. Locked eye-to-eye, they stared at each other for an uncomfortable amount of time. Then, Abby drew a long breath through her nose and leaned against the back of the booth.

She crossed her arms and exhaled through her teeth. "I'm not going to do this with you, George. I'm thirty years old. You are well aware of how many men have tried to take me on a date in the last six years. Of those, how many have I gone out with?"

He stared.

"How many?" she demanded.

"None," he said. "That I know of."

"That's right," she huffed. "None."

He glanced at me and then at her. "What's that got to do with anything?"

"After six years, I've found someone that likes me because of *me*. And, it just so happens that he's honest, genuine, funny, and has a big heart." She said, her voice laced with attitude. "Now, if you'd be so kind as to get us a few menus, I'd like to eat. I'm so hungry I feel like I might pass out."

"Up all-night talking made you hungry?" He shifted his eyes to meet mine. "While you were *talking*, did you wear protection?"

"Yes, Sir. I did," I responded. "Always."

His jaw tightened. His muscles tensed. I prepared to block the punch I was sure he would throw.

Instead, he gave a sharp nod. "Let me get a few menus."

While he stomped to the back of the restaurant, I moved to the other side of the booth and let out a sigh. "That went better than expected."

"Basically, I have two dads," she replied.

I motioned toward the kitchen. "Does he always walk like that?"

"All the time."

"So, he's not mad?" I asked.

"Oh, I think he's mad," she said with a laugh. "But he always walks like that."

"What's he like?" I asked.

"He's just like he is right now, all the time," she replied.

"No," I said. "What *does* he like. What does he do in his spare time?"

"Well, he likes to go up north and hunt. And he likes to fish. Oh, and he likes fast cars. Old-school fast cars, not the new stuff."

The easiest way to win a man over was to have something in common with him. If there was one thing I liked almost as much as fucking, it was driving a fast car. The rumpity-rump of a carbureted engine with a racing cam in it was music to my ears. As he made his way back to the table, I grinned and cracked my knuckles.

"Watch this," I said.

George handed Abby her menu, and then held mine in front of me. When I reached for it, he pulled it away.

"One hair. Just one," he said through his teeth. "That's all you'll have to harm on her for me to hunt you down and put my thumbs through your eye sockets."

"George!" Abby shouted.

"That's all I've got to say," he said. "I made my point."

I reached toward the menu and paused. "What's your recommendation?"

"Depends on what you like," he snapped. "I can't decide for you."

"I was taught to eat what's put in front of me," I responded. "Just send me whatever you think your specialty is."

"I'll have the Abby and a glass of water," Abby said, handing her menu across the table. "I see you've got it on the menu now. Thank you for that, by the way."

"If you didn't abandon this place, you'd know it was on the menu," George grumbled.

"You named something after her?" I asked.

"Best sandwich on the menu," George gloated. "According to her."

I raised my index finger. "Bring me your specialty and one of those, too. I'd like to try it. Water to drink, please."

"Isn't that cute," Abby said. "Porter's going to eat an Abby."

George took a step away from the table and crossed his arms so violently air shot from his lungs. "We don't allow sexual innuendos in the diner," he said though clenched teeth. "They're inappropriate."

"So's dropping the f-bomb, and you toss it around like you're saying *hi*," Abby responded.

"Your food will be up in a minute." He turned away with a huff.

When he was out of sight, I looked at Abby. "Jesus. You're being rude as hell. Are you *trying* to piss him off?"

"No, I'm just trying to let him know this is real. That it's not a fling, or whatever. Throwing it in his face is the best way to get him to accept it, believe me."

I shrugged. "You know him better than I do."

"You asked me what George liked to do with his time, and then you said *watch this*. You didn't do anything. What was that about?" she asked.

"I was going to say something to him, but I never got a chance," I explained. "I will, though."

"What were you going to say?"

"I was going to tell him about my Mustang." I reached for my phone. "I just finished building it."

"An old one, or a new one?"

"Old."

She smiled. "I love old mustangs."

"I wondered if that was the case," I said. "Based on a comment you made in one of your videos."

She squinted. "Which one?"

I had yet to talk to her about it. After getting to know her more, I really didn't see much value in it.

"The gym rat video."

"You saw that?" She covered her face with her hands. "You're not mad?"

"I was. I'm not now."

She lowered her hands. "I was just…it was parody, or whatever."

"I figured as much," I said as I scrolled through the photos on my phone.

"What about that video made you think I liked Mustangs?"

"You mentioned *Gone in Sixty Seconds*." I selected a photo from my gallery and handed her my phone. "The star of the show was Eleanor, the sixty-seven Mustang."

She chuckled as she accepted the phone. "Eleanor wasn't a *Mustang*. Eleanor was a sixty-seven Shelby GT500. Eleanor is my all-time favorite--"

I cleared my throat and nodded toward the phone.

Her eyebrows raised. "What?"

"Take a look at the picture."

She looked at the phone. "The screen's black."

"Zero-nine-one-seven," I said, giving her the unlock code.

She unlocked the phone and swiped her thumb over the screen. When she saw the photo, her eyes went wide.

"Holy F-ing Moses" she screeched. "It's *her*!"

"Exact reproduction," I said with a smile. "Built it from the ground up with my bare hands."

She took another look. "Oh. My God."

"Four-link suspension, a stroked four-twenty-eight, six-speed, roll cage, the whole enchilada. Almost nine hundred horsepower. Drives like a dream."

"You *drive* it?" she gasped.

"Every chance I get."

"Gone in Sixty Seconds was my dad's all-time favorite movie," she said excitedly. "I was thirteen when he took me to see it. He bought in on VHS when it came out. We wore out the tape, watching it. Then, he got a DVD. I've seen that movie a hundred times."

I grinned. "The guys I ride with and I went to see it when we were fourteen. That movie got me interested in cars. I wasn't old enough to drive at the time, but I told myself while I watched the movie that one day I would have *that* car. Took me almost eighteen years to get it built, but there it is."

She stared at the phone's screen. "Can I go for a ride in it?"

"You can drive it."

Her mouth flopped open. "You'll let me drive it?"

"Sure."

She lurched across table and gave me a kiss.

The clank of plates being against the end of the table caused us to break the embrace. Before Abby was back in her seat, George shot her a glare. "Public displays of affection are frowned upon. It makes the customers uneasy."

Abby cleared the screen on my phone, turned it to face George, and cocked an eyebrow. "He's letting me drive this. That's why I gave him a kiss."

George looked the picture. His eyes shot from the phone to me. "That's yours?"

"Built it with my own two hands," I said proudly.

He reached for the phone, and then hesitated. "May I?"

"Sure."

He admired the photo for a moment, and then handed it to me with reluctance. "I've got a sixty-three Mercury Marauder fastback I've been working on for years. One of these days, I'll have that ole girl done."

"I'm handy with a wrench," I said. "Might be able to teach you a few tricks when it comes to horsepower, too."

He waved his hand toward the restaurant. "All the men I know are handy with a rifle, and that's about it. Tough to find anyone these days that knows how to build an engine. That's what I'm down to. Motor and transmission."

"A weekend's work," I said.

He chuckled. "For you, maybe."

"Well, I'll volunteer to help." I reached for my plates and then met his gaze. "If you want it, that is."

"If you can build a car like that," he said. "I'd be honored."

"Just say the word," I said. "I'll make the time."

"I appreciate it." He looked at each of us and then grinned from ear to ear. "Let me know if there's anything I can get you. Enjoy your lunch."

"I love you, George," Abby said.

"I love you, Abby," he replied.

After he walked away, Abby looked at me and smiled. "Well, you won him over."

"A way to a man's heart is having a common bond with him," I said.

"And, the way to a woman's heart," she picked up her sandwich and took a bite. "Is by trusting her."

"What do you mean?"

"When you gave me the code to your phone?" A soft smile formed on her face. "I melted."

"Transparency is the only way something like this will work," I said.

"I agree," she said. "Thank you."

I knew, however, there were some things I'd never be able to tell Abby. And that, more than anything else, bothered me.

15

ABBY

W e'd reached the two-week milestone. It wasn't much by most people's standards, but by mine, it was a huge accomplishment. Excluding Kelvin, I hadn't been with a man long enough to realize what his eye color was.

After staying up and watching two episodes of *The Marvelous Mrs. Maisel*, we fell asleep in each other's arms. It seemed Porter was looking for exactly what I thought I wanted, which thrilled me to no end. But, because I was a girl, I twisted the fact that he liked to lie by my side in bed into a potential problem with our quickly developing relationship.

"Do you like sex, love sex, or see it as something that, I didn't know, kind of has to accompany a relationship or whatever?" I asked.

He looked up from lacing his boots. "What do you mean?"

"Sex. Do you like having sex?"

Boot laces in hand, he gave a slight shrug. "Love it, why?"

An involuntary sigh escaped me. "Just wondering."

He finished tying his boots and stood. "What's on your mind, Abby?"

"Nothing."

It was Saturday morning. On the previous night, we'd been on a dinner date. When we got home, we watched television and then went to bed together, all without having sex. I was thrilled that he often stayed all-night and loved sleeping with him. I probably didn't want to worry about his sincerity, sexual appetite, or his loyalty, but I did, nonetheless.

I worried that I wasn't sexy enough to cause him to want me. I wondered if there was someone else. It was also possible that we weren't sexually compatible, me desiring sex on a more frequent basis than he was willing to give.

In fact, the possibilities of potential problems were endless.

"You're standing there with a blank look on your face," he said. "And, you've done that thing with your hair twice in the last thirty seconds."

I started to object to his statement, and then realized I was scratching my nose with my index finger.

"I just. What," I stammered. "What happened last night?"

His brow wrinkled. "What are you talking about? What happened with what? We watched that show, and you fell asleep with your head on my chest."

We were getting ready to leave in an all-day motorcycle ride, and I didn't want to ruin it. I desperately needed to know why he didn't like me enough to have sex and had to ask.

I prepared for the inevitable. I was too short, had no boobs, and talked too much. In anticipation of the reasons he was sure to give, my gaze dropped to the floor between us.

"We didn't have sex last night," I whined.

His eyes narrowed. "And?"

"Well, I'm wondering if you're attracted to me like that? You know, sexually."

He spit out a laugh. "You're being serious?"

I bit against my lower lip and nodded. I was on the verge of tears and hoped I could manage to keep from crying. I desperately wanted things between Porter and I to work, but not if he didn't want me as much as I wanted him.

He sauntered from the living room to where I was standing in the kitchen, and then stood right in front of me. Through thin eyes he glared at me until I felt small, and unimportant.

"You're wondering if I'm sexually attracted to you?" he asked.

A verbal response would have started the waterworks, leaving a nod as my only means of acknowledgement. I nodded.

"Do you remember telling me you didn't want this to be about sex?" His brows raised. "On the night this 'relationship' started?"

I didn't remember saying that, specifically, but I vaguely recalled making a few references that may have been construed as such. I gave another series of nods in agreement.

"You said your former boyfriend saw you as 'someone to screw and nothing more'." He raised his index finger. "Then, you said, 'when the anger faded, I realized no one put me in that relationship but me. I decided the next time I decided to commit to someone, it was going to be because I wanted to be in a *relationship* with them. Not because I wanted sex'."

It sounded familiar, but it didn't make complete sense. The way Porter worded it, it sounded like I wanted to be in a sex-less relationship. At best, one with minimal sex. That wasn't at all what I wanted.

"If that's what I said," I murmured. "I don't think it's what I meant."

His eyes thinned. "How am I supposed to know what you mean if you don't tell me what you're truly thinking?"

"You're spinning this on me," I said, nearly in tears. "All I wanted to know was if you were attracted to me. If you think I'm sexy. If you like having sex with me."

He was standing six feet away. He quickly closed the distance between us. With his eyes locked on mine, he unbuckled his belt and wrestled with his jeans. Then, he leaned forward. The side of his face lightly brushed against mine. His mouth came to rest beside my ear.

"Grab my cock," he breathed.

His warm breath encompassed my ear. My pussy tingled. A prickling sensation crawled up my neck. My face went flush. While I struggled to process his request, he bit my earlobe. My pussy began to throb with every beat of my heart. Lost in the heavenly feeling, I simply forgot what it was he had asked of me.

"Grab. My. Cock. Abby," he whispered.

With my heart in my throat, I reached between his legs. Much to my satisfaction, he was rock-hard. I gripped the rigid shaft firmly in my hand.

He leaned away and cocked one eyebrow. "Does that feel like I'm attracted to you?"

I nodded. "Uh huh."

With lightning-fast hands, he pushed against one shoulder and pulled on the other, spinning me around in the process. Then, in one fluid motion, he flipped my dress over my hips, yanked down my panties, and pressed my chest against the cold granite countertop.

I felt the tip of his cock press against my wet folds. His animalistic approach to sex had me soaking wet and brimming with desire. My hands blindly searched the cold countertop for something to grip ahold of. Without further warning, he shoved his entire length into me in one savage thrust.

The air shot from my lungs as my hips slammed against the island's edge. His hands groped at my boobs. Waves of emotion surged through my body, reminding me of the magic we shared when he was inside of me. While he tweaked my sensitive nipples between his thumb and forefingers, two more violent thrusts followed, the second of which brought me to a quick climax.

He held himself deep inside of me during the orgasm. My body tensed and released repeatedly, erasing what little doubt I had developed regarding Porter's sexual desires. I felt his cock swell. In response, my pussy tightened around his throbbing shaft.

Then, while I was in mid-climax, he withdrew himself completely. A carnal groan bellowed from his inner being. Warm droplets coated my lower back, butt, and thighs.

The entire process took less than a minute but scored a solid ten by my sexual ratings scale.

I lifted my chest from the countertop and turned to face him. While struggling to catch my breath, I held my dress at my waist with shaking hands.

Porter wetted a handful of paper towels and wiped the cum away. After tossing them in the trash, he looked at me admiringly.

Between his muscular thighs, his semi-hard cock hung heavily. A droplet of cum clung to the tip as a reminder of what had just happened. His worn denim jeans were just above his knees and his boots were laced tightly to his feet.

"What...what was that...about?" I asked between breaths.

"By my watch, that took fifty seconds," he said. "Do you really need to ask yourself if I'm attracted to you?"

After that display of affection, I had no doubts. I shook my head. "I'm sorry."

He gripped his half-hard cock in one hand and wiped the cum droplet away from the tip with the index finger of his other. With his finger extended, he reached toward my face, offering me the cum-covered digit.

I took the full length of his finger into my mouth and sucked the salty droplet from the tip. With my tongue encompassing his calloused flesh, I opened my mouth slightly. He withdrew his hand slowly, watching intently as each inch of his finger slid past my lips.

"I like fucking just as much as you do." He leaned forward and gave me a soft kiss. "You need to decide if you'd rather spend quality time together, or fuck. You can't have both."

I disagreed wholeheartedly. "Fucking *is* quality time."

"Guess we won't be watching the rest of *The Marvelous Mrs. Maisel*, then. Will we?" he asked with a laugh.

We'd watched the first five episodes from the comfort of my bed. It was a great show, and I hated to think about missing the ending. "I don't see why we can't do both," I offered. "You can screw me from behind while we're facing the TV. Like the Canadians do during the Stanley Cup playoffs."

"That's one of the things I like about you, Abby." He kissed me again. "You're a problem solver."

"I'm a girl," I said. "We create problems when there's actually nothing to worry about. It's part of what makes us interesting creatures."

He pulled up his pants. "If creating problems is part of being a woman, I don't see how that's to anyone's benefit."

"Finding the solution is the fun part," I said. "It usually ends with us getting something we want."

He buckled his belt and gave me a look. "So, you're manipulative?"

"Absolutely not," I lied.

His eyes narrowed. "You didn't just coerce me into having sex?"

I did, but I wasn't going to give him the satisfaction of thinking I'd manipulated him. "No. You screwed me to prove a point. *You* manipulated *me*. You asked me to grab your cock, remember?"

"Oh." He looked away. "Yeah, that's right. I did, didn't I?"

"So, in summary, you manipulated me into having sex this morning. That means that you need to give it to me without me asking for it tonight. You know, to make up for your manipulative actions this morning."

He met my gaze. "Huh?"

I had him right where I wanted him. "Just nod your head."

He shrugged. "Sounds good to me."

I gave him a kiss on my way to the bathroom. Being in a relationship with Porter was going to be fun, at least until he figured out who was manipulating who.

16

GHOST

Although I'd been in California for thirteen years, I'd never spent much time at the beach. After meeting Abby, I'd sat and watched the sunset no less than a dozen times. The event had become somewhat of a ritual for us. One I truly enjoyed.

We were seated side by side on the upper deck of her home, facing the ocean. Three weeks had quickly passed since the day I first kissed her, which made our relationship the longest one I'd ever had. Pleased that everything was working in our favor, I stared at the indigo body of water and waited for the sun to melt into it.

"Do you think this is peaceful?" she asked.

I glanced in her direction. "Sitting here?"

Peering through the lenses of her Aviator sunglasses, she sipped her glass of tea. "Watching the sunset. Smelling the ocean. Sitting here."

With the sound of the waves within earshot and the air so thick with salt water it could be tasted, I didn't worry about my condition, cancer, or what the future might hold. Somehow, the ocean transported me to a place where either my problems didn't matter, or they simply didn't exist.

"It's comforting," I said.

She shifted her attention back to the horizon. "When I was sick, I used to sit out here and pray. Sometimes I'd fall asleep in this chair."

I had no desire to say a prayer to a God I wasn't sure existed. Falling asleep with the sound of the ocean in the distance sounded like a good idea, though.

"We should do that sometime," I said.

"Do what?"

"Fall asleep out here. I bet I'd feel refreshed in the morning."

"We can tonight, if you want."

I closed my eyes and listened to the waves washing ashore. "Let's do it."

I found myself doing things with Abby I never would have dreamed of before we met. I wondered how much of the differences I saw in myself were a result of being with her, and how much was driven by knowing my future was uncertain. That my time on earth was very likely limited to a much shorter timespan than most men my age.

It seemed I was willing to be far more accepting of life since I met her. I'd never describe myself as an angry man, but my life had become a pool of serenity since meeting Abby. Pinpointing what caused the change in me was impossible, so I simply accepted the changes as simply being part of what one received from a relationship.

"You know what?" I opened my eyes and turned to face her. "I like this."

"What?" She asked. "Sitting out here waiting for the sun to set?"

"No, being in a relationship."

She looked at me and lifted her glasses, revealing her majestic blue eyes. "Me, too."

After a lingering glance, she smiled. I liked it when she smiled. It let me know she was pleased with life or with me. I liked thinking it was a little of both. Eventually, she turned to face the horizon. Out of the corner of my eye, I watched as she brushed her hair behind her ear and did the nose scratching thing.

"What do you like about it the most?" she asked.

"About what?"

"Our relationship, silly."

"Just one thing?" I asked. "or do you want me to give you a list?"

"Let's stick with one. The best one."

"Waking up next to you," I said. "Same question to you."

With her eyes fixed straight ahead, she responded. "Being appreciated. And waking up in your arms."

I glared at her. "You said one answer. That's not fair."

She glanced at me and lifted her glasses. "Women can't give one answer to a question like that. It's impossible."

"Fine. I'll give another, then."

With her glasses held against her forehead, she fixed her eyes on mine. "Okay."

I thought about it for a moment. Explaining what I felt in Abby's presence was impossible. When I was with her an inner sense of balance enveloped me, leaving me feeling as if I was acting in harmony with her. It was as if we were one being.

Explaining *that* and not seeming like a complete idiot would be impossible. I opted to keep it simple. "I like how you make me feel."

"How do I make you feel?" she asked. "Explain it to me."

I should have seen it coming. Beating around the bush with Abby didn't work well. After another moment's thought, I sighed. "I can't."

"Well, that's dumb."

I didn't like that I couldn't explain to her how she made me feel. I shifted my eyes to the setting sun, and then back to her. "Stand up."

"Huh?"

I stood. "Stand up."

She did as I asked. I draped my arms over her shoulders, looked her in the eyes, and then kissed her.

The kiss was long, passionate, and included me gripping her little ass firmly in my hands. When our lips parted, her sunglasses fell from her forehead down onto the bridge of her nose.

"How did that feel?" I asked.

She lifted her glasses. "Awesome."

"Okay," I said. "You make me feel *awesome*."

She lowered her glasses. "I'll accept that. Awesome is as good as it gets. You make me feel awesome, too."

"Thank you."

She leaned onto the handrail and faced the ocean. "There it goes."

I draped my arms over her shoulders. "We almost missed it."

"There will always be another tomorrow," she said.

There were no assurances that tomorrow would ever come, but I didn't argue with her. I simply enjoyed the sunset while I held her in my arms. As a myriad of colors merged into the sea, I dreamed of a life filled with as many tomorrows as a man could imagine.

He simply picked them off a *tomorrow tree*, like apples. Each piece of fruit was one more tomorrow. Beyond each tree was another, just like it, as far as the eye could see. A land where my relationship with Abby lasted as long as there was fruit to pick from the trees.

And the trees went on forever.

ABBY

Porter and I were days away from being together one month. I'd convinced myself if we could last that long, we could last forever.

Lying on my back with my head resting against the arm of the couch, I faced Porter, who was on the opposite end, positioned in the same fashion, facing me. My legs were draped over his thighs and my feet rested on his hips. A cluster of grapes was resting on my chest, and a cluster rested on his.

I plucked a grape from the stem, took aim, and paused.

"It doesn't look like you're ready," I said. "Are you ready?"

"Uh Uh," he muttered.

"Is that a yes?"

"Damn it. I can't respond with my mouth stretched wide open. I was ready. Just toss the damned thing."

I flipped the grape into the air. After reaching its apex, it began to fall toward Porter's face. With wide eyes he studied it, and then snatched it from mid-air.

"Are you part frog?" I asked. "You snatched that thing with precision."

He swallowed. "I told you."

He picked a grape from his cluster and raised it. "Damn. What kind of grapes are these? They're good."

"Cotton Candy."

His brows knitted together. "Cotton Candy grapes?"

"Yep."

He looked at me in disbelief. "Really?"

"What do they taste like?" I asked, my tone sarcastic.

"Cotton Candy."

"That's because they're Cotton Candy grapes." I tilted my head back. "Whenever you're ready, I'm ready."

He tossed the grape with expert precision. I watched intently as it rose, and then fell. With a wide-open mouth, I positioned myself beneath the falling piece of fruit, only to be hit in the chin by it.

"Damn it," I said as it rolled into my arm pit.

I reached for the grape and hoisted it into the air.

"One to zero," he said. "And, you can't re-throw a grape. Get a new one."

"Who says I can't re-throw a grape? There aren't rules."

"I'm not eating a grape that smacked you in the chin. Get a clean one," he insisted.

I laughed out loud.

"What?" he asked.

"You stick your tongue in a hole that I piss out of." I chuckled so hard I had to catch my breath. "And you're worried about a grape that hit me in the face?"

"Fine," he said. "Throw the damned thing."

I tossed the grape *at* him not *to* him. Nonetheless, he somehow managed to catch it in his mouth. After chewing it, he gave me a cross look.

"What the hell, Abby? You threw that fucker."

"I didn't know we had rules about speed."

He scowled at me.

"Okay, let me make a few mental notes. No dirty grapes. Nothing over five miles an hour. Alright, I think I'm good for the next one."

He picked a grape from his bunch and raised it. "Ready?"

I nodded.

"Two to zero," he said.

He lobbed the grape into the air.

I leaned left, and then right. Despite being certain I was well within the grape's path, it fell against my upper lip and then ricocheted off the arm of the couch. As it rolled across the floor, Porter laughed.

"Your fat lips get in the way."

"You like them when they're wrapped around your dick, Dick."

"No need to call names." He checked his watch. "This is just a friendly game."

"How much time do we have?" I asked.

"Three or four minutes."

"Is it three or is it four?"

He glanced at his watch. "Three and twenty seconds."

I pulled a grape from the bunch and flipped it into the air carelessly, and without warning. Using his eight-pack of stomach muscles, Porter did a sit up, catching the grape in mid-flight.

"Is there anything you're not good at?" I asked.

"I'm sure there's something," he said. "It looks like this isn't it, though."

"You suck," I said.

He inspected the grapes, chose a small one, and then raised it. "I picked a little one. Smaller should be easier, right?"

"Throw it, I'll tell you in a minute."

"Just open your mouth wide, and don't move. I'll throw it right in there."

I opened my mouth wide enough to throw a cat into it. He tossed the grape with a flick of his wrist. It shot right into my mouth without so much as grazing a tooth, flew right past my tongue, and then got lodged in my windpipe.

My eyes bulged. I tried to cough but couldn't. I wanted to give the universal signal for *I'm choking, help me*, but had no idea what it was. After pounding my fist into my chest twice, frantically, Porter must have realized the threat was real.

He leaped from his end of the couch, yanked me to my feet, and spun me halfway around. I felt a surge of pressure against my chest. I coughed and watched the grape shoot from my mouth and then bounce across the living room floor.

"Holy crap," I gasped. "I almost died."

"You didn't even come close," he said, releasing me from his grasp. "Three to zero. Time's up. You lost."

"I can't go pick that crap up," I said. "I almost died."

"You choked on a grape, and it's over. We had a bet. The loser of this grape toss has to dive to the Chinese place and pick up the food."

"The loser is recovering from almost choking to death," I said. "You go get it."

"What good did it do to play the game?" he asked. "If you're going to cheat and stay home while I go get the food?"

There were a million and a half people in the city of San Diego. Of those, roughly half were men. Of that population of seven hundred and fifty thousand men, I doubted there were more than one who would agree to a grape toss contest with the loser picking up the Chinese take-out.

Porter was quickly finding his way into my heart. Deep into my heart. He was so much more than what he appeared to be on the surface.

"How about we both go?" I asked.

He twisted his mouth to the side. "If I go, I'll feel like a loser, but I didn't lose."

"Come on," I whined. "I don't want to go alone."

"Suck my cock after dinner?" he asked.

His cock was huge, and my mouth was small. Sucking it was nothing short of jaw-breaking torture. But, if that's what it took to get him to go with me, so be it.

"Sure" I said.

"Promise?"

I extended my hand.

He shook it, grinning the entire time.

I scrunched my nose. "What?"

"Who's manipulating who, now?" he asked with a laugh.

I tried to act stupid. "What are you talking about?"

"That bullshit in the kitchen last week, after I bent your little ass over the island to prove a point."

"I wasn't manipulating you," I lied.

"And, I'm not manipulating you now."

"You are, too," I argued.

"Manipulation is tricking someone into doing something. I won the grape tossing contest fair and square. You tried to claim you damned near choked to death, hoping I'd get the food out of sheer pity. I agreed, but only if you'd suck my cock later. You agreed to the blowjob offer, because you wanted my company on the ride to China-Go. This deal is as legit as the day is long. Zero manipulation." He snatched his keys from the end table. "You ready to go?"

It sounded pretty legit.

I nodded. "I guess so."

On the way to the door, I had a brainstorm.

"How about when we get home, we have a contest to see how many peas we can pluck out of the fried rice using chopsticks? If you lose, you lick my pussy."

He opened the door. "Sounds good. What do I get if I win?"

There was no way he could win. "Two blowjobs," I said.

"One tonight, one tomorrow?"

"Sure."

I stepped through the door and onto the stairwell, all but tripping over a box that had been placed in front of the door.

He nodded toward the Zappos box. "What the fuck is that?"

I pushed the box inside the door with my foot. "New pair of Chucks. My old ones are getting raggedy."

"What's it doing up here?" he asked.

"The UPS guy always comes up the back steps. He knows I sit back here, and he likes to chat. I think he feels like he's kicking it with a celebrity."

He nodded, and then pulled the door closed. "So, do we have a deal?" he asked. "Chopsticks tricks for blowjobs?"

"You haven't been practicing, have you?"

"Nope," he said.

I laughed. "You're going to lose. You can't use chopsticks for shit."

"What's the punishment, again?"

I locked the door. "Licking my pussy."

"Damn it," he said. "Looks like you've manipulated me again."

I paused and looked at him, confused as to who was manipulating who. Truth be known, I think Porter was manipulating me into manipulating him into having hot sex. But, he was doing so willingly, and knowingly.

Which, in my mind, meant that I was the one being manipulated.

I shrugged it off and followed him down the stairs, wondering if I could ever win at anything with him.

Anything at all.

GHOST

To describe our MC as an Outlaw Motorcycle Club would be an understatement. We were an outlaw club, but beyond that, *we* were outlaws. Being an outlaw and appearing to be otherwise wasn't an easy task. Not expressing emotion was crucial to our way of life, and to protecting our identity. I had the ability to look into the eyes of the devil himself without showing emotion. Remaining stoic had become second nature for me.

Until I met Abby.

Positioned between the door frame and the window, I rang the doorbell. Despite the cool morning air, I wiped sweat from my brow while I waited for her to open the door.

The door swung open. Wearing running shoes, nylon shorts, and a tight-fitting tee shirt that said *Nevertheless. She Persisted* on the front of it, she looked adorable. She always looked adorable.

"Oh, Wow." She leaned forward and kissed me. "You're early. Come in."

It had been exactly one month since we kissed that day at the pie shop. I stepped through the doorway and revealed the hand that I'd nervously been hiding behind my back. Upon seeing my surprise, she gave me a bug-eyed look.

"Oh my God. Are those." Her blue eyes met mine. "They're for me?"

Seeing the excitement in her eyes was reassurance that she liked the flowers as much as I hoped she would. Expressing my feelings wasn't easy, which made conveying how much I cared for her a difficult thing to do.

I wanted to say that being with her made me feel different than I'd ever felt. That comfort washed over me completely when she was in my presence. Nothing else seemed to matter after meeting her, but I couldn't find the words to tell her without feeling foolish.

So, a gift of flowers and a simple card was my only hope.

Beaming with pride, I handed her the vase of flowers. "They are."

She raised them to her nose and inhaled a slow breath. "They're beautiful."

"One of the fellas has a nursery," I said. "His Ol'…his wife has a green thumb. She picked them out special for me. She told me what they were, but I can't remember what they're called. Inside of the Mustang smells good as fuck, though."

She looked the flowers over. "Some of them are tulips, I know that. I'm not too familiar with the rest of them, this is the first time I've ever had flowers."

Seeming to be in a trance, she walked toward the kitchen and set the vase on the center of the island. She adjusted the stems, turned the arrangement in a circle, and then stepped back and gave it a long look.

"They smell so good." She wiped her eyes with the heel of her palm and then met my gaze. "I'm sorry. This is just…I've always wanted this to happen."

A tear welled at the corner of her eye. I placed my hands on either side of her face and wiped her eyes with my thumbs. "So, those are tears of happiness?"

She nodded. "They are."

I kissed her. "I hate to see you cry, but I'm glad you're happy."

Kissing Abby was indescribable. The things in my life that once seemed important became irrelevant after I kissed her the first time. All that mattered following that kiss was kissing her again.

"You're amazing." She hugged me.

"I'm not that amazing," I said. "It's kind of like an anniversary, or whatever. I thought I needed to do *something*."

She leaned away. Her expression changed from joyous to one of surprise. "That's what these are for?"

"Yeah, like a celebration, or whatever." I shrugged. "I didn't know what else to do. Thought maybe we could get dinner."

She grinned from ear to ear. "At nine in the morning?"

I chuckled. "No. I was just excited. Hell, I couldn't sleep last night when I got home. I came over as soon as I thought you'd be done running."

She raised her index finger. "I'll be right back."

She bounded across the living room like a lion chasing a gazelle. She returned just as fast, with her hand hidden behind her back. "I got you something too I couldn't decide whether to give it to you or not because I thought maybe I was being sappy or whatever and it's been on my dresser since the day before yesterday and last night I was thinking I was an idiot for getting it but now I know that you and I are like peanut butter and jelly or whatever maybe peas and carrots I always thought that was a cute line from that movie." She extended her hand. "Here."

I laughed at her breathless explanation and then looked at what she'd handed me. A pale-yellow envelope with a bulge in the center. I grinned upon seeing it and reached into my back pocket. I pulled out the card I'd purchased and handed it to her.

She smiled. "Open yours first."

I opened the envelope, pulled out the card, and then reached inside. After removing the gift, I looked it over. A weathered piece of hammered brass had been formed into a bracelet. In the center, it had one word stamped.

Believe.

"I know you like to wear bracelets," she said. "I had a lady make that one special for you. It looks old, but it's not. I measured your wrist by wrapping my hand around it. I hope it fits."

I tried to think of the last time someone gave me a gift. I couldn't. I studied it for a moment, and then slipped it onto my right wrist.

"Believe." I looked at her. "I like that."

"In anything, and everything," she said. "If it can be done, you can do it. We can do it. All we have to do is believe. Remember that."

I rubbed the bracelet with my thumb. "I will."

"Read the card," she said.

The card had a photo of a pile of shit on the front of it. I chuckled at her selection and opened it. Printed inside, it said, *you are not a turd.* I laughed again, and the read the elegant hand-written script.

Ghost Porter-Porter,

I know how and when our relationship began is a matter of opinion, but I'll give you mine. I'm sure it isn't what you want to hear (because it involves God) but I've always had a problem with saying what comes to mind, and this is what came to mind.

Here we go.

I think God put you in my life because you were exactly what I needed. Consequently, I'm exactly what you need, too. You may not know it, but I am. I make you happy. I can see it in your eyes.

If you can't see the joy that you bring me when you look into mine, it's because you're too busy paying me compliments (which I adore, btw). We've been together a month. I know it's only the beginning, but something as devastatingly beautiful as the Grand Canyon started with one trickle of water flowing across the desert.

We have a beautiful future together, I'm sure of it. All we have to do is continue believing this is where we belong.

Believe.

Abby

With a lump in my throat and a swollen heart, I looked up.

"B-T-W means 'by the way'," she said. "I was going to cross it out and spell it, but I didn't want the card to look crappy."

"I knew what it meant," I said, my voice straining from the emotion I was feeling. "Read." I cleared my throat. "Read mine."

Mine wasn't as delicately written as hers. When she finished reading it, she laid it beside the flower vase.

She inhaled a long breath, and then let it out. "You asked me not to hurt you," she said. "After we kissed. Remember that?"

"I do."

She brushed her hair behind her ear and then scratched her nose. "I need to ask you to do something for me."

I grinned. "Okay."

"Don't leave me. Please. No matter what happens between us, don't make me live a day without you. If there's ever something I do that makes you angry or sad or whatever, just tell me. I'll fix it. There's no reason for us not to be together, ever. Doing this." She pointed to herself and then to me. "It's easy. Too easy. I don't even have to try. I'm just my stupid self and you accept me. Don't--"

"I won't." I said.

"I can't imagine what I'd do if--"

"I won't," I assured her. "Don't worry. I'm not leaving. Now, or ever. I lay in my bed at night and think of you. I read and re-read your text messages. I'll probably sleep with this card under my pillow. It's crazy, but I can't imagine living a life without you."

"Neither can I," she said. "So, it's settled."

"What's settled?"

"You're stuck with me."

I slipped my arms around her waist and pulled her tight to my chest. I knew I'd never leave her. I didn't have it in me. I feared, however that she'd one day leave me.

Every other woman I loved had.

Why would she be any different?

ABBY

George sat down across from me and gave me a quick look over. "It's been a long damn time since you came in here for advice."

"Who says I'm here for advice?"

"We're empty." He waved his hands toward the vacant seats. "It's three o' clock. Too early for dinner, and too late for lunch. You're here to talk."

It aggravated me that he knew me that well. "No, I came in for something to eat."

He rubbed his hands together. "What'll you have? Pancakes? The Abby? Your other favorite? Apples and grilled cheese?"

"I'm not hungry," I admitted. "You're right. I wanted to talk."

"Is everything okay?"

"It's perfect." My shoulders slumped. "That's the problem."

His eyes narrowed. "Perfect is a problem?"

"I don't feel like I deserve this. I worry that it's all going to come crashing down. That he's going to leave me. That it's too good to be true. He's too good to be true. This entire thing is too good to be true. That there's no way this can last. That--"

"Take a breath" He reached across the table and cupped my hand in his. "In through the nose, and out through the mouth. You're going to hyperventilate if you're not careful."

"I get worked up when he's gone," I said. "I don't know what the problem is. It's like I can't function without him."

He squeezed my hand and smiled. "Solution sounds simple to me."

"What do you mean?"

"Spend more time together," he said.

We saw each other every day. I didn't want to smother him and give him a reason to reject me. But. When he was gone, my mind went fifty different directions, developing possibilities of what might happen to prevent him from ever returning. Everything from changing his mind about being in a relationship to wrecking his motorcycle. I remained stuck in my pattern of worrying until he returned.

It wasn't that I didn't trust him, because I did. When he was away, I simply couldn't believe I deserved something as special as what we had.

I let out a breath. "I see him every day. If we had normal jobs, we wouldn't see each other this much. Sometimes I see him two or three times a day. It's not that. It's just. I get worked up when he's away. When he's gone, I can't believe I deserve what it is we have when he's with me."

"It doesn't matter if he's with you or he's gone, Abby. You still have it." He looked at me like I was crazy. "Did you give him that bracelet that Lawson's wife made for you?"

"I did."

"What did it say on it?"

"You know what it said."

"What did it say, Abby?" He arched one brow. "Remind me."

"Believe," I responded. "It said, *believe*."

"Sounds to me that you need to take some of your own advice," he said with a dry laugh. "Believe, Abby. Believe you're worthy of him. Believe he's in this for all the right reasons. Believe that he feels the same way about you that you feel about him. Believe that your lives collided for a reason. That the man above gave you an opportunity, and that for once you were paying attention and recognized what it was he put in front of you."

I nodded. "I'm trying."

"I don't like too many people, and I like this guy. It has nothing to do with cars, if that's what you're wondering. Deep down in my gut, I believe Porter's a good man. I can't assure you of what the future holds, but I can tell you this: your odds of succeeding are greater with him than they were with--"

"Don't even say his name," I said.

"Well, you were with *him* for six years, and we never had a talk like this."

"I was in that relationship for sex. I didn't care about him. I was a fool and got wrapped up in the comfort of having sex and thought that was enough. I learned that it wasn't."

Sex was the only thing I had in common with Kelvin. If we weren't screwing, I didn't see much value in having him around. In fact, when we were done having sex, I often wanted him to leave.

"Exclude the sex," he said. "Why are you in this relationship?"

I thought for some time before speaking. The answer was easy for me to understand, but not so easy to convey. George released my hand and relaxed against the back of the booth while he waited for me to respond. After an awkward silence, I decided it wasn't one reason, it was many.

"Well, for one, when he kissed me the first time it was better than sex. Every time we kiss it's like that. It's crazy. And, he makes me laugh. He gives compliments without me asking for them. He puts his hand on my waist when we walk. It just rests there, reminding me that he's with me. I can be myself when I'm with him and he accepts me, even though I'm a dork. He laughs with me, not at me. I don't have to ask him if he cares about me, he shows me. Then, there's this part of him that seems broken, and I feel like I'm fixing it. He gave me a card the other day, and it said, 'When I'm with you, you're all that matters. When you're away, you're all that matters. Abby, you're all that matters'. I guess that kind of sums it up. I feel the same way."

He smiled. "Sounds like love."

"I like him a lot," I admitted. "But I don't think it's love. Not yet."

He chuckled. "Why not? Are you afraid if you admit it that he might find out? That he'll run away?"

I was. I nodded subconsciously but didn't respond. George studied my face. When the silence got awkward, he continued.

"For any relationship to survive, honesty is required," he said. "From what he wrote in that card, I'd guess that he feels the same way. I recommend you tell him exactly how you feel. It'll probably make you feel better. It might make him feel better, too."

"Not saying something isn't being dishonest," I said.

He leaned forward and looked me in the eyes. "Through the windows behind me, you watch a man rob the bakery across the street. He runs out, gun in one hand and a bag of money in the other. The police come in here afterward and say, 'We'd like for anyone who saw anything to step forward'. You choose to maintain silence. Are you being honest?"

I shrugged. "Kind of. I mean, they didn't ask if I saw anything. They just said *we'd like for you to step forward*."

He reached under his apron, pulled out his phone, and messed with the screen for a minute. Then, he turned it to face me.

hon·est – *adjective*: free of deceit and untruthfulness; sincere

He set the phone aside. "I'll ask it a different way. Would maintaining silence in the scenario I gave you be honest, based on the true definition of honesty?"

I shook my head. "No."

"I'll just rephrase my statement about relationships," he said. "*For any relationship to survive, it must be free of deceit*."

After George's speech I felt obligated to have a talk with Porter. It didn't make the thought of doing so comforting, though. The possibility of rejection was real. If I said nothing, I was safe. But, I was also being deceptive.

I hated being wrong.

"We're going out to eat tonight," I said. "I'll see how it goes. Maybe I'll have a talk with him."

He smiled. "If the time is right."

I reached across the table. "I love you, George."

"Love you too, Abby."

20

PORTER

I connected the linkage to the carburetor and checked the cable, making certain it was smooth and without any kinks in the travel. After double-checking electrical connections, I looked at George.

"I think we're ready to give it a try."

He looked the car over, exhaled a slow breath, and shook his head. "I can't believe you've got this thing ready to run in two weekends." He glanced at me. "Do you really think it'll start?"

"What do you mean?"

He nodded toward the engine. "Do you really think it'll run?"

"I *know* it'll run," I said. "Get in and turn the key."

"Fucker's been sitting in here for four years." He opened the car's door and climbed inside. "Seems like more of a dream than reality. Had this thing shipped here from Okinawa Island, Japan."

He'd twice told me the story about a Colonel who bought the car stateside during the onset of the Vietnam war, and then had it shipped to the Marine base on the island of Okinawa. Then, over the years, it had been sold to multiple Marines, one of which blew the engine in a drunken display of tire burnouts. He purchased the car with the blown engine and in need of bodywork, later shipping it home immediately prior to retiring.

Beaming with pride, he got in the driver's seat, crossed the fingers of his left hand, and turned the key. On the third rotation, the sound of raw horsepower echoed off the walls of his garage.

"Hold it at one thousand RPM for a minute or so," I shouted, reaching for the oil pressure gauge.

"Holy shit!" he howled. "She runs!"

While I verified the oil pressure, he stared at the tachometer. A face-splitting smile gave hint as to the pleasure he derived from finally having the car in operating order. Personally, I got my satisfaction out of building the engine from scratch.

Knowing that I took hundreds of parts and assembled them into a running engine with my bare hands gave me a sense of worth. The engine would extract three times the horsepower of a Detroit manufactured equivalent and be ten times as reliable.

"Take it to about eighteen hundred," I shouted.

The engine's RPM increased. The vintage metal signs he'd hung on the garage walls began to vibrate and shake. A quick check of the gauge confirmed we had great oil pressure.

"What's the temp?" I asked.

"Two hundred," he shouted.

I visually checked for oil and water leaks and found none.

"Shut her down," I said.

He turned off the engine and opened the door. "Look," he said, extending his arm. His hand was shaking. "I'm shaking like an infantry private in a combat zone."

"What are you nervous about?" I asked.

"Shit," he scoffed. "This isn't nerves. I've got nerves of steel. This is sheer excitement."

"Let me look her over for leaks and you can take her for a spin."

"I'd tell you to feel my heart," he said. "But that'd be weird. Fucker's about to jump out of my chest."

"Wait till you romp this fucker at a twenty mile an hour roll," I said.

"What'll she do from a stop light?" he asked.

"If you don't have a sticky tire, it'll just send you sideways," I said.

"This thing's going to be a monster on horsepower with the cam I chose. You said you wanted it *hot*, so it's hot."

He tried to hide his smile but didn't even come close. "What if I put some sticky tires on it?"

"Get some Mickey Thompson's on it, and it'll probably yank that left tire off the ground when you take off."

His eyes went wide. "You think so?"

"I know so."

"But, it'll pass emissions?"

I nodded. "With flying colors."

While George paced the garage, I spent the next thirty minutes checking connections, re-tightening fasteners, and checking for leaks. After double-checking everything, I climbed from beneath the car, removed my rubber gloves, and tossed them aside.

"Let's see what she'll do," I said.

He extended his hand. "In case I'm too excited to remember when we get back, just want you to know how much I appreciate your help."

I shook his hand. "Least I could do, considering you're Abby's best friend."

"She sure thinks the world of you," he said.

"I'd say the feeling's mutual," I said. "Can't imagine life without her in it."

I walked around the car and got in on the passenger side. He climbed in the driver's seat and glanced over his shoulder. "You guys go out to eat last night?"

"Had steaks up in Oceanside at a seafood joint," I responded. "Great ribeye."

He reached for the key, paused, and then looked at me again. "She have much to say?"

I chuckled at the thought. "She's always got a lot to say. Non-stop talk out of that girl. One of the things I like about her is that a man never has to worry what she's thinking. She'll tell you."

He grinned a half-assed grin and started the car. When he shifted it into reverse, he grinned. "Love how that cam sounds at an idle. If this son-of-a-bitch could talk, it'd be saying, 'don't bother trying to race me, I'll kick your ass."

"I'm sure it would."

He drove slowly until we were at the highway on-ramp. After checking for traffic ahead, he looked at me. "It's okay to stomp it?"

"Don't take it above five thousand RPM for five hundred miles. That's all."

He nodded. "Okay. I'm gonna gun it."

I knew exactly what the car would feel like. I'd built dozens of high horsepower Ford engines. He, on the other hand, had refused to drive Eleanor, and only had an idea of what he believed the car would feel like. I was anxious to see the look on his face when he saw the car's true potential.

We were rolling uphill at fifteen or twenty miles an hour. I glanced over my shoulder and made sure no one was behind us. "Don't be afraid of it," I said. "Just stomp it all the way to the floor and keep your eye on the tach. Shift at five thousand."

He clenched his jaw, gripped the shifter knob tightly, and mashed the gas pedal. The car didn't hesitate to react.

Both back tires gripped firm on the hot Southern California pavement. The engine's horsepower was converted to energy, and that energy was beyond what I – or George – was ready for.

The car shot forward like a rocket, slamming both of us against the seat backs. In an instant, George shifted gears expertly. After the car slid sideways a few inches, the tires gripped, once again causing the engine's power to smash us against the seats. After shifting into third gear, he was well over one hundred miles an hour, and not to the highway entrance.

He released the gas pedal.

"Holy shit! That power's crazier than hell." He glanced in my direction. "I think you've got a gift, Son."

"Few things I'm good at," I said with a smile. "Cars is one of them."

"Yet you're managing car washes," he said. "Abby told me that, and I about had a heart attack."

"It pays the bills."

"My fucking heart is pounding," he exclaimed. "Did you hear this ole girl screaming out the tailpipes?"

"Sounds like she belongs on a race track," I said.

"I'll drive her from work from time to time," he said. "Watch people drool over it. Other'n that, she'll be out at the track, racing for side bets."

"Well, you've got the shifting down. All you might need is a few suspension tweaks."

"Know anyone who can tweak a suspension?"

"Other than me?" I asked.

He laughed. "Should have known."

We took the next exit ramp, and drove back to his house slowly, and without incident. Through the quiet neighborhood he lived in, the car's exhaust turned a few heads, which George seemed to like.

When each person looked, he waved like a politician on parade. Seeing his joy couldn't have pleased me more. When we came to a stop in the garage, he turned off the engine and looked at me.

"Set the bullshit aside, Porter. What do I owe you?"

I opened the door. "Stack of pancakes."

After getting out, he peered over the top of the car. "I'm not fucking around," he growled. "I need to pay you something. You did in two weekends what I couldn't do in years. I got quotes to build this thing, and after everyone saw that box of loose parts, the numbers were in the ten-grand range. Couldn't ever seem to afford that much. Let me give you a couple grand, at least."

"Wouldn't even consider it," I replied. "Friend of Abby's is a friend of mine, and this is what friends do for one another."

He shook his head. "You're one of a kind."

I laughed. "So are you. I thought on the day we met that you were going to be a prick. But you're all bark and no bite."

"Oh, believe me," he said. "I bite, and bite hard. Abby's got a damned good head on her shoulders, and if she thought you were a good enough man to come into my diner, I knew I needed to give you a chance."

"I appreciate it."

"She's a special girl," he said. "Hard to understand what drives her to do what she does, but she's driven. Can't help but respect her."

I opened the car's hood. "You mean the YouTube stuff?"

"No, I was meaning the charity. She's not one to brag, but I sure brag about her," he said. "Last year she had a fundraiser for raising drug awareness amongst teens. Said she's match two dollars for every dollar donated. Damned girl gave four million of her own money to charity. Year before she did the same thing for breast cancer. Year before that was to build a soup kitchen for the homeless. And, all she can do is talk about how I have that pancake fundraiser. She acts like I'm a saint. Truth be known, that girl is a gift from God if there ever was one."

I forced a smile and ducked under the hood. "She's a gift, alright."

He leaned over the fender. "Say something to offend you?"

I shook my head. "No, why?"

"If there's one thing I learned to do after fifteen years at war, it's how to read people. Something I said tasted foul."

"I'm not a big God person, that's all. Don't care if you are, I'm just not what I'd call a believer."

"Everyone needs something to believe in." He gazed at the engine for a moment, and then looked up. "In boot camp they asked, 'Are you catholic or protestant?' I said, 'Neither.' They said, 'You're one or the other, pick one. So, I picked protestant. I always struggled with God's existence, at least until I was in combat. I found God one afternoon when I was on the receiving end of a Kalashnikov in Afghanistan. Kalashnikovs don't jam for what it's worth. Ever. His did. I don't know who he was praying to, but my God answered my prayer."

He let out a long breath. "He went on to meet his maker. That night, while I was staring up at the stars, I somehow came to believe. Ever since, I've been a believer."

I felt like laughing but didn't dare. "No offense, but having a guy's gun jam made you believe in God?"

"I think I was just looking for a reason," he said. "On that day I found it. If a man doesn't believe in God, he's left to believe he *is* God. I've got news for you. You're not."

I chuckled. "Never thought I was."

He turned away, returning in a moment with two beers. He handed me one. After I accepted it, I tilted the neck of the bottle toward him. "Here's to fast cars, battlefield miracles, and having something to believe in."

He clanked his bottle against mine.

I took a drink and then raised my clenched fist. "For now, I'm going to believe in this brass bracelet."

He gave a nod. "As long as you've got *something* to believe in."

I began checking for coolant leaks. After enough time passed that I felt like I could change the subject, I did, deciding to speak about something we both had in common.

Abby.

"I'm grateful as hell that Abby came into my life," I said. "I've been blind to what it's like have someone care about me – other than family – and I haven't had any family for thirteen years or so. Hard to put into words how much she means to me."

He sipped his beer, and then silently studied me for a moment while I checked for leaks.

"You've got something to say, just say it," I said without looking up. "Never been much for having a man stare at me and not speak."

"She loves you," he said. "But she's scared to death to tell you. Don't know if it's my place to do so, but I guess I just did."

I sprung upright, banging the back of my head on the hood when I did so. "Son of a bitch," I shouted. "That hurt like hell."

"Finding out she loves you?" He chuckled. "Or hitting your head?"

"Maybe both." I rubbed the back of my head with the palm of my hand. "Did she tell you that?"

"More or less," he said.

I'd felt like I loved Abby, but also feared telling her how I felt. Confiding my feelings wasn't easy, especially when it came to love. One way to get tossed to the curb would be to tell her I loved her if she didn't love me. *More or less* wasn't much of an indication of love, though.

I looked at him as if he'd taken a liberty he shouldn't have. "More or less?"

"We talked about you yesterday, at length," he said. "She loves you. I thought she was going to tell you last night. It's why I asked about your dinner."

"Maybe she decided she doesn't," I said.

He took a long drink of his beer, and then lowered the bottle. "She's scared to death of losing you. I know that."

"I know how that feels. I can't seem to convince myself I deserve her. I can tell you that much."

"In my fifty some years on earth, I learned this," he said. "When it comes to living life, we all get what we deserve. Nothing more, nothing less. If you don't believe me, maybe you ought to have another look at that bracelet of yours."

I glanced at my wrist. It was nothing more than a piece of brass with a word stamped into the face of the metal. But, for the time being, it was all I had. I studied the inscription. Abby may have deserved me, but I wasn't convinced I deserved her. Not yet, at least. Before I could truly believe, I needed to tell her the truth.

The entire truth.

If she accepted me when I was done, our relationship was meant to be.

21

ABBY

As a teen I was preached to about what types of boys to avoid. My parents weren't overly strict, but they wanted me to succeed in whatever endeavors I chose. Success, in their eyes, couldn't be achieved unless I selected the right man to be at my side.

If I chose the wrong man, I'd be destined for failure. Or, so they led me to believe. Nonetheless, I was attracted to bad boys. The kids who were always in trouble. The boys who fought after school. The hellions who were ostracized by everyone else in school for their actions or beliefs. The kids who wore black, sat alone in the lunch room, and wore a scowl from first period until the dismissal bell rang.

Those were the boys I liked.

No, no, and *hell no* was my father's common response to my expressions of attraction to the opposite sex. As I grew older, I developed much more than a fascination with bad boys. They were my only desire. I blamed my attraction partially on my father's insistence that I avoid those types, and, in part because he was a staunch pacifist.

When I was in first grade, a man bumped into my mother while we were waiting in line to be seated at a restaurant. The collision was an accident, but it all but knocked my mother on the floor. When the man regained his footing, he looked at my mother, and then my father.

He was big and rough-looking. He wore a messy beard and a baseball cap, and his jeans had holes in them.

His brown eyes then looked my mother up and down. He reached for the bill of his cap and grinned. "Nice tits."

I understood what he said, but at the time, I didn't comprehend the magnitude of it. My parents fought about it during our meal, with my mother asking why my father hadn't said – or did – anything when the man ran into her, or when he made the remark.

My father explained that nothing was worth fighting for. Men shouldn't fight one another, they should learn to love one another, he said. It sounded like a good explanation at the time, but as I grew older, I realized exactly what my mother meant.

I didn't take a vow to never fall in love with a pacifist, but my subconscious mind must have, because I was attracted to the exact opposite man my father was. I desperately wanted to be the significant other to a man who had the ability – and desire – to stand up for me. During my younger years I dreamed of being in a similar situation as my mother and having my beau make clear what was acceptable behavior.

Porter and I were walking side by side toward the movie theater's ticket counter when I saw him. I clung to Porter's side and diverted my gaze, hoping to go unnoticed as he walked past us. I considered saying something to Porter, but by the time I thought of what to say, it was too late. He paused several feet in front of us, turned to face me, and stared.

"Abby." His voice floated to us on a cloud of desire. "Oh my God, it's you."

"Who's that?" Porter asked under his breath.

"One of life's bad F-ing choices," I said. "Keep walking."

I acted as if I didn't see him or hear him. After we'd taken a few strides, he turned, took a few quick steps and intercepted us.

Crap.

"Abby, I never heard back from you after the last time we saw each other," he said. "What happened."

Luke Westham was a professional football player for the former

San Diego Chargers. The team had recently been moved to Los Angeles, and my hope was that Luke went with them, for good.

He was an obsessed fan of my YouTube channel who had emailed me relentlessly over a six-month period. I finally agreed to meet him for a cup of coffee. That was all it took for me to decide he was a wacko. Ten minutes into our meeting, he was talking about getting married and having babies.

I couldn't get away from him fast enough. The strange messages that followed caused me to block his email address and block him on social media. It didn't prevent him from setting up alternate Facebook profiles and email addresses – with false names – and contacting me through them.

He was one of my worst nightmares. In fact, getting rid of him completely was number one hundred and eighty-four on my list.

I put on a face of surprise. "Oh, hi. It's Luke, right? I almost didn't recognize you."

"I never heard back from you," he said, his tone bitter.

Yes, you did. I told you I'd get a restraining order if you didn't leave me alone.

I swallowed my desire to spew proof of his mental instability and choose to go a safer route.

"This is my boyfriend, Porter," I said.

He gave Porter a dismissive look, and then looked at me dreamily. "When do you want to get together? I miss seeing you."

"You only saw me once," I snapped back. "For ten minutes. Three years ago."

Porter cleared his throat. "Excuse us, please. We're running a few minutes late."

Luke shot Porter a quick glare and then reached for my left arm. "Don't go. We haven't even had a chance to catch up."

Oh my God this weirdo's hand is on me. Help! Help! His skin is touching my skin.

Porter grabbed Luke's arm by the wrist. By the look on Luke's face, Porter wasn't being gentle either.

"I said we're running late," Porter seethed as he shoved Luke's arm to the side. "Excuse us, please."

Luke puffed his steroid-enhanced chest. "I wasn't done talking to her, asshole."

I didn't know much, but I knew those were fighting words. But, there was never a *fight*. Not to speak of, anyway. It was more of a show of speed versus stupidity, I guess. The word *asshole* no more than cleared Luke's lips, and Porter stepped in front of me.

The rest, I didn't see. I mean, I was there, and I was watching, but *seeing* it would have required recording it and playing it back in slow motion. Hearing it was enough to cause me to cringe. I mentally jumped for joy later, but the cringing came first.

Porter's hands became a blur. A series of horrid crunching sounds followed. Luke's legs turned to noodles, and he crumbled into a three-hundred-pound wad of useless flesh at Porter's feet.

"Did you kill him?" I gasped.

"I hope so." Porter chuckled. "He was an irritating prick."

A crowd began to gather between us and the ticket counter. "Holy shit," I heard someone say. "Did you see that?"

A man stepped through the crowd and looked at Luke, who was attempting – unsuccessfully – to rise to his feet.

"That's Luke Westham," the man said excitedly. "You knocked out Luke Westham."

"He needed knocked out," Porter replied.

Porter looked at me. "Who the fuck's Luke Westham?"

"He's a running back for the LA Chargers," I responded. "And, he's some weirdo that was stalking me. I almost got a restraining order against him. I swear, I only met him for a cup of coffee a few years ago, that's it."

"He was a fucking weirdo, that's for sure," he said with a laugh.

I'm sure women exist who would have been appalled by what happened. I wasn't one of them. The fact that Porter knocked out a pro football player because he had acted disrespectfully made me swoon.

As I proudly took a position at Porter's side, a few of the people who gathered helped Luke to his feet.

"Shit," Porter said, looking at his watch. "The movie started already."

I looked at the crowd that had gathered and realized it would only be a matter of time before the movie theater's security arrived. "Can we just do something else?"

"You sure you're okay with that?" he asked. "I know you wanted to see that movie."

"We can do anything," I said. "As long as we're together."

It didn't matter what we were doing, I'd be doing it with the man of my dreams. Simply knowing he was willing to stand up for me was enough to make me weak in the knees.

Not as weak in the knees as Luke Westham, but close.

"Where'd you learn to fight like that?" I sucked a mouthful of chocolate malt through the oversized straw. "Chuck Norris hasn't got anything on you."

He pressed the heels of his palms to his temples. "I can't drink any more of that thing."

I paused from drinking, but left the straw in my mouth, just in case I wanted more. "Ice cream headache?"

He nodded.

"So," I raised my eyebrows. "Are you going to answer me?"

"I'm thinking."

I sucked another ounce of cold deliciousness from the cup. "About whether or not you want to answer me?"

He no more than lowered his hands and winced from the pain. "Something like that."

"Are you okay?"

"I'll be fine."

"Your hands were a blur. I was just wondering if you were some Kung Fu master or some crap. That was awesome. I don't hate people, but I come really close to hating Luke, just so you know."

"He'd be an easy one to hate," he replied.

Since the incident at the movie theater, Porter seemed sidetracked and incapable of focusing. "Are you sure you're okay?" I asked. "You seem off, or whatever."

"I'm thinking."

I sucked on the straw until my cheeks caved in, gaining another mouthful of the perfect blend of chocolate and malted milk. With the straw resting on the tip of my tongue, I looked up. "About?"

He stared at the entrance for a while, and then looked at me. "I'm not who you think I am," he said, his voice filled with regret. "Not entirely."

My heart fell into the pit of my stomach. I pushed the malt to the side. "What do you mean?"

He glanced over each shoulder and then held my gaze. "I need to tell you some things about me."

I felt sick. The malted milk rose until it tickled the back of my throat.

I swallowed heavily. "Okay."

"The motorcycle club I ride with is an outlaw club," he said.

I waited for him to continue, but he didn't. I'd heard the *Outlaw MC* term before but wasn't completely sure what it meant. I didn't think it was all that bad, though. Not when compared to other things.

"What does that mean?" I asked. "In terms I can understand."

"Well, it means the members of our club fall within the one percent of riders that aren't willing to live by the rules of society. But, with us, there's more to it than that."

So far, I was relieved with what he'd revealed. There was obviously more he wanted to say, and I wanted to listen to anything he was willing to offer me.

"If you want to explain," I said. "I'll listen."

He nodded. "I can't go into detail, but I can speak in general terms."

Anything was better than nothing. His reluctance to continue made me more nervous than anything. His opening statement of *I'm not the man you think I am* still had my stomach in a knot.

"Okay. I mean, I'd just like to know more about 'I'm not the man you think I am'. When you said that, it made my stomach do flips."

His jaw tightened. He looked away, toward the ice cream cooler that was on the far wall. While he stared blankly at it, he began to speak. His voice was quiet, barely above a whisper. It was almost as if he was narrating a movie.

"I had a few run-ins with the law when I was a kid. Nothing much to speak of. Fighting, and riding a scooter through town without a license. I realized at a young age that I liked outsmarting the cops. I liked outrunning them even more. By the time I was a senior in high school, I'd been in a handful of high-speed chases with the cops and had never been caught. I'd stolen an old car from a salvage yard, built an engine for it in shop class, and kept it hidden on my grandparent's farm, in a windrow of trees. My friends and I would take it out, raise hell, and get the cops to try and catch us. The thrill of outrunning them gave me a high that nothing else could match. Although they tried, they never caught me once. The local cop referred to the guy in the sixty-five Fairlane as *a Ghost*. The name stuck, and I became 'Ghost'."

A sigh of relief shot from my lungs. "That's cool how you got your nickname. You had me scared there for a minute. I thought there was going to be more to it than that."

"There is," he said without looking at me. "Gimme a minute."

My stomach started churning.

"Four of my closest friends and I moved here after we graduated school, and we started this motorcycle club. We didn't abide by the law. In fact, we broke the law." He shifted his eyes to meet mine. "Intentionally."

I acted indifferent, waiting for him to elaborate. My stone-faced expression allowed him to continue without much pause.

"In our outlaw endeavors, we needed to escape quickly. I was, of course, the driver. Crime after crime, year after year, I never got caught. I became the club's good luck charm. The getaway driver. *The Ghost*." He looked at me. "That's who I am. I'm a biker, an outlaw, and a getaway driver."

The thought of him being a criminal was exciting. It also scared the shit out of me. The first question I asked him when we met was if he was a real biker. I didn't expect him to be a model citizen, nor did I want him to be. I didn't expect him to be a getaway driver for a group of outlaws, either.

I took a moment to digest what he'd said, and then drew a shallow breath. "Can I ask what kind of things you guys do?"

He shook his head. "I can't discuss club business."

His response sent me right back to feeling sick. The thought of losing him was real, and I didn't like it one bit. He was either going to need to trust me, or chance losing me. I couldn't be part of mass-murder plot or turn the other cheek if they were shooting gas station attendants in failed robbery attempts.

There were, however, some scenarios I could accept. Stealing truckloads of cigarettes and selling them on the black market was fine. Manufacturing methamphetamines wasn't. My mind was going a thousand different directions and I wasn't thinking clearly.

My eyes welled with tears. "Porter, I'm scared shitless right now, and I don't want this, or anything, to come between us. Can you. Can you give an example of what you're talking about? If you can't, we might need to quit seeing one another."

I couldn't believe the words that came out of my mouth. I wanted to take them back, but it was too late.

His expressionless look changed to one of worry.

With a tight jaw, he studied me.

"I need you to trust me," I begged. 'You can't expect me to accept who you are if you won't tell me who you truly are. I've hidden nothing from you. Be truthful with me and let me make a decision based on the truth."

He continued to stare. Fear clouded his eyes, leaving them dull and without much emotion other than distress.

"Do you trust me?" I asked.

He nodded.

"Prove it," I demanded. "Prove you trust me."

He blew out a long exhaustive breath, and then met my gaze.

"Every one of us takes a stance against drug dealers, and what their dope does to society. It's pretty common for us to rob drug dealers."

"At gunpoint?" I asked.

He shook his head. "We're professionals. Did you watch *Ocean's Eleven*?"

I'd seen the movie more than once. If the crimes depicted in the movies were what his club was doing, it was going to go from bad to good in instant.

"We're kind of like that," he explained. "A computer expert to manipulate the alarms. Explosives expert to divert attention. A weapons expert just in case. A man damned good at planning to put everything together. A getaway driver to make a quick escape."

"And you split the money?" I asked.

He chuckled. "We give more than half of it to charity. The club's president is like Robin Hood. He doesn't do it for the thrill, or for the financial gain. He does it for the betterment of mankind. When we rob drug dealers, we burn the dope in the desert, just to make sure it doesn't end up on the streets. He gives the money away like candy to the unfortunate."

"So, you don't manage car washes?" I asked.

"No," he responded. "That's true. I do manage car washes."

"And you rob drug dealers?"

He laced his fingers and leaned forward. "The last job we did was this: a woman had her retirement account compromised, and two million dollars of her savings was taken. The financial institution wasn't able to find it, but we did. We recovered the money and gave it to her."

I was fascinated. I shouldn't have been, but I was. "Cyber banking stuff?"

He shook his head. "No. Someone drained her accounts and converted it to cash. Then, he took the cash home and had it in his safe. We recovered it."

"So, you physically took it back? That kind of recovery?"

He nodded. "Correct."

I braced myself for the fact that at least one of them was a murderer. "What did you do to the guy that took it?"

"Advised him to keep his mouth shut, or we'd turn him in to the law for the crime."

It sounded like he was more of a vigilante than a criminal. Granted, he was committing crimes, but they weren't crimes against humanity. My gaze dropped to the table as I absorbed everything he'd said. While I tried to make sense of it all, he cleared his throat.

"For what it's worth, the club has a rule," he said. "We have a hands-off policy when it comes to women and the elderly. Men, on the other hand, are subject to the wrath of the club."

I looked up. "But only as a last resort?"

He nodded. "Correct."

"Would you consider walking away from the club?" I asked.

"I'm considering it now," he said. "I haven't made up my mind. I needed to come clean with you and see what you said. But, I need you to accept me, regardless of the choice I make. This has been killing me, Abby. I can give you as much time as you need. Either way, I understand."

I didn't need any time. I'd already made my decision. It wasn't solely based on the fact that I loved Porter, but my love for him played a huge part in my ability to accept him for who he was. He was committing crimes in the eyes of the law, but they were crimes that many law-abiding citizens would commit if they were able.

"I'd prefer you walk away," I said. "But only because I don't want you to get hurt. If you choose not to, I can accept that. We'll need to talk about it more, I'm sure, but I can accept it. Is there anything else?"

"Are you sure?" he asked.

Love is the key to coloring outside the lines. My prompt acceptance of my criminal boyfriend's activities was proof. Losing him wasn't something I was willing to risk. I managed to find a way to accept everything he'd said. I didn't like the thought of him being hurt while robbing a drug dealer, but for the time being I'd reserve hope that he'd find a way to walk away from the club.

I offered a crooked smile and a nod. "Yes."

"You're one hundred percent sure?" he asked.

"Yes."

Both eyebrows raised. "Abby?"

I sighed. "Yeah?"

"I love you."

"Pardon me?" I blinked a few times. "I thought you said *I love you.*"

"I did," he said. "When I admitted it to myself, I knew I had to tell you everything. Now that I have, it's time for me to be honest. I love you, and I can't imagine living a single day without you. I want you in my life, now and forever."

I covered my mouth with my hand to prevent hyperventilation. After a moment of heavy breathing, I lowered my hand. "I love you, too I really do I think I have for a long time but I was too afraid to admit it I'm glad you finally said something because it was eating me up inside I went to talk to George about it God I love you."

He stood and stretched his arms wide.

I wanted to attack him like a rabid spider monkey.

He swept me from my feet and spun me around, so my back was to the wall. Then, he kissed me like I'd never been kissed. I couldn't remember if Disney princes and princesses kissed, but if they did, their kisses would have been like that kiss.

It was the perfect kiss. From the perfect man. On the perfect night. After the perfect fight to preserve our perfect relationship. And then, the perfect revelation.

He loved me.

And, he told me so in the perfect place.

My favorite ice cream parlor.

When our mouths parted, I began to cry.

He wiped my tears away and looked into my eyes. "What's wrong?"

"Number two on my list," I blubbered. "I did it."

"*We* did it," he said.

I couldn't wait to tell my mother and George. My father would shit a complete brick, but I didn't care. He'd have to find a way to get over it.

"I can't wait to tell George," I blurted.

"Can we tell him together?" he asked.

As far as I was concerned, we needed to start doing everything together. Except for pooping. Pooping was an alone activity, even if I was in love.

I nodded eagerly. "When do you want to?"

He looked at his watch. "How about now?"

"What time is it?"

His mouth twisted into a smirk. "He closes in fifteen minutes."

It was twenty-five minutes away, maybe more, depending on traffic. "Guess it's a good thing I fell in love with a getaway driver," I said. "You want to show me how you earned that nickname, Ghost?"

GHOST

Despite my triple-digit high-speed run to the diner, the door was locked when we arrived. By my watch, we were a few minutes early. Abby, as excited as a kid on Christmas day, pounded on the door as if she was trying to knock it down.

"He's in the back," she said. "He always cleans the kitchen last."

George peered over the ledge of the pass-through opening. After recognizing us, he shook his head and turned away. A moment later, he burst through the swinging doors and into the dining area.

With his arms swinging at his sides and his head held high, he marched to the front door and removed the keys from his pocket.

After fumbling with the lock for a moment, he pushed the door open just wide enough to fit his head in the crack. He glared at Abby. "What in the name of fuck is going on?" He shifted his eyes to me and grinned. "Evening, Porter."

I gave a nod. "George."

Abby tossed her hands high in the air. "We're in love."

He glanced at each of us and then fixed his eyes on Abby. "You two have been drooling over each other since the first day you brought him in here. I'm not dirtying up my kitchen to celebrate something that I've been knowing for the last month or so."

"Stop being so grumpy," she said. "I'm excited."

"I'm excited, too." He grinned a cheesy tooth-revealing grin. "See?"

She put her hands on her hips. "We saw Luke Westham at the Mission Valley Theater. He grabbed my arm and called Porter an asshole. Porter knocked him out cold."

He looked at me and arched one of his oversized eyebrows. "The creepy running back for the Chargers?"

"That's the one," I said.

"I'd planned on kicking that dip-shit's ass myself, but he never cashed in the free lunch vouchers I sent him on Facebook." He pushed the door open. "Well, hell's bells, get your asses in here. That's cause for celebration."

Abby walked past him and turned around. "You sent him lunch vouchers?"

"Four or five times after that last series of emails he sent you. Told him he was a random winner. Offered all you can eat pancakes and ham for free. Son-of-a-bitch never showed up. Figured Lawson and I would tune him up if he did."

I laughed. "Which one's Lawson?"

"Tall kid with the scar on his face."

That would have been a fight worth seeing. Lawson was at least six-feet-six, and weighed two fifty, easily. His hands came to rest right beside his knees, which would have given him a six-inch reach on the football player.

I chuckled. "You could have sold tickets to that fight."

"If they would have sold tickets to yours, there'd be a bunch of people wanting refunds," Abby said with a laugh.

"Why's that?" George asked.

"He hit him five times in two seconds, and then Luke fell in a pile," Abby said. "It was over before it started."

George offered his hand. "Good work, Porter."

I shook his hand. "He got what he deserved."

"So." He looked at Abby. "What'll it be?"

"To celebrate the fight?"

He smiled a genuine smile. "Wasn't falling in love item number two on the list?"

"It was."

"Technically, we're closed," he said. "As long as no money changes hands, we can have a glass of champagne."

"You've got champagne?" Abby asked excitedly.

"Got a couple of bottles in the back for such an occasion," he said.

Abby looked at me.

I shrugged. "I've never been in love with anyone. It's a pretty big deal for me."

"Big deal for me, too," George said, shifting his eyes from Abby to me as he spoke. "Be right back."

In a few minutes, we were seated in Abby's favorite booth, right next to the kitchen. Each of us had a ruby red plastic tumbler filled with champagne. George raised his over the center of the table.

"Raise your glass for these two lost souls, for they've finally found their fate. May this toast keep them as one, 'till they reunite at heaven's gate."

We clanked our glasses together and took a drink.

Abby lowered her glass. "I like that. Where'd it come from?"

"I made it up," George said.

"Just now?" she asked.

"Just now."

I liked what he said, short of the heaven's gate thing. Nonetheless, I offered a smile and a nod. "That was nice."

"I'm about two percent Irish, according to that ancestry DNA thing," he said. "The Irish always give witty toasts. I thought I'd make something up. Rolled off the tongue pretty easily."

"I liked it," Abby said.

"I hope this lasts forever," George said. "If anyone deserves it, it's the two of you."

Forever ended when either of our clocks stopped ticking. Although we were the same age, my forever and Abby's forever weren't the same. Since meeting Abby, I'd avoided questions about my condition, all but lying to her – and to myself – about the cancer that ate away at my chance of having a meaningful forever with her.

Admitting that I loved her opened a floodgate of emotion, and of possibilities. I could see my future with her, and I liked what I saw. It was time for me to cast my insecurities aside, become a responsible lover, and seek treatment for my cancer. I owed it to her, and to myself, to take care of my health the best that I was able.

I took a silent sip of what remained of my champagne, hoping my decision wasn't made too late.

23

ABBY

I sat in the waiting room of the cancer center with my purse in my lap and my heart in my throat. I'd give any amount of money to fix Porter's condition, but I had no idea what it was or what he needed. He never spoke of the doctor, of his appointments, or of his recovery. He hated going to the meetings, and over the course of the time that we'd been together, had only gone to two.

During a visit to his doctor two days prior, they scheduled another appointment at once. I was all too familiar with the research center, and knew if his appointment was there, that his condition wasn't as good as I hoped it would be.

Over the last seven weeks I'd told myself he was getting better. I convinced myself of it. In my mind, if he said nothing, it meant things were improving. I now felt like an ostrich that had buried its head in the sand.

The unique smell of the research center brought back memories of my frequent visits. With them came a flood of recollections from my lengthy recovery. Losing weight until I weighed eighty-five pounds. Being covered in bruises. Vomiting day in, day out. Losing my hair. Praying. Losing my faith. Praying some more.

Flushing the toilet twice became a habit that was difficult to break.

I feared the chemicals would remain in my body forever. Then, after deciding I couldn't go another round of therapy, I was told I had beaten the dreaded disease.

I was a true survivor.

My father said *it's not the dog in the fight, it's the fight in the dog.* My mother agreed, telling stories of how I was stubborn, even as a toddler.

Now worried sick, I clutched my stomach and waited for Porter to return. I decided no matter what, he was going to have to start confiding in me exactly what his condition was. I was not going to allow him to shelter me from the truth any longer. We were a team, and we were going to get through the treatments together, regardless of the outcome of each visit.

Just like George said, deception was the same as a lie. Porter not telling me about his doctor visits was the same as telling me an untruth. If he loved me – and I was sure that he did – he could tell me everything. He *needed* to tell me everything. If he did, as a team, we could get through anything.

I clutched my purse, closed my eyes, and drew a deep breath.

It's me again, the girl with the potty mouth. I need another favor. I don't ask for much. In fact, I've asked for nothing since I was in this room last. Considering what you did for me, I need to ask that you consider doing something for the man I love.

He's not close to you, and I know he won't ask for anything. That doesn't prevent me from asking that you bless him. I'd give anything to have you place your healing hand on his shoulder.

Anything.

If you're able, and if you see him as fit for a better life on earth than in heaven, please consider blessing him with the power of healing. Despite some of the choices he's made in life, he's a good man.

If you choose to answer this prayer, I reserve hope that it gives him the faith he needs to become closer to you.

In your name I pray.

Amen.

I opened my eyes.

I watched the minutes on my cell phone's clock tick past, until another hour had passed. I checked the status of the purse I'd ordered online. I scrolled through my recent Instagram posts. I Googled *brain tumors* and read data until I was sick. I looked on Amazon for a new bicycle. I picked the sand out of the split soles of my beloved Converse. I twirled my hair. Just when I was on the verge of breaking down, the door beside me creaked open.

I looked up. Porter stepped through the threshold and into the room. Glassy-eyed and expressionless, he pulled the door closed behind him. His eyes met mine.

A tear rolled down his cheek.

I stood and turned to face him.

His upper body fell against the wall. He began to cry. "I can't get my legs to work."

I joined him, blubbering for what I knew not. I knew, however, that I must remain strong for him. I somehow managed to walk the few steps that separated us. With tears rolling down both cheeks, Porter fell into my arms.

While I held the man I so dearly loved against my chest, I said one more prayer. Not for healing, or for a miracle, but for strength.

Strength that I knew he'd require to do something as simple as take a single step.

After the quick prayer, I motioned toward the door. "Come on, sweetheart. We're going home."

24

GHOST

I was in shock. I took two steps, stumbled, and braced myself against the wall. "Give me a minute. I can't get my legs to work."

"Come on, sweetheart," she said. "We're going home."

I wanted to run all the way back to her house, screaming the entire way. Hand in hand, we'd run up the stairs – two at a time – and out onto the deck. We'd watch the sunset while we kissed and sipped champagne.

But I couldn't take one single step. Since seeing the results of the scan, my legs were made of rubber.

I loved her with every ounce of my being. Her forever had somehow managed to grab ahold of my forever and take it with it, whisking it past the one obstacle that prevented us from having a future together.

My outlook now included a long, prosperous life of loving one another.

"Do I need to get a wheelchair?" she asked.

"Just…" I paused and drew a breath. "Look at me."

She turned to face me. Tears streamed down her face. I wondered what she must be thinking, and realized she feared the worst.

"The scan. They did two of them," I said, my voice cracking from emotion. "Three, actually."

She bit against her lower lip and nodded. "We'll get another opinion. We can fly you to Houston. Come on, let's go. I hate this place. It stinks in here. The doctors are stupid, too. They don't know shit."

"The tumor," I muttered. "It's…it's gone."

She stopped in her tracks. "Gone?" Her eyes shot wide. "As in *gone*?"

"Gone. Completely." I pressed my palms to my thighs and struggled to catch my breath. "After the third test…they said what they believed was cancer was nothing but…an odd brain swelling. It was brought on from hitting my head…too many times. I've got a free bill of health. Well, kind of."

She raised both fists, looked at the ceiling, and shouted *thank you*.

"Holy shit." I drew a long breath and then shook my head. "I can't believe this is over."

"You don't have to come back?" she asked. "No more tests? They're sure?"

"That's what took so long. They couldn't believe it, either."

"It's a miracle," she said. "An answered prayer. Let's celebrate."

She could believe what she wanted to believe. I knew it was nothing more than a misdiagnosis. A doctor pressed for time, attempting to make as much money as he could from HMO payments, scouring a series of images and making a rash judgement.

Prayer, or no prayer, the outcome would be the same. It wasn't close to a miracle. It was simple science. I hit my head, my brain swelled. According to the doctor, the three concussions I'd suffered hadn't left me with much room for any more.

"I can't hit my head again," I said. "They said it could cause severe damage. Brain damage."

"There'll be no more fights with football players." She adjusted her purse and gestured toward the door. "I can tell you that much."

I drew one last breath of the medicinal air, took her hand in mine, and smiled. "Let's go plan our life together."

ABBY

I'd spent nearly two months acting as if Porter's condition wasn't an issue, while in the back of my mind the possibility of him truly being sick festered like an infectious wound. Now that the nightmare was over, it was time, as Porter said, to plan our life together.

With Porter dressed in a new pair of swim shorts and me in a two-piece bikini, we sat on the deck and talked about renting surfboards.

"I'm still processing it," he said. "It's crazy. After a scare like that, you look at life completely different. Completely."

Following my successful cancer treatment, the sky was bluer, trees were greener, and the air smelled fresher. I couldn't spend enough time outdoors enjoying all of God's offerings. I bought a bicycle, a pair of running shoes, and a shopping cart filled with running outfits.

Within six months, I was running three days a week and riding my bicycle more than I drove. I focused on my YouTube channel, doing one high-quality video a week. I watched as my followers increased from two hundred thousand to over twenty million.

Everything changed following my recovery.

Everything.

"I know exactly what you're talking about," I said. "After my tests came back clean, I kept waiting for the other foot to drop, but it never did. After that, I looked at life as a true gift. My to-do list grew from fifty things to two hundred in about a month."

"What's left on it?"

"Two things," I responded. "There were three the other day, but I think we got one of them resolved."

"What's that?" he asked. "I don't remember you saying anything."

"One hundred and eighty-four. Rid myself of Luke Westham for good. At one point, I thought I was going to have to move to the Atlantic coast and change my name to Jennifer."

Porter let out a laugh. "We've seen the last of him, believe me. He got embarrassed in front of a room full of people that recognized him. He won't show his face again. He's too fucking embarrassed."

As Porter stated, being embarrassed was going to keep Luke away from me for a lifetime. Yet, I was supposed to agree to try and surf, which would undoubtedly end in me being made a fool of. I hated feeling like I'd been embarrassed. It was what had kept *surfing* on my to-do list for almost a decade.

"Yeah." I let out a sigh of relief that I'd been holding in for three years. "I think I'll draw a line through one eighty-four for sure."

"So, what's left on your list?"

"If I can get past these jitters and surf, I'll be down to one."

"Which is what?"

I scrunched my nose. "Get a tattoo."

"What's kept you from doing that?"

I liked looking at tattoos on other people, even the crappy ones. When it came to place one on my skin, I wanted it to be simple, perfect, and something I'd never get sick of. As much thought as I'd given it over the years, I couldn't come up with anything that I was comfortable getting.

"Not knowing what I'd want to add to my body that I'd be comfortable keeping forever."

He finished his champagne. "Have you got any ideas yet?"

"A few," I said. "Nothing I'm really excited about, though."

"We'll have to think about that." He gazed over the handrail, toward the beach. The mid-day sun had just cleared the deck's canopy, and the weather was perfect for the beach. "So, do you want to try and surf?"

"Maybe later."

He closed his eyes and drew a long breath through his nose. "I'm going to relax, then."

"I'm nervous about falling off the board," I said.

"You're falling into water. It doesn't hurt."

"It'll be embarrassing."

"Only if you let it be."

"If people see me, it'll be embarrassing."

"It's only embarrassing if you lack self-esteem. It's not a big deal. Fall off, get back on. Fall off, get back on. Then, one day, you don't fall off."

"You don't get embarrassed, do you?"

"Haven't yet."

"Ever fallen off a bike?" I asked.

"Bicycle?"

"Yeah."

"Many times," he said.

"Did people see you?"

"Yep."

"It wasn't embarrassing?"

"Nope. I didn't let it be. The difference between me and you is that I don't give a fuck what people think. Now that we're getting on with our lives, you should try adopting that philosophy."

It sounded easy, but it wasn't. If I fell off the surf board, people would laugh. Then, I'd feel embarrassed. Actually, I wouldn't be surprised if someone video taped it and posted it on YouTube.

It seemed I couldn't go anywhere and maintain anonymity.

I stared toward the beach for a moment. Two men paddled out and caught a wave, then rode it back to shore. Neither of them fell off, and no one seemed to care. I wanted to check surfing off my list, but a small part of me feared the inevitable.

After Porter's release from the doctor, I'd been filled with nervous energy. I was itching to live a life free of restrictions, inhibitions, and the threat of cancer. I glanced in his direction. Still sitting with his eyes closed, he looked peaceful. I, on the other hand, was yearning to do *something*. Something other than surf.

"Can I play with your dick while you're relaxing?"

He tilted his head to the side and opened one eye. "If it'll make you happy."

I found pleasure in doing anything with Porter. Doing things with Porter's dick took my pleasure to an entirely different level.

I'd see more dicks in one weekend than most girls would see in a lifetime career in the porn industry. Stiff dick pics flooded my inbox, as did five-second-long videos of men stroking themselves.

Porter's dick stood out from the tens of thousands of dicks that had burned cock-shaped lesions on my corneas over the years. It was long, thick, and as straight as a rocket. I was fascinated by it.

It was the one dick – the only dick – I'd ever seen that was pretty.

I slid off the edge of my chair, duck-walked to his side, and reached into the leg of his shorts. After gripping the semi-soft shaft, I looked him in the eyes.

They were closed.

I stroked his cock gently, fascinated by its ability to grow to four times the original size. In a few strokes, it was as hard as steel. His eyes, however, remained closed.

"Does it hurt?" I asked. "When it's all bound up in your shorts like that?"

"Nope."

He was shirtless, shoeless, and freshly shaven. I wanted him to toss the shorts and let me play with his dick. Other than the fact that his cock was hard, he didn't seem too interested in my little dick game.

"It's trying to stand up, but it can't." With the shaft gripped firmly in my hand, I wiggled it back and forth, watching the peak of the fabric tent move as I did so. "It's restricted. Like putting on a size two when you need a size six. It can't feel good."

"It's not a big deal," he said dryly.

I peered into the leg of his shorts. His dick was pointing toward the beach at a forty-five-degree angle, limited in travel by the fabric of his swim shorts, which were stretched to the limit.

"You're pitching a nylon tent," I said. "It looks like it hurts."

He opened one eye. "Okay. It hurts."

"Does it really?" I asked excitedly.

"No."

I sighed. "Okay."

"What do you want me to say, Abby?" he asked. "Dicks aren't as delicate as you might think. It doesn't hurt."

I squeezed it as hard as I could. "What about now?"

"Nope."

I bent it downward, toward his chair's seat. When it felt like it was going to snap off in my hands, I stopped. "What about that? That has to hurt."

"It's not comfortable," he said without emotion. "But it doesn't hurt."

Frustrated, I released his dick and tugged against the leg of his shorts. "If we're not going to surf right now, can we take these guys off?"

One eye opened. "Is that what all that was about? You want to take my shorts off? Why didn't you just ask?"

"That's not how girls do things. We beat around the bush until the man gets the hint."

"Fine." He untied the shorts, wrestled them over his stiff dick, and tossed them aside. Being naked was obviously comfortable for him, because he nonchalantly sat and propped his legs onto the wicker ottoman no differently than if he were clothed. He closed his eyes. "There. Problem solved."

I was disappointed that I hadn't suggested he spend all his outside time sans clothes. As I admired his naked beauty, I made a mental note to require that he be naked in the future.

Tanned and covered in muscles from his knees to his neck, he looked like he belonged in the risqué display of the art studio on Beverly Hills Boulevard, in Los Angeles. With a watering mouth and a wandering mind, I shifted my eyes from his rigid dick to the beach, which was a few hundred yards away.

From our second-story vantage point, we could see everything below, but it wasn't easy for passersby to see us. I looked left, and then right. My neighbor's homes weren't as tall as mine, and it was equally impossible for them to see us.

Satisfied that we were secluded enough to allow me to play with his dick without repercussion, I began to stroke it. The velvety smooth skin amazed me, considering what it encompassed was as hard as a Porter's bulging muscles.

"I really like you," I whispered.

"You talking to me?" he asked.

"No, I was taking to him."

"To my cock?"

"I like him," I said.

With his eyes still closed, he nodded in acknowledgement. "He likes you, too."

I increased my speed and tightened my grip a little.

"That feels good," he said under his breath.

I compared my dainty hand to the size of his massive shaft, and soon got lost in the rhythm of providing Porter pleasure.

"I want to watch you come," I whispered.

"Are you talking to me, or to him?"

"Both of you."

"Keep doing that, and you'll get exactly what you're after."

The thought of it excited me. I'd never watched cum spurt from the tip of his dick – or any dick, for that matter. If such wayward things were going to occupy our days in the future, my life was truly going to be filled with blessings.

I developed a predictable rhythm, stroking his dick as if it were mine, doing what I felt I'd want done if I were a man. He seemed unaffected by the gesture, which satisfied me and bothered me both. His lack of interest left me feeling like I was doing something wrong, or that my dick stroking skills were mediocre at best.

But. I was free to do as I wished, without fear of repercussion or retribution. He truly didn't give a fuck. Hell, he could have been asleep for all I knew.

I licked the tip of his dick as I stroked it, circling my tongue around the swollen tip. Then, I wrapped my full lips around the head, encompassing it fully. I knew having my mouth on his cock drove him crazy, and that was exactly what I hoped for. After another minute or so of sucking and licking, I lifted my head.

"Are you going to come for me?"

"He is," Porter breathed.

I continued my pace, licking and kissing as I stroked the entire length from base to tip. After a long period of forcing my mouth over the head and onto the shaft, his back arched a little. Then, a little more.

The thought of seeing him come was wreaking havoc on me. Tingling in all the right places and driven by a passion to satisfy the man I loved, I maintained my pace, hoping for an end result that pleased him deeply.

His breathing became labored. Excited for the grand finale, I sat up straight and fixed my eyes on the tip.

With his eyes closed and his hands dangling loosely at his sides, Porter continued his expression of indifference. It fascinated me that he could maintain such an emotionless position on the outside but be brimming with sexual excitement on the inside.

"I'm going to lose it in a minute," he whispered. "Fuck this is hot."

"Come for me, baby," I said softly.

I nudged my purse to the side in hope of getting a better view of the fountain of cum that was sure to blow from the tip at any moment. Then, a light bulb illuminated in my feeble mind. I reached into my purse, grabbed my phone, and opened Instagram's Boomerang app.

With his cock in one hand and my phone in the other, I waited to start my ten-second recording of Porter's climax.

As his breathing changed to choppy and unpredictable, I stroked with one hand, and pointed my phone with the other. His hips raised, lifting his ass from the seat cushion. Then, the muscles in his legs flexed.

Excited beyond belief, I pressed the *record* button.

Two seconds into my rudimentary pornographic production, a stream of cum shot from the tip of his dick. Another followed. Watching through the phone's screen, I grinned from ear to ear, knowing I satisfied my man to no end – and that caught every morsel of the climactic ending on film.

When I lowered the phone, Porter was giving me a side-eyed look. "What the fuck are you doing?"

"Oh," I gasped. "I thought you were sleeping, or whatever."

"Relaxing," he breathed. "I was relaxing."

"I was just." I released his dick and raised my phone. "I was making a Boomerang."

"A video of me busting a nut?"

"Uhhm." I grinned. "Yeah."

He rolled his eyes. "Don't be putting that shit on Instagram."

Instagram had a strict policy against nudity, which included Boomerang videos of skinny women in sundresses jacking off musclebound hunks with big dicks.

A shame, but true.

"They won't let me," I said. "It's porn. It's for personal use. Just for me. I'll pleasure myself while watching it."

He lowered himself onto the seat cushion. "That was pretty awesome, by the way."

"Getting a handy at noon?"

"Yep." He crossed his arms and closed his eyes. "After you give me a kiss, and I take a little nap. I'll be ready to surf."

I leaned over and kissed him, thankful that our relationship was so open and loving that I could choke his cock for research purposes and not have to worry about him taking exception to my ridiculous idea. My future with Porter was an open book, limited by nothing more than our imaginations, and my imagination was vast.

After repositioning myself beside his chair, I touched my phone's screen with my thumb and started the Boomerang, which was nothing more than a ten-second video on *loop.*

On the video, Porter's abs and chest were visible in the

background, as was my hand stroking his cock. Two seconds into it, cum blasted from the tip, twice. Then, it repeated itself.

It was the most awesome, no-nonsense piece of pornography to ever exist. Brief, and to the point. I watched it play, repeatedly, a dozen times. I loved satisfying him sexually, and the video stood of proof of my abilities.

"UPS delivery," a voice said from my left side.

"OhmyGod!" I screeched, nearly jumping out of my skin.

I hadn't even heard him come up the steps. A mere five feet from us, the UPS delivery man stood with a box in his hands.

Without opening his eyes or covering his still semi-rigid dick, Porter raised his left hand and pointed at the space beside his chair. "Leave it right there."

"Need a signature, Sir."

"Got a pen?" Porter asked.

"You can sign with the stylus."

Naked as the day he was born, Porter leaned forward, opened his eyes, and accepted the electronic signature pad. After signing it, he stood and handed the device to the stone-faced delivery man.

The man handed Porter a brown box. "Have a nice day."

"I'm in the process of it," Porter replied with a nod.

While my phone continued to re-play the money shot video, I gawked at the transaction in disbelief. Only Porter could do such a thing without an ounce of emotion or sliver of embarrassment.

He handed me the box. "If I can do that without turning red, you can try and surf. All it requires is a little confidence. You're a badass, Abby. Get out there, get on a board, and *be a badass*."

Porter had a way of building my confidence through compliments. Two years in our future, I'd be overflowing with self-assurance, I was sure of it. I grinned at the possibilities that were on our relationship's horizon.

"Fine," I said. "Let's go check another one off the list."

GHOST

I didn't have parents to introduce Abby to, but I had five brothers and two sisters-in-law. "Remember," I said. "Everything we talked about is hush-hush. Even when you meet their girlfriends, you know nothing about the club's business."

"I've got it," she said. "Don't worry. I'm not going to say anything."

While she buckled the strap on her helmet, another thing crossed my mind. "Don't mention the cancer, either."

"Mine?"

"No, mine."

Her eyebrows raised. "What do you mean?"

"Don't mention it."

"Okay. What if one of them brings it up?"

"They won't."

"What if they do?"

"They don't know about it."

"You *still* haven't told them?" She gave me a bug-eyed look. "Any of them?"

"Nope."

"I'm just glad my prayers were answered," she said. "And that it's over. But, I won't bring it up."

My physical condition had nothing to do with prayers, and everything to do with science. I didn't miraculously recover from cancer. I'd been misdiagnosed by a doctor who had his head in his ass. Giving God credit for something that no God has control over was ridiculous.

I wiped the lenses of my sunglasses. "Do you really think *your God* answered your prayers? That you prayed, and that he changed me from having a brain tumor to having nothing?"

She nodded. "I do."

I chuckled. "Ohhh-kay."

She stepped away from the motorcycle and gave me a shitty look. "You're going to tell me after all of that, after going from a brain tumor that was so bad your migraines kept you from sleeping to being completely cured, that you still don't believe there's a God looking over you? And, that the very same God didn't answer the prayers that I asked of him while you were in there getting your tests done?"

"I'm sorry." I put on my glasses. "I don't."

"I'm not going to preach to you about it," she said. "But will you let me believe what I believe?"

I shrugged. "Sure."

The ride to Goose's home was silent. Discussions between believers and non-believers never ended well, which was why I'd refused to participate in them in the past. Refusing with Abby was impossible, so I had to accept that such discussions may create tension between us.

Her beliefs, however, weren't going to become my beliefs. For the time being, I believed in my bracelet, and that was enough to get me through each day.

After coming to a stop in Goose's drive, Abby pulled off her helmet and lifted her leg over the seat. "It smells good."

"Goose is a great cook. Basically, the guy's a chef. He can cook anything. Wait 'till you taste his smoked turkey. It's awesome."

She hung her helmet on the handlebars. "Awesome is the best something can be. You know that, right?"

"Wait 'till you taste it. You'll agree."

Apparently, we were done discussing God. I liked that Abby gave me my space when it came to religion. I hoped she realized it wasn't my intention to argue about it. Convincing me of the existence of God wasn't something she – or anyone else – was going to do. In time, I hoped she could find a way to accept that my position on the matter wasn't something that was going to change.

Goose's home was a small ranch with an ornate yard that stood out from the rest of the homes on the block. His green thumb was obvious, as his yard was filled with greenery, flowers, and various shrubs that only he could get to grow in Southern California's climate.

We walked up the drive and to the gate that led to the back yard. As soon as we came into view of everyone in attendance, all eyes were on us. I'd warned the fellas not to swarm her, but I feared they would, regardless. Partially due to her celebrity status, and in part because I had settled down with one woman, I suspected we'd be the center of attention.

Twenty feet into to the yard, Tito stepped off the deck and greeted us.

"Tito," he extended his hand. "Pleasure to meet you."

"I'm Abby," she said. "Are you the cook?"

He shook his head. "Brother Goose is the cook." He gestured toward the back deck. "He's the one wearing the apron with the lobster on it."

Abby glanced in Goose's direction. He stood beside the grille, talking to Baker and Cash.

"Oh," she said. "Whatever he's cooking smells wonderful."

"He's not cooking seafood, is he?" I asked.

"It's kind of a hodgepodge," Tito said. "Baker wanted seafood, and everyone else wanted barbeque. So, we're having oysters, lobster, turkey, brisket, and grilled fish of some sort. Maybe trout, I don't know."

"I love seafood," Abby said with a smile.

Baker, Cash, Goose, and Reno craned their necks in our direction. Baker's girlfriend Andy, and Cash's wife Kimberly stepped off the deck together, and began walking in our direction.

"Hi," Andy said. "I'm Andy."

Andy was as solid as any woman on earth. She'd entered the club through an odd series of circumstances, but had proven her devotion to the club, and to Baker repeatedly through her actions. There weren't many people on earth that I'd give my endorsement, but Andy was sure one of them.

"Abby," Abby said. "Nice to meet you."

Kimberly shook Abby's hand, and commented on her new Converse, saying that the shoe had made a recent comeback.

"It's all I wear," Abby said. "Chucks and a dress have become my signature outfit."

"It looks great on you," Andy said.

Abby smiled. "Thank you."

"Come on," Andy said. "I'll introduce you to everyone."

"I can introduce her," I said.

Andy gave me a look. "Go hang with your brothers and let the girls have their time together."

"Fine."

I didn't consciously hold back on my relationship with Abby, but for some reason, I hadn't introduced her to the club. After being given a clean bill of health, the first thing I wanted to do was bring our relationship to light.

I suspected an inner fear of dying prevented me from outwardly admitting that I was in a relationship, and that I was sick. Admitting one required admitting the other. Keeping my diagnosis from the club was easier if I kept Abby from the club.

"So, this is what you've been doing with your time over the last two months," Tito said.

"Pretty much," I responded.

Seeing Abby interact with the girls opened a new window of opportunity in our relationship. As I watched her meet the rest of the fellas, I envisioned trips across country with her on the back of the bike, sharing one of my favorite activities.

Connecticut in the fall with Cash and Kimberly would be quite an experience. During the trip the women would develop a bond that would be unbreakable, comparable to the bond the men had developed since childhood.

Since Cash and Kimberly adopted their child, Cash's mother moved from Montana to San Diego to be closer to the baby. She was a loving grandmother, a babysitter, and the club's voice of reason.

"Is Erin bringing the baby later?" I asked.

"I haven't heard," Tito responded. "Maybe."

Kimberly and Cash opened a nursery, which had been Kimberly's dream for some time. It was an immediate success, consuming much of Cash's time and all of Kimberly's time. Their baby and Cash's mother, Erin, had become fixtures in the nursery's office, staying in a nursery Cash had built within the office.

Seeing Cash happily married gave me reason to believe I could to the same. I knew, beyond a doubt, that I would never want anyone but Abby. I'd given her my entire heart, and she, in turn, had given me hers.

I worried that two months into a relationship was far too early to propose marriage, but not expressing my intentions to her – when marriage was all I could think about – seemed dishonest to me.

And, as I had said since the beginning, I wanted to maintain complete transparency.

"Can you keep your little mouth shut?" I asked.

"About what?" Tito asked.

"About whatever I want to talk about."

Reno stepped off the deck and started to walk in our direction. I raised my index finger. "Give us a minute, Brother Reno."

He paused and gave a nod.

"Sure," Tito said. "Why?"

"Because, I want to talk to you about some shit, privately. And, privately means *privately*."

"It'll remain between us," Tito assured me.

While I watched Andy and Abby wander through Goose's lushly landscaped yard talking, I turned to face Tito. He was a walking dictionary, had received a scholarship to MIT – which he declined – and a genius.

Beyond that, he had a good head on his shoulders.

"I'm going to ask you something," I explained. "But I don't want the statistical answer, or the Google response. I can Google shit. I want your opinion, because I respect you."

"Okay."

"Abby and I have been seeing each other for two months, basically. We've both admitted that we're in love with each other. I can't imagine living a day without her, and I want her to fully understand how much she means to me. How soon is too soon to get married?"

"The national average time to date prior to marriage is about three years," he said.

"Damn it, Tito. I said I wanted to know--"

"But," he interrupted, raising his hand between us. "I don't think three years is required to realize you're in love with that one woman who makes a difference in your life that only she can make."

"So, you think it's not too early? Not to get married," I said. "But to propose marriage."

"To get engaged?" he asked.

"Yeah. Engaged."

"An engagement is the promise of marriage. Personally, I don't see the problem with doing that as soon as you're certain that the woman in question is *that* woman. Postponing that marriage to allow a lengthy engagement is probably a good idea. It would allow the two parties to learn each other's faults and weaknesses, and to build on the relationship. Then, when they're married, there's very little that might go wrong."

"Gives time to plan it and make sure everyone can attend and stuff, too," I added.

He smiled. "Absolutely."

I narrowed my gaze. "What?"

"Are you going to ask her?"

"That's none of your business," I said.

"You already revealed your cards, Ghost. Personally, I think it's quite charming. To take a guy like you, who has struggled with relationships for one reason or another, and form him into a loving caring--"

"Stop," I insisted. "I don't want to hear it."

"Hear what?"

"All that wishy-washy shit. I love her. She loves me. I can't imagine life without her. That's the beginning and the end of it. Nobody formed me into anything. I finally found the girl that makes a difference in my life, and in my way of looking at love. It's that simple."

He shrugged. "Okay."

"Now, keep you little mouth shut," I said. "Let's go mingle."

He gestured toward the deck. "After you."

We joined the rest of the men on the deck while the women sat by the fountain that Goose built in the center of the yard. While they discussed decorating ideas, clothing, and makeup, we talked about camshafts, horsepower, and blowjobs.

"She can't fit much more than the tip in her mouth," I said. "That's it."

"It's not a blowjob, then," Cash said. "It's a rim job."

Baker burst into laughter. "A rim job is when a woman licks your butthole, genius."

Cash's eyes went thin. "I thought a rim job was when a girl licked the head of your dick?"

Baker shook his head. "Nope."

Cash looked at Tito.

"A rim job is just as Baker said it was," Tito said. "It's when a man or a woman licks the area surrounding the anus, or the anus' *rim*."

"What is it when she licks the head of your dick, then?" Cash asked.

"A shitty blowjob," Reno said with a laugh.

"She's got a little mouth and I've got a big dick," I said. "It's fine with me."

"Girls with little mouths have little twats," Reno said.

"Where the fuck did you hear that?" Baker asked.

Reno crossed his arms. "It's true."

"That's bullshit," Baker huffed. "Andy's got a big mouth, and her twat is the size of a dime."

Reno looked at me. "What about the movie star? She got a big twat?"

I rolled my eyes. "For the sake of ending this stupid conversation, I'll reply. *No.*"

"She's got a little bitty fucker, doesn't she?" he asked.

I cocked an eyebrow.

He raised his hands and turned his palms to face me. "I don't need to know."

"No," I responded. "You sure don't."

"Kim can swallow a baseball bat," Cash offered. "Without gagging."

"Never understood why all girls couldn't do that," Reno said. "Deep throating a dick is a man's dream come true."

"Not mine," I said. "I don't give half a fuck about what Abby can or can't swallow."

"She must have other talents," Reno said. "Really good ones."

"Yeah." I looked the men over. "She's got one really good talent."

Ten eyes widened in wonder of my revelation. I hadn't planned on revealing my feelings to the entire club, but I was caught up in the moment and felt the need to clarify matters.

"She's good at loving me," I said. "And, when you're truly in love with someone, you accept them wholeheartedly."

I waited for the fallout.

No one laughed. No one made a snide comment, and no one questioned my devotion to her. After a few silent seconds passed, Baker patted me on the shoulder.

"Love is a beautiful thing, Brother Ghost," he said. "Half the men standing here know that first hand. The other half? They'll wonder until the day they find what it is that we've been blessed with. Only then will they understand."

There was a reason Baker was the president of the club, and he'd just reminded everyone why. His character, his demeanor, and his ability to speak from the heart when needed was second to none.

I raised my bottle of beer and tilted the neck toward him. Cash lifted his bottle, and Baker followed. I glanced at Abby and then at the men.

"To love," I said.

The two men clanked the necks of their bottles against mine and chimed the toast in unison.

"To love."

ABBY

S ince becoming successful in my career, I'd not really had a girlfriend that I spent time with beyond the reach of social media. It sounded terrible to say, but I feared women who tried to befriend me were doing so in the hope of gaining an increased social media presence, or for financial gain.

I'd seen it happen too many times with other celebrities to question whether my fears were justified or not. Due to those reservations, George had become my closest friend. Nothing, however, could match the joy of having a female companion.

Andy picked up a piece of sushi with her chopsticks, dipped it into her soy sauce, and poked it into her mouth. "This place is awesome."

"I love that word," I said.

"Which one?" she asked.

"*Awesome*. It's one of my all-time favorite words." I chose a piece of sushi, paused, and looked at her.

She was beautiful, curvaceous, and had curly hair and perfect olive-colored skin. I had straight hair, sticks for legs, and was so pale-skinned that I should be the one with the nickname *Ghost*.

I wasn't envious of her, I simply wanted there to be things we had in common with one another. A common thread that we shared between us beyond having bikers for boyfriends.

"Let's say you're at a buffet, and there's all this food. Some of it is good, and some of it is so-so, and then there's one that is just perfect. What word would you use to describe the perfect one?" I asked.

"I don't eat at buffets," she said. "They're a breeding ground for bacteria, and you don't know where they get their food. I like places like this that make food fresh and don't use preservatives."

"Okay. You're at an all-you-can-eat sushi bar. And the itamae sets six different items in front of you. One stands out as being miles ahead of the rest in flavor. What one word do you use to later describe it to your friends. Good? great? Best? Fantastic? You know, something like that?"

"I'd say it was awesome, why?"

"I just love that word."

She smiled. "I like it, too."

At that moment, I decided Andy and I could be great friends. She was a property manager, which I found fascinating. She didn't bother me about my job, ask a bunch of questions about my income, or even ask where I lived, for that matter.

She simply enjoyed shopping with me and getting a bite to eat.

"How'd you meet Ghost," she asked.

Porter and I had talked about it and decided to tell everyone we met while he was getting his CAT scan for his head injury. It was as close to the truth as we could get without telling an out-and-out lie.

"I met him when he hurt himself at the gym," I said.

"Oh," she said. "At the gym?"

"No. At the hospital."

She looked puzzled. "Oh."

"How did you and Baker meet?" I asked.

The corners of her mouth curled up. "Well, he stays in Old Town, in a three-story building that attaches to every other three-story building on that block. So, it was on my first day as the property manager of the building that attaches to his, and he came up to see if we had any condos to rent, short-term. He said he needed it for a temporary home while his was being worked on. Personally, I think it was a ploy. A few minutes later we went up to look at a space I had for rent. He looked the space over, we hit it off, and that was pretty much it."

I liked hearing how people got together. "How'd you guys start dating?"

She reached for a piece of sushi. "When he looked at the property."

I felt that I must have missed something. "So, he looked at the property, and then what?"

She scanned the restaurant, and then leaned forward. "He, like, ripped off my cloths and bent me over the kitchen countertop."

I slapped my hand on the countertop. "Get outta here. Seriously?"

She gave the Brownie salute. "Dead serious."

"Oh. Wow. That's pretty awesome." I set my chopsticks aside. "Porter and I had been out a few times, and then he took me for a piece of pecan pie at some cute little town up north."

"Julian Pie Company?" she asked.

"Yep, that's it. Have you been there?"

She nodded. "We ride up there all the time. I love the pie. The Rhubarb is awesome. Add a scoop of cinnamon-vanilla ice cream and it's scrumptious."

"So, that Kimberly girl. What's she like? Is she fun, too?"

"She is the best," she said. "She doesn't talk much at first, but once she starts, look out. She's so funny. Her husband, Cash? His mother's Irish. Like, Irish as F. She has this accent, it's like she's not even speaking English. She always says Irish sayings and stuff. They're a riot to listen to. Kimberly and Cash arguing about flowers, which, by the way, he knows *nothing* about. And Erin, Cash's mom, arguing about *everything* and sneaking drinks of whiskey from under the desk. It's hilarious. You've got to go to the nursery."

"I'd love to."

"Seriously, we should go some time. It's better than going to the movies."

"OhmyGod," I shouted. "Listen to this. We went to the movies, and there's this guy, Luke Westham, and he--"

"The football player?" she asked.

"Yeah. He's such a psycho," I blurted. "So, anyway. He stalked me for a while, and I blocked him on Facebook, and on everything else sand--"

"Luke Westham is a stalker?"

"Yeah, but don't tell anybody."

She did the Brownie salute again. "I won't."

"Okay. So, we went in the movies, and that creep was in there. He looked at me and was like, *oh my God, how have you been?* And I was like, *uhhm, go away, creep.* So, he walked up and grabbed my arm. Porter punched him like ten times in two seconds and knocked him out cold. And everyone gathered around and said, *oh my God, you knocked out Luke Westham.* And Porter said, *who the fuck's Luke Westham?* It was the best thing, ever."

She laughed. "Baker pinched a guy's throat in Target one night. At first, I didn't know what to think, and then I decided it's nice having a guy stick up for me."

"Like, pinched his skin?" I wrinkled my nose. "I don't get it."

"No. He grabbed his windpipe or whatever. You know, pinched it. The guy was looking down my shirt. I had on this top that I loved, but I hated it too, because it creeps up in the back and down in the front, and it had creeped way down. In the front. The guy was staring into my cleavage. Baker made sure he knew not to do it again."

Kelvin wouldn't have hurt a fly, nor would he have stuck up for me in a similar situation. Having someone who was willing and able to do so, even if they didn't ever do it, was a good feeling.

"I like these guys," I said. "They're all pretty nice."

"They're basically brothers," she said. "They all moved here from Montana after high school. They're inseparable."

"I like it. It's like a big family."

"Exactly," she said. "That's *exactly* what it's like. A huge family. Barbeques. Trips on the motorcycles together. Racing cars at the racetrack. Just hanging out. Now, you're part of it. Do you like to ride?"

"On the motorcycle?"

"Uh huh."

"I love it," I said. "Love, love, love it."

"Me, too."

It was crazy. My life had gone from great to awesome after meeting Porter. I was in love, which I never thought was going to happen. I had a new girlfriend who wasn't an attention whore, and the possibility of having another who had a nursery and a funny Irish mother-in-law.

I'd spoken to my parents about Porter, but not at length. I needed to do just that, and to schedule a time for Porter and I to go visit them.

"Have you met Baker's parents?" I asked.

"They're not alive any longer," she said.

"Oh. Has he met yours?"

Her face went solemn. "They're both deceased. I was raised by my aunt."

"I'm so sorry," I said.

She put on a slight smile. "Has Ghost met yours?"

I'd talked to my mother at length about Porter, but not my father. I suspected my mother may have mentioned him to my father, but she hadn't said one way or another. I remained nervous about revealing the news to my father, as I knew he'd react unfavorably.

"Not yet," I said. "But he's going to."

"They'll like him," she said. "He's pretty to look at. Parents like pretty boys."

I'd never really thought of him that way, but he was pretty. My mother would love him. My father? Well, that was a different story altogether.

GHOST

George sat down across from me and looked at me like I'd forgotten to bring the turkey to the Thanksgiving dinner. "Where's your better half?"

"She's not feeling good. It's either a bad piece of sushi, or a rotten oyster. We had seafood on Sunday and on Monday she ate raw fish with one of the girls."

"One of what girls?"

"One of my friend's wives."

"She needs more women in her life." He looked me over. "You're not here to eat, are you?"

"Why do you ask that?"

He cocked an eyebrow. "Why are you answering a question with a question?"

I shrugged. "I planned on eating, yeah."

"What's troubling you?" he asked.

"Who says something's bothering--"

He cleared his throat. "I'm like the know-it-all bartender. Except I'm not a bartender."

I chuckled. "So, you're just a know-it-all?"

"The all-knowing diner owner." He leaned against the back of the booth and crossed his arms. "I know there's something you want to talk about. I guess that leaves the only question as being *what is it*?"

It wasn't going to be easy to talk about no matter how long I waited, so I decided to do what Abby often did, and just blurt my thoughts out onto the table.

I wished I was all-knowing like George, but I wasn't. All I knew was that I loved Abby, and that the love I felt for her had me wanting to commit to spend the rest of my life with her.

I drew a long breath and spit out the entire sentence as I exhaled. "I want to ask Abby to marry me, and I don't want to do it without talking to you about it first."

He pressed his clenched fist into his open palm and rested his chin on top of his hands. "Marry her, huh?"

He took it better than I imagined he would. Relieved that he didn't give argument, I continued spewing my thoughts. "Yes, Sir. I mean, yes, George. Yes, I want to marry her."

"Why do you want to marry her?"

"Because I love her."

"A man doesn't marry every woman he falls in love with." He raised both brows. "What makes her special?"

"Everything about her is special."

"You want to marry her because of *everything about her*?"

"I want to marry her because I know beyond a shadow of a doubt that I want to spend every day of the rest of my life with her. It's hard to explain, but I *know* it. Every day. Forever. I can't imagine life any other way. And, if I know that, truly know it, asking her to marry me is the only way to express to her how I feel. We can wait as long as she wants to get married, but I want to put a ring on her finger. I want to make that commitment to her."

He looked over his shoulder.

"Lawson!" he yelled. "Turn around the sign and lock the door. We're closed of the rest of the night."

"Closed?" Lawson asked.

"Closed," George said.

"Aye-aye, Top," Lawson said.

George faced me. "You're sure about this?"

"Right now? Sitting here? I'm worried about leaving her at home. I want to take care of her. Hell, she's not even *sick*, she just feels crappy. And, I can't think of leaving her alone." I laughed. "Yeah, I'm sure."

He pursed his lips and studied me for a few seconds. "So, you're asking my permission?"

"Kind of. She says she has two fathers, you and her dad. I'm asking you first, and then I'm going to ask you if you know how to get ahold of him."

He grinned. "She said that?"

"Said what?"

"That she has two dads?"

"She's said it more than once."

"I'm glad she looks at me like a dad, because I look at her as a daughter." He exhaled a heavy breath and looked me in the eyes. "I can't imagine her being with anyone but you, Porter. I remember the day she came in here telling me she loved you. I was pretty damned happy for both of you. Her wedding day will be a day that I'll cherish for ever and ever, I can tell you that much. She's like the daughter I'll never have. If you're seeking my blessing, you've got it. I'm convinced this can't be anything but right. "

"She thinks the world of you," I said.

"You need help with money for the ring?" he asked.

"Appreciate it, but I've got it covered."

"You sure?"

"Positive."

"What are your thoughts about kids?" he asked.

I laughed. "Three months ago, I couldn't imagine a life with kids in it. Now? Hell, it's always on my mind. I want to have kids with her and give our children the family life that I never had a chance of having. A mother and a father, both at home, both taking part in everything. I lay in bed at night and think about it."

"What about the club?"

I sighed. "I'm thinking when we decide to have kids that I'm going to walk away from it. There was a time and a place for it, and those men will always be brothers to me, but I can't imagine having kids and staying in the club will be a good thing. I want our children to be my only focus other than her."

"I like the way you think, Porter."

"Do you know how to get ahold of her father?" I asked.

"I do."

"Mind telling me?"

"For this occasion, I don't mind at all."

As nervous a virgin at a prison rodeo, I held the phone to my ear and hoped he answered. If he didn't, I doubted I'd have the courage to call him again for some time. After losing count of how many times it rang, he answered.

"This is Anderson," he said.

"Mister Northrop?"

"This is Anderson, yes."

"Sir, my name is Porter Reeves. This might seem like an odd telephone call, but if you've got a moment, I'd like to talk to you."

"Is Abby alright?"

I was surprised that he'd made the connection. "Yes, Sir. She's fine. She's got a little bit of a stomach ache, and she's at home. I'm away from there right now. Actually, I'm at George's diner. I got your number from him."

"Is everything okay?" he asked.

"Yes, Sir. Everything's just fine. I uhhm. Well, I'm calling for your permission."

"My permission?" He chuckled. "She already told us she rides on that motorcycle of yours. I guess I'll tell you I'm pleased that California's a state that requires the use of helmets."

"Not for that, Sir. For something else."

"She speaks highly of you, Porter. What can I help you with?"

"Sir, I'd like to marry your daughter. Not right away, but whenever she's comfortable with it. Maybe a year down the road, maybe two.

Heck, it might be six months. Whatever she, and you, Sir, are comfortable with. But I'd like your permission to ask her to marry me. I guess I'd like to propose to her. You know, give her a ring."

The phone fell silent for a moment.

"Hold on a moment, will you, Porter?"

"Yes, Sir."

I heard muffled voices for a moment, and then he returned.

"Porter?"

"Yes, Sir?"

"Anna and I would be thrilled if you'd like to ask Abby to marry you. When are you planning on doing it?"

"In the next few days, I think. I need to get a ring and everything."

"Well, you certainly have our blessing on the matter. Don't rush. Things like this take time and planning."

"Yes, Sir."

"Porter?"

"Yes, Sir?"

"We're pleased with her decision to see you. I'd like for you to know that. She speaks highly of you, as does George. In fact, George said you're one of the finest men he's ever had the opportunity to meet, and he's met a few."

I was shocked that he had talked to George about me, but it didn't last long. If I had a daughter a special as Abby, I'd want to know everything abou the man who was seeing her as well.

"Thank you, Sir."

"When the two of you get time, you need to come see us. Connecticut's only a few hours by plane."

I laughed to myself. "Actually, we're planning a trip up there this fall."

"Well, we look forward to meeting you. Keep us posted on the engagement, will you?"

"Yes, Sir. I will."

"I'm sure Abby will call her mother as soon as she settles down."

"I'm sure you're right."

"Is there anything else?"

"No, Sir."

"Have a nice evening, Porter. Keep this number. If you need anything else, don't hesitate to call."

"Thank you, Sir. Same to you."

After hanging up, I peered over the top of the booth and searched the restaurant for George. Helping a couple to a few menus, he glanced in my direction. He gave me the thumbs up, and then the thumbs down. A shrug followed.

I gave the thumbs up.

He grinned and returned the gesture.

I had one more task to resolve. Well, two, actually.

I looked at the salesman in disbelief. "You either take cash, or you don't. Which is it? If you don't, I can make other arrangements, I just need some time."

"We do take cash, Sir. I am not, however, certain that we can take *that much* cash."

"Who do you need to ask to find out?"

He raised his index finger. "Hold on one moment, please."

A gray-haired man who walked like he'd taken a college course on the subject paraded down the corridor in front of my thirty-something salesman.

After reaching the counter's edge, he extended his hand. "Gilthrop Wilshire, Mister Reeves. It's a pleasure to meet you."

I shook his hand. "It's a pleasure. I was telling…"

I looked at the salesman, who was standing behind him.

"Winston," he said.

"I was telling Winston I expected to pay cash for the ring. He said last night that you took cash, and I said I'd be back tonight. He either didn't believe me, or he misunderstood that I'd be returning with cash."

"Which ring do you have your eye on?" he asked.

I pointed to it. "The custom ring at the corner of the upper case."

He smiled. "All of our rings are custom. Let me get it."

He removed the ring and set it on top of the counter. "Is this the one?"

"That's it."

"Would you like to look at it?" he asked.

"I've looked at it. I've held it. I slipped it onto the tip of my pinkie finger. I'd like to take it home."

He inspected the ring, and then blinked a few times. "Mister Reeves, this example is a four-carat, VVS one clarity, D color, that's a brilliant cut with excellent table, depth, and girdle. It's four forty-three. That's four hundred forty-three thousand. Call it four hundred forty for arguments sake."

"Will you take four hundred and forty for it?"

He nodded. "We certainly would."

I tossed my backpack onto the display case. "I'll need to get three grand out of there, then."

He looked at the backpack, and then at me. "Would you like to come into my office?"

"Sure."

He lifted a wooden pass-through gate, and I followed him to his office. Thirty minutes later, I was preparing to leave with the ring.

"I'll come back for all the certificate paperwork tomorrow. I'm on my motorcycle, and I don't want it to get bent. She might want to do something with it, frame it or whatever. I don't know," I said excitedly.

"No rush," he said with a smile. "We'll keep it under lock and key."

"Thank you," I said. "I'm sure she'll love it."

"I'm sure she will," he agreed. "Let us know how the engagement goes, will you?"

After she agreed to marry me, I'd be so proud I'd feel like telling the world, Gilthrop Wilshire included.

I admired the ring one last time, and then closed the box. "I sure will."

ABBY

Over my shoulder, I stared at the watery horizon and waited. When the next swell was fifty yards behind me, and approaching fast, Porter shouted.

"Paddle, Abby. Paddle like fuck!"

I looked at him, at the swell, and then did just as he'd taught me. With my eyes fixed on the shore, I paddled with my hands, attempting to match the wave's speed. As the board started to rise, I pushed my chest off the board and quickly rose to my feet.

Ho-lee-shit.

I glanced to my left. Porter was beside me, twenty yards away, with my GoPro attached to some goofy piece of elastic that was strapped to his head.

"I'm surfing!" I screamed. "I'm F-ing surfing!"

"Looking good, baby!" he shouted.

As quickly as it began, it was over. The wave diminished to nothing. The board, and I, came to a stop in the shallow water.

After getting to a depth where I could stand up, I looked at Porter. "I want to do it again."

"We can do it all day," he said. "If you want."

"Will you take that stupid thing off your head?"

"Nope. I'm recording our life together." He gestured toward the horizon. "Let's catch another."

We surfed until I was no longer capable of standing. I couldn't believe it was so easy, or that I'd waited as long as I had to attempt it. I found it humorous that it took Porter getting a handy in front of the UPS man to convince me to finally do it.

After successfully getting up on a board, I suspected my future days would be filled with nothing more than binge watching Netflix, eating, having sex with Porter, watching the sunset, and surfing.

"I'm famished," I said as I walked ashore. "We need to eat."

"We need to get these boards back," he said.

"You can return that one," I said. "I'm keeping this bad boy."

"It's a rental, you have to return it."

I poked the nose of the board into the sand like I'd seen surfers do from my deck. "I'll buy it from him. He's not getting it back. It's my lucky board."

Porter did the same with his. "Buy a *better* board."

I slapped my hand against the rag-tag looking piece of rental shit. "There is no better board than mine."

He shook his head. "Fine. If it works, keep it."

"I intend to."

He peeled the GoPro off his head and rested it on top of the board. "Is your stomach better?"

I flopped onto the sand and let out a sigh. "It's good enough to eat non-seafood. I swear, I felt like shit for a week. I still feel weak, but not that bad."

Either the oysters at Goose's or the sashimi at my favorite sushi place made me so sick I couldn't get out of bed for five days. I was doing much better but still felt tired. The thought of anything seafood related made me feel nauseous.

"The diner?" he asked.

The Devil Dog Diner was comfort food if there ever was any.

"Pancakes sound good," I said. "Those would be easy to digest."

He reached for his board. "Let's get cleaned up and go to George's then."

I glared. "Hold on a minute, Mister fast hands. Give me a minute to get up. Jeez. I'm worn out. It's not every day I surf for six hours."

He looked at his watch. "Five."

"Six since we rented these piece of shit boards."

He gestured toward the chipped piece of fiberglass. "The piece of shit board you're keeping?"

I laughed. "I'm not keeping this piece of shit. If you've got good footage of me riding it, that's enough. I am buying a board, though."

Surfing would require nothing more than walking off my porch and to the beach, which was a matter of feet away from my home. It would be a new activity to add to my list of things to do with Porter on a regular basis.

"Come on," he said. "Let's go eat."

An hour later, we'd cleaned up, changed clothes, and were seated in my favorite booth at George's place. It was three in the afternoon. As always in the middle of the day, the place was empty.

George handed Porter a menu. "So, other than surfing, there's no other *new* news, is there?"

Porter snatched the menu from George's hand. "Not *yet*."

I looked at George. "Like what?"

"Like." He shrugged. "Anything."

I glanced at Porter. He was glaring at George. I shifted my eyes to George. He had an ear-to-ear grin on his face and was staring blankly at me.

"What the F is going on?" I asked openly.

"Nothing," Porter blurted.

"Just delivering menus," George chided.

I alternated glances between them. "I don't know what you two of you are doing, but you can stop it right now. You're creeping me out."

"Take your time looking over the menus," George said with a smile. "I'll be back as soon as you give me a wave."

I squinted. "Give you a wave? Since when do we wave you in from the outfield?" I handed him the menu. "I'll have pancakes. Times three, please."

Porter handed his menu to George. "I'll have the same, thank you."

"Ham?" George asked.

"Please," I responded.

He looked at Porter. "Bacon?"

"Please."

"Short stack with ham, and a short stack with bacon," George said cheerily. "You'll have plenty of time to talk, we'll have to mix the batter."

"You always mix the batter," I said. "It's one of the reasons I eat here, remember?"

George grinned and turned toward the kitchen.

"Is it me, or are you two acting like a couple of goofballs?"

"Acting normal," Porter replied.

"You're acting normal?"

He nodded. "Perfectly."

"I think you and George are up to something," I said.

"Nope," he responded. "We're up to nothing."

"Really?"

"Absolutely. Nothing at all. Everything's normal."

"Any *new* news?" I asked mockingly.

He shook his head. "Nope."

"I was mocking George," I said.

"Oh."

I took a drink of my water and studied him. My birthday wasn't for three months, and Porter's wasn't for seven. George didn't celebrate birthdays, but his was in January, which was five months away.

So, a surprise party was out of the question.

I wondered if they might be planning a big fundraiser or a special dinner with the bike club. Maybe, I decided, Porter was quitting the club, which I really didn't want him to do, now that I'd met everyone.

"Have you given any thought to quitting the club?" I asked.

"A little," he said.

"Don't," I said. "I like everyone. And, I don't want you to lose that fellowhip, or whatever it's called."

"Okay. Well, we can talk about that."

"Let's talk about it, then."

"Not now," he said.

I cocked my head to the side. "What do you want to talk about *now*?"

He glanced toward the kitchen and then shrugged. "I don't know."

I gestured toward the back of the diner with my eyes. "Do you want to check with George and see what he wants you to talk about?"

"No."

"I'm going to figure out what you two nut buckets are doing. You know that, right?"

"I'm not doing anything."

"Yes, you are. And I know it." I extended my hand. "Your phone, please."

He wiggled to the side of the booth, pulled out his phone, and handed it to me. His mouth twisted into a grin.

I opened his text messages, scrolled through them, and saw nothing out of the ordinary. I handed him the phone. "I'm going to figure it out, believe me."

"There's nothing to figure out."

"Pancake delivery," George said, sounding like a he was trying out for an Aunt Jemima commercial.

He set the plates in front of us. "Any new revelations?"

"No!" Porter blurted.

I looked at the steaming pancakes, and then at George. "What. The. F. Is. Going. On?"

"Nothing."

I looked at Porter and raised a brow.

He shrugged. "Nothing."

I picked up my fork and pointed it to George. "I'm." I pointed it at Porter. "Going to." Then, back to George. "Figure." Back to Porter. "You two." Then, to George. "Out."

George shrugged and turned toward the kitchen. "Nothing to figure out."

I looked at Porter. He was already half done with his pancakes and shoveling them into his mouth at a breakneck pace.

"I don't know what you two knuckleheads are up to, but if it includes embarrassing me, there'll be hell to pay," I fumed. "Remember, I have a video of you blowing your load over the edge of the deck."

"It won't embarrass you," he said.

"*What* won't embarrass me?"

He cut another section of pancakes from the stack. "What's going on."

I scratched my arm feverishly. "What *is* going on?"

"Oh," he said. "Nothing."

I glared at him while I poured syrup on my pancakes. I had no idea what he was planning, but when I found out, he was going to pay dearly for disrupting an otherwise peaceful mid-day meal.

Because I didn't like surprises.

At all.

GHOST

B aker gazed out the window of his office, looking at who knows what. I knew not to talk to him while he was peering through the glass. It was the time that he took every day to relax. Staring out the window while music played was his means of escape.

The same as Abby and me sitting on her deck watching the sunset.

I sat in the chair on the opposite side of his desk and enjoyed the music that was playing. When the song ended, he turned around.

Upon seeing me, he gave a nod. "How's it going, Brother Ghost?"

"Going good, thanks."

He stroked his beard as he looked me over. "What brings you in? Hell, you haven't been up here in ages."

"Just wanting to talk."

"About?"

"Well, first, what was that song that was playing? I liked it?"

"Peter Gabriel. *In Your Eyes.*"

I recognized the artist as being the singer of Abby's favorite song. "Have you heard *Solsbury Hill*? Same guy, I guess."

"I have," he said. "You've never heard it?"

"She was going to play it for me but hasn't got around to it. Just wondered what it was about. I liked that last one."

He reached for his phone, fucked with it for a moment, and then set it on his desk. In a few seconds, a song began to play.

I closed my eyes and listened intently. I didn't perceive the song as spiritual, as Abby had described it. To me, it was more of a revelation about a man who was finding himself. When the song ended, I opened my eyes.

"What's that about, in your opinion?"

"It's about him finding himself after he quit the band he'd been playing in. He talks about making it from day to day, and how his life was in a rut. He talks about his life being filled with people who had no etiquette, and how he was going to find his own way. It's about taking your own inventory and moving on without the baggage. That's what I hear, anyway."

"Good tune. Kind of timeless," I said.

"I agree." He turned down the music and stood. "I know you're not here to talk music. How's the girl?"

"Abby? She's great, thanks."

"Didn't wreck the car, did you?"

"Nope."

I crossed my arms and looked around the room. "Bought a ring."

"I'm guessing it's not a clunky sterling silver set-up with a skull on it, is it?"

I laughed. "Nope."

"You're proposing to her?"

"Planning on it."

"It's a good feeling. Committing to a woman you love. I proposed to Andy on Christmas morning."

"Do you have any regrets?"

"About becoming engaged? Hell no."

"No," I said. "About how you did it? On Christmas morning?"

He shook his head. "No. Why would I?"

I shrugged. "I don't know. I've been carrying this ring around for three or four days and can't seem to find the right time to give it to her."

He chuckled. "Sounds to me like you're having second thoughts."

"Not at all," I said. "I just don't want to do it at the wrong time, and I don't want some cliché bullshit attached to my memory of it. Or, to hers."

"Not at Christmas, then?"

"Nothing against you, Brother, but no."

He stroked his beard. "Do it at a time that's natural. You know the feeling you get when you just feel like kissing her? Like, out of the blue?"

"Yeah, it happens all the time, why?"

"Give it to her at one of those times," he said. "It'll feel natural. Or, in one of those moments when you're laying in bed admiring her. When she does something cute. When she, and you, are least expecting it. It'll feel natural. Who gives a fuck about the story that's attached to it. Do it for you, and for her, not for the story you'll tell about it later."

I nodded. "Good point."

"Everything else okay?" he asked. "Is she still sick?"

"She's better. Fucking oysters."

"Didn't bother me. Cash puked out his butt for two days. Must have been some bad ones in there. Hell, he flew them in from Louisiana, fresh. It's not the Goose's fault."

"Not blaming him," I said. "Just one of those deals."

He studied me for a moment, and then grinned. "Finally lifted that ass of yours off that wallet."

"What?"

"Other than building that fucking Mustang, you haven't spent a dollar since high school. Took you thirteen years to build that car. As far as I can figure, that's five hundred bucks a month, give or take. Hell, that's the interest you're receiving off our first job. You don't even own a house, you rent one. You're so tight, you squeak when you walk."

"Don't like spending money."

"Did it hurt? To come up off some of that cash?"

He was right. I was frugal. Spending money seemed like a waste to me. I grew up without it, and now that I had some, I cherished it.

Buying a new pair of jeans troubled me so much I'd often wait until they had holes so big my junk was falling out.

Spending it on Abby's ring didn't bother me one bit.

I shook my head. "Didn't feel a thing."

"Spend a chunk?"

"Half a million."

His eyes went wide. "Jesus. Must be some ring."

"It's a nice fucker."

"Got it with you?"

I laughed as I reached into my pocket. "Been carrying it for days."

I handed him the box.

He opened the box and looked the ring over. "I take it back," he said.

"What's that? About me being a tight ass?"

"No." He handed me the ring. "About proposing. You need to make sure she's got something soft under her when you do it, because she's likely to faint. That's one hell of a rock, Ghost."

"Hope she likes it."

"She'd like it if it was a polished coffee bean. That girl's eyes light up when you start to speak. Andy said she didn't shut up for five minutes when they went out. Talked about you the entire time."

"Feeling's mutual," I said.

"Looking at doing a job in Bakersfield," he said. "Some child pornography kingpin. Fucking creep runs a website where he sells videos and shit. Been making millions for years and hasn't been caught. We'll talk about it Wednesday. If it goes the way I'm thinking, you'll make enough to pay for that ring two times over. After we're done, Tito's going to open up a back door on the guy's website and let the feds get him."

I had no desire to do a job. The risk of getting caught, which had always been a thrill to me, lingered over me as a reminder of losing Abby. It was a risk I wasn't willing to take. At least not at that moment.

"Sounds interesting." I stood. "Think I'm going to do some tuning on the X5M, get it ready for the upcoming job."

He stood. "Let me know how the proposal goes."

"Will do, Brother."

I turned toward the door, feeling no more certain of when I was going – or how I was going – to propose.

But I knew one thing for sure.

I didn't want to do another job as a Devil's Disciple.

ABBY

George's diner was frigid. While I waited for him to greet me, I sat on my hands, hoping to warm them up. When he arrived at the table, he was overly excited to see me.

He sat down across from me and motioned toward my lap. "Why are you hiding your hands? Let me see your hands, Abby."

"They're cold."

"Let me see them."

"What is wrong with you?" I gave him a look. "I'm not hiding anything."

"Let me see them."

I raised my hands. "It's like Antarctica in here."

He looked my hands over and then sighed.

"What?"

"Well, you've been talking about a tattoo, I thought maybe you got one."

"On my hand?"

He shrugged. "Hand, wrist, arm. Who knows."

"No new revelations?" he asked.

"Like what?"

"Anything."

"Nope. Just laying around. Trying to feel better. All I can eat is pancakes."

"Where's Porter?"

"Making his rounds. Seeing Baker and checking the pumps on the carwashes in Oceanside."

He rested his chin in his hands and looked me over, smiling the entire time.

I giggled. "You're acting weird."

"Do you want children?"

It seemed like a strange time for that specific question, but I liked that he asked it. "I do," I said. "Three."

"Boys? Girls?"

"Some of each. I don't care. But I want one in the middle, and one on each end. Maybe the boy would be oldest, so he could protect the other two."

"Porter and I were talking the other day. Might not be my place to tell you, but I'm doing it anyway. He wants kids. The thought of you two having kids excites the hell out of me. They'd be like grandkids to me."

My heart swelled. "He said that?"

"He sure did."

We hadn't talked about it, but I'd hoped he wanted children. Having children with him would be the best gift ever. I could see us spending all our time on the beach building sandcastles and teaching them to surf.

"I like thinking about that."

"So do I," he said.

"Why didn't your marriage work?" I asked.

His gaze dropped to the table. "I got married to please my mother."

"Did you love her?"

He looked up and shook his head. "Not in the way you're thinking."

"You didn't even love her?"

"Not in the sense you're thinking. I loved her, but I didn't love her like a wife. We were friends more than anything. We had been since we were kids."

"Then, after you got divorced, you went in the Marines?"

He smiled. "I was twenty-one. Oldest kid in my platoon. Everyone looked up to me. Best decision I ever made. I guess, in some respects, I married the Corps."

"Do you think you'll ever fall in love?"

"I haven't got time." He looked around the diner and then met my gaze. "I love you, though. I love Porter, too. Love all the people that work for me."

"Can I ask you something? Something serious?"

"Sure."

"Are you sure?"

"Abby, you can ask me anything."

"Anything?"

He reached for my hand. "Anything."

"Are you…are you…do you think you might be gay?"

He glanced over each shoulder, and then smiled. "I'm surprised it took you this long to ask. Yes, I am."

"Holy crap?" I screeched. "Really?"

"No." He chuckled. "I'm kidding."

"You're serious, though? You're gay?"

"I am."

I felt happy and sad at the same time. I was happy that he told me the truth, and of the possibility of him finding someone to love, but sad that he'd chosen to hide it from me, and from everyone else as far as I knew.

"Why do you hide it?" I asked.

"I didn't have a choice in the military," he said. "It would have ended my career."

"What about now?"

"It's a choice I make, I suppose. It's not as easy as you'd think to reveal something like that. Everyone looks at you differently."

"Not everyone," I said. "Just some people."

"How do you think Porter would react?"

"Just like I am," I said. "He'd ask you why you're not in a relationship."

"I doubt that."

I crossed my arms and gave him a look. "I don't."

"I like the way things are right now," he said. "Everyone's happy. I'll keep things like this until the good Lord tells me to make a change."

I shrugged. "I can't argue with that. Thanks for telling me, though."

"It feels good to admit it. I haven't done it with too many people." He smiled. "Pancakes?"

"Yes, please."

"Ham?"

"Please."

"Give me a few minutes?"

"I'll be right here."

As I finished my meal, Porter showed up. He came in, gave me a kiss, and took a seat across from me.

"I need some elbow room," he said. "I'm going to get the Abby and that double burger."

"Are you pregnant?"

"Not yet," he said with a laugh. "But we can keep trying."

"That reminds me of something. At what point did we decide to have unprotected sex? That kind of just happened."

"Oh." He blushed. "Sorry."

I held the last bite of pancakes in front of my mouth. "What's going on with that?"

"Maybe I subconsciously want to have kids."

I arched an eyebrow. "Subconsciously?"

"Uh huh."

I smiled. "Me, too. Maybe that's why I haven't said anything until now."

"You want them?" He leaned forward. "Kids?"

"Three. Boys and girls."

He smiled. "Same here. Maybe four. Two and two."

"You don't get to pick what they are," I said with a laugh.

"In a perfect world, I'd like four."

"We don't live in a perfect world," I said.

He sighed. "I get reminded of that every day."

"What does that mean?"

He shook his head. "It means people do stupid things, and I have to read about it and hear about it. I'm sick of it."

"Like what?"

"Shooting up schools. Killing people at concerts. Kidnapping their students and driving across country. You name it."

"It's sad."

"It's worse than that."

George walked up beside me and gave me a look. I gave him one right back. "Have a seat."

"Too busy." He looked at Porter. "What'll it be, my man?"

"Sit. Down," I huffed.

"I've got too much going on."

"You're all but empty," I said. "Sit!"

He sat beside me, at the edge of the booth. I elbowed him in the ribs, hoping he'd give the big reveal to Porter. He did nothing but elbow me right back.

"What's the deal with you two?" Porter asked.

"George has something to tell you."

"No. I don't."

"Yes, you do."

"No. I don't."

"I love you, George," I said.

"I love you, too."

I let out an exaggerated sigh.

George leaned against the back of the booth, crossed his arms, and huffed out a sigh.

"What?" Porter asked.

"I'm gay," George whispered.

"Yeah," Porter said. "I figured you were."

George looked at me and then at Porter. "What do you mean *you figured I was?*"

"You're fifty-three, unmarried, and your garage is the tidiest place I've ever been in my life. Then, when I was wiring up the tachometer in your car, I found a business card underneath the carpet below the glove box. It was a manager's card from one of the bars in town."

George's face went stark white. "I wondered where that went."

"Can I get the double burger and the Abby?" Porter asked. "I'm starving."

"You're not bothered by it?" George asked.

Porter's eyes narrowed. "By what?"

"Me being gay?"

Porter laughed. "You bothered by me being heterosexual?"

George laughed. "No."

"Well," I'm only bothered by one thing, and you being gay isn't it," Porter said.

"What's that?"

"My hunger," Porter said. "Haven't eaten since last night."

George stood. "One double burger and one Abby coming right up."

Porter stood and opened his arms. "Give me a hug."

George looked at me, and then at Porter.

"I want in on this," I said.

While the three of us hugged to celebrate George's *coming out*, I decided that I wanted to marry Porter and have his children.

He truly was the best man God could offer me.

All I had to do was wait. Wait, and hope that he felt the same way about me.

GHOST

I'd carried the ring in my left front pocket for six days, waiting for the perfect time to propose to Abby. I didn't want the event to be driven by my enthusiasm alone. It needed to be the perfect time and place, naturally. Planning it seemed far too cliché and wasn't what I'd come to envision.

Abby's admitted hatred of surprises didn't help matters. Over the last few days, she'd suspected something was going on, and had scratched her left arm to the point it had a rash covering it from her wrist to her elbow.

She glanced at me and grinned. "I can't believe it's over. No more to-do list. It's done. Kaput."

I looked at the half-finished tattoo. The letters B, E, L, and I were complete, and the artist was filling in the outline for the E.

"The tattoo's *half* done," I said. "So, the list is almost complete."

She winced in pain. "It'll be complete here in a few minutes."

"Are you going to make another?"

"Nope. We're just going to live life. No lists."

"Sounds good to me."

She decided to get the word *believe* tattooed on her wrist. It seemed appropriate, considering she had it inscribed on my bracelet. I'd come to look at the bracelet as more than a gift, viewing it as a symbol of power, strength, and support.

I found myself studying it, using it as a reminder that my life, albeit different, was wandering down the only path that it was destined to travel upon. I truly believed Abby was the final item on my unwritten *to-do* list.

In thirty minutes, the artist was done with the tattoo. "Let your arm hang at your side and look in the mirror," he said. "See what you think."

Abby rose from the chair, walked to the full-length mirror, and turned her wrist until the reflection revealed the delicate script.

"I love it," she said.

He smiled. "Cool."

She returned to the chair, sat down, and reached for her purse. "How much was it, again?"

"Tag me in an Instagram post with a picture of it, and it's free," he said.

She pulled out her wallet and fished through the bills. After removing two one-hundred-dollar bills, she handed them to him. "Here, take this. I'll tag you on a post. What's your username?"

"At Turner Made."

"I'll do it right now," she said with a smile.

She took a photo with her phone, made an Instagram post, and put several hashtags on it. After posting it, she stood. "There you go."

He wrapped her tattoo with a protective wrap, instructed her on aftercare, and gave the tattoo one last inspection. "Looks good."

"I'm not a tattoo virgin anymore." She opened her arms wide. "Do you hug?"

He stroked his beard nervously. "If he's cool with it, I'm cool with it."

"He's cool with it," she said with a dismissive wave of her hand. "Give me a hug."

While they hugged, his phone, which was sitting on top of a large red tool box, was buzzing like a bee. When she released him, he reached for it.

"Holy shit." He turned his phone to face her. "Look at this."

I looked at the phone but saw nothing but a picture of a tattoo machine.

"What?" Abby asked.

He moved the phone closer. "My followers."

The number of followers listed on his Instagram page was changing right before our eyes. In the time that he held it in front of us, the number changed from five thousand to seven thousand, and was steadily climbing.

"You did an awesome job. Tagging you in that post was the least I could do," she said. "Maybe you'll get some business out of it."

He flashed the peace sign. "Thanks, Abby."

She returned the gesture and stepped to my side. "Do you like it?"

I gave the artist a wave and turned toward the door. "I love it."

"Me, too."

"That other guy was a dip-shit," I said. "I can't believe he wouldn't tattoo you."

She chuckled. "Since when is Benadryl a narcotic?"

The first tattoo studio we'd gone to asked that she fill out a questionnaire. One of the questions asked if she had taken any medication in the last twenty-four hours. She listed Benadryl, which she'd been taking for the rash on her arm, and Pepto-Bismol, which she'd been taking for her upset stomach. The artist refused to tattoo her because of her recent use of Benadryl.

I shrugged. "I think he just didn't want to do it and used that as an excuse."

"There's a reason for everything," she said. "It brought us here, and Steve was awesome."

I didn't agree with the everything happens for a reason remark, but I did agree that Steve did an awesome job.

"Agreed," I said. "Want to grab something to eat?"

"I'm exhausted," she murmured, yawning as she spoke. "I think the whole tattoo thing wore me out. Can we just go home, and eat something there? I'm scared to eat restaurant food, anyway."

Her stomach had been a disaster for the last ten days. If she didn't take Pepto-Bismol regularly, she was miserable. A light meal, relaxing, and getting some sleep was probably in her best interest, anyway.

"Sounds good," I replied.

An hour later, we were laying in her bed watching television. Six months prior, I didn't give a shit about what was on TV and hadn't so much as turned mine on in years. Now, Abby and I had no less than half a dozen shows we enjoyed regularly. I looked forward to the time that we watched television together, as most of it was done from the comfort of her bed.

"I guess I ought to change my address," I said. "I'm never at home."

She nestled against me, resting her head against my chest. "You should just move in."

"You'd get sick of me," I replied.

She swung her hand toward me in a joking manner. I flinched, and when I did, her hand smacked me dead in the nuts.

I folded up like a cheap suit as pain shot from my groin to my stomach. I writhed in pain from side-to-side, eventually coming to a rest with my eyes fixed on hers.

"Son-of-a-bitch," I howled.

"I'm so F-ing sorry," she huffed. "Oh my God."

She nodded toward my crotch, which was currently being protected by my hands. "Get your dick out, please. I want to apologize to him."

"He's broken."

"I want to fix him."

With slight reluctance, I pushed my shorts past my knees, exposing my shriveled, and very sore, manhood.

She looked at my shorts and let out a sigh. "Toss 'em on the floor."

I grinned. "Sure thing, sweetheart."

I did as she asked and tossed my shorts beside the bed. After fluffing her pillow, she lowered herself onto her back. Then, with her eyes fixed on the television, she blindly searched for my cock until she found it.

She gripped it lightly. A slow, predictable stroke followed. In seconds, I'd recovered fully from the nut-punch, and was as hard as the diamond ring that remained in the left front pocket of my jeans.

I studied her as she stroked my rigid shaft. Her eyes were fixed on the television, squinted into a smile. A slight grin gave hint to the satisfaction she obtained from either what she was watching or what she was doing.

Abby lived her life without excuses. She didn't need them. She was an old soul with the heart of a princess and the imagination of a budding teen. I'd always seen beauty as something that masked one's faults.

Part of Abby's beauty was that she didn't conceal her faults. She handed them to me on a silver platter, giving me the freedom to inspect them thoroughly. *Knowing* Abby allowed me to accept her for who she truly was. I respected her for being genuine, and true to herself.

For several moments' time, I admired her as she lay at my side, smiling. Meeting her had changed my life completely. We now had an open book ahead of us, limited by nothing more than our imaginations and the sixty years of time we were sure to spend together.

While she continued to slowly stroke me while she was focused on the television, I reached over the edge of the bed and fumbled to find my jeans. It was the perfect time for me to propose. Later, when we were asked when and where the proposal came, we wouldn't be able to tell the truth.

We'd have to make up something, all the while knowing when and where it *really* happened. It would be the imperfect proposal for two imperfectly perfect people.

My jeans were six inches out of my reach. I stretched as far as I could, nearly reaching them, only to have Abby respond by yanking on my root and reminding me of my obligations.

"What the F are you doing?" she asked.

"I was--"

"You're not going anywhere," she whispered. "Relax. I want to ride my little friend and show him how much I love him."

We embraced in a passionate kiss. Kissing Abby took my mind to a place where only we existed, and it was there that we remained until long after the kissing stopped.

When our mouths parted, she looked at me and smiled. "I'm going to climb you like a tree, " she said in a playfully sultry voice.

I found the remark out of context. "I'm flat on my back," I argued. "You're not going to climb--"

"Fine," she snapped. "I'll ride you like a pony."

"Horse," I said. "I'm not a pony, I'm a horse."

"Pogo stick." She straddled me and glanced over her shoulder. "I'm going to ride this dick like a pogo stick."

With her back facing me, she positioned herself over my rigid shaft. After a few test runs of grinding her wet mound all over the tip, I was ready to explode. I placed my hand on the small of her back, gripping her lightly as she slowly guided me into her.

Exercising caution, she gyrated her hips, taking a little more of my length with each careful stroke. My eyes fell closed, relishing in the satisfaction of having our bodies become one.

Her wetness rose and fell along the length of my shaft in perfect timing, like that of an expertly crafted Swiss watch's movement. After a few strokes, I felt her tightness encompass me fully.

I opened my eyes.

Like a dancer who was performing in perfect timing with a song, Abby pumped her hips fore and aft, to music only she could hear. My eyes became fixed on the valley between the cheeks of her perfectly shaped ass. As she rose, revealing the length of my pleasure, my heart took pause.

When she reached the tip, she hesitated and glanced over her shoulder. I drew a quick breath. Her body was perfectly proportioned, and her skin silky smooth. Watching her devour me, inch by inch, was a pleasure in itself.

With our eyes locked, she ground herself against me, taking my entire shaft in one thrust of her hips. There, with me buried inside of her, she remained, smiling at her accomplishment. In a moment she began to contract.

Proving we were connected by much more than our touching flesh, her climax brought on mine. She milked me of my juices without moving a single muscle of her body.

As she wailed out her satisfaction, I, too, groaned in satisfaction.

With her work done, she collapsed against my body, laying her back against my chest. Still inside of her, I wrapped my arms around her and held her against me.

"How do you feel?" I asked.

"Magical," she responded.

"Stomach?"

"Better."

"Wrist? How's the tattoo."

"Don't even know it's there," she breathed.

I kissed her neck. "That was incredible."

"You're incredible."

"You want to shower?"

"Not right now," she said. "I want to lay here and rest for a minute. I like your skin."

I laughed. "I like your skin, too."

"I love you, Porter."

"I love you, too."

The minute she spoke never expired from the clock. Within seconds, she was snoring, dead asleep.

I chose to let her sleep for a few minutes. She needed the rest. Since the seafood incident, she'd been exhausted.

I thought of Connecticut in the fall. The leaves. The cool air. Abby's laughter. Her parent's joy. The pride she'd wear on her face when she showed them the ring.

The pride I'd feel when she explained how I gave her the ring. How she learned, on that day, to accept some surprises as being a good thing.

In that moment of slumber, I decided I'd waited long enough. When she awoke, I'd give her the ring.

No exceptions.

I closed my eyes and nestled myself in the relief of knowing our proposal was on the horizon. I clutched her body tight to mine, hoping for another moment of feeling our skins become one.

And, it was there that I fell asleep.

GHOST

I opened my eyes and looked around the room. Confused as to what had happened, I glanced at the television. The *Samsung* screen saver bounced from one corner of the television to the other.

I rolled to the side to wake Abby up. "Abby," I tapped her on the shoulder. "Abby, wake up. We fell asleep."

I pressed my hand against her arm and immediately yanked it away.

Her skin was hot to the touch.

Not warm.

Hot.

I leaned over her, gripped her shoulders, and shook her. "Abby, wake up. We need to get you in the bath, you've got a fever."

She didn't respond.

Fuck.

I shook her again. "Abby!"

She was limp in my hands.

I took her pulse. It was faint, but she was alive. I scrambled to find my phone, found it in my jeans pocket, and then dialed 911.

"Nine-one-one, state your emergency."

Racing against a clock I couldn't see, I stumbled across the floor as I tried to get into my jeans. Panic-stricken and afraid, I responded.

"This is Porter Reeves. She's non-responsive. She's hot to the touch. She won't." I glanced in her direction. Her hair was matted and stuck to her face. "She's got a horrible fever. I need an ambulance."

"Slow down," she said. "Who is *she*?"

"Abby Northrop. Uptown Abby. My fiancé. She's. She's passed out."

"Has she taken any drugs that you know of?"

I placed my hand on her cheek. If I didn't do something quickly, she was going to die.

"Listen lady, I don't have time for this shit. I'm headed to Mercy. Tell whoever you've got to tell I'm in a sixty-seven Mustang. Gray. License plate reads ELEANOR. Don't try and pull me over, because I won't. I'm taking her in there *now*."

I rested the phone between my shoulder and my cheek, picked up her naked body, and lifted her from the bed.

"Tell them to get ready."

"Sir, I'm sending an ambulance. Will you verify the address? You're on Mission Boulevard?"

"I'm headed out the door right now."

"Sir, stay where you are. I'm dispatching an ambulance."

It would take fifteen minutes for an ambulance to navigate traffic, and an additional fifteen minutes for it to get back to Mercy. I knew alternate routes. I was a better driver than any ambulance attendant.

If things went to hell, I'd have her there in ten minutes, tops.

"No!" I shouted. "There's no time. I'm headed in your direction. Tell them I'm coming. Have people ready at the emergency room."

"Sir, please. Stay—"

"I'm headed down the steps now," I mumbled. "Forget the ambulance."

"Does she have a pulse?" she asked.

With Abby in my arms, I took the steps two at a time. "It's faint."

"Sir, stay on the line. I'll have a response team in wait at the entrance. Can you answer a few questions?"

When I landed on the bottom step, the phone slipped from between my shoulder and cheek, and landed on the driveway. After trying to bend over and get it, I gave up.

There wasn't time.

I carefully placed her in the passenger seat, strapped her harness in place, and ran around the car.

I hopped in the driver's seat, not bothering with my harness. "Hold on, Baby." I said. "We're going for a little ride."

I shoved the shifter in reverse, did a one-eighty maneuver, and shifted into first gear before the car came to a stop. After releasing the clutch, I hammered the gas.

We shot out of the driveway and into the street. I fishtailed for sixty feet, then hit second gear. Then third. Fourth. Fifth. Sixth.

In triple-digit speeds, I flew up Mission Boulevard, then onto West Mission Bay Drive.

"Don't worry, Baby. I'll get you there in time," I assured her. "Almost there."

I took the entrance to the eight at one hundred and forty miles an hour, speeding onto the highway between a truck and a minivan, and then taking the middle lane, which was empty.

In and out of cars I swerved, keeping an open lane ahead. "Five minutes, Sweetheart. Five minutes. Hold on."

In five minutes we were at the one sixty-three exit. "Hard right, Baby. Hold on."

With my heart in my throat, I took the exit sideways, but in control. Scripps Mercy was only minutes away, and every minute counted.

I simply needed her to hold on.

"Baby. I bought you a ring. It's in my pocket. After they get you to a room, guess what? I'm going to propose to you. We're going to have kids and play on the beach and I'm going to walk away from the club and we're never going to have to worry about anything ever stopping us from living life. I love you so much, Baby."

"Baby?" I looked at her. "Baby? Did you hear me?"

I took the Washington exit and flew toward fifth. As smoke poured from the back tires, I blasted up fifth toward the hospital's entrance.

"It's right here, Baby," I blubbered. "We made it."

No less than ten men were standing in front of the emergency room entrance. I hoped like hell they were there for Abby. As I slid to a stop right at their side, I realized she was completely naked.

I yanked my door open.

"Abby Northrop?" someone asked.

I pulled the passenger door open. "Yes. She needs a blanket," I shouted, lifting her from the seat. "She's naked."

I turned around. "Where do I--"

"Sir," a doctor said. "We'll take her."

A rolling bed was between me and the door. People came from every direction. Monitors, wires, and hoses were being attached to her faster than I could comprehend what was going on. Then, as they began to rush her into the hospital, it dawned on me that there was nothing I could do.

Nothing.

"Is she alive?" I shouted.

A man glanced over his shoulder as they ran toward the double door. "Yes," he responded. Yes, she is."

GHOST

I'd been pacing the waiting room floor for five hours. George sat at the end of a row of chairs with his head in his hands, in and out of sleep.

Andy stared out the window as she held Kimberly's hand. The remaining members, short of Baker had fallen asleep. Baker paced the floor at the opposite side of the room.

I couldn't sleep. Hell, I couldn't relax. Not until I saw Abby.

We'd received two updates, both of which gave us no useful information, only that she was alive and fighting to stay alive. They had no idea what was wrong with her. I feared that lack of knowledge wasn't in my – or in Abby's – favor.

"Coffee?" I asked.

"No, thank you." George looked up. "I've had so much I'm on the verge of a heart attack."

I sat down beside him. "Yeah. Me, too."

"I've prayed so much I don't know what else to say," he said. "It's in His hands now."

I spit out a laugh, and then regretted it. I didn't want to be disrespectful to George, but praying seemed a little far-fetched. Abby didn't need a prayer, she needed a competent doctor. I second-guessed my decision to drive to Scripps and wondered if I should have taken her elsewhere.

"Her parents are on their way," George said. "Terrible this is how you're going to meet them."

"Sorry about that," I said. "I wasn't trying to be disrespectful about you praying. I just…"

He placed his hand on my shoulder. "Believe me, I understand."

"If it works for you, keep it up."

He offered a crumpled smile. "I will."

I wondered about food poisoning, some type of parasite, or even if she might have had an allergic reaction but guessed the hospital's staff would have already checked such things. We'd given them all the information we thought they could use about her recent health, and nothing seemed to help.

I wondered if she might have ingested something from the ocean on the day we surfed. While I continued to grasp at straws, George lowered his head into his cupped hands.

I didn't need her in perfect health. I didn't care if she had a fever. I just needed to see her. I wanted to give her the ring, lift her spirits, and have her pull out of the funk she was in. She was a fighter. She'd proven it at least once in her life, when she beat cancer.

I felt guilty for having recovered from my brain tumor. I would trade brain cancer for her health any day, and it sickened me that I couldn't. That there wasn't a way that I could fix her. It was my duty to fix her. I was her protector, and I couldn't do my job.

With my eyes fixed on a flickering lamp in the distant parking lot, I sat with our engagement ring in my pocket and my heart in my throat. The pain of not being able to change anything enveloped me.

I wadded into a ball. Feeling small and incapable, I began to softly cry. After a moment, I closed my eyes. I needed to look rested when she saw me. I needed to be strong.

"Mister Reeves?"

"Mister Reeves?"

"Mister Reeves!"

I jumped from my seat. A doctor I didn't recognize stood in front of us. I nudged George. "Someone's here."

He crossed his arms and raised his brows slightly. "Mister Reeves?"

"Porter Reeves, yes, Sir." I shoved my hand into my left pocket and squeezed the ring in my hand. "What's the latest, Doc?"

"Mister Reeves, we've done everything we can," His gaze dropped. "I'm sorry--"

My face flashed hot with anger. "Everything you can?" I scoffed. "Do we need to take her somewhere else? What? You're giving up? Where is she? I'll take her somewhere else."

"Mister Reeves." He lifted his chin. "She's gone. I'm sorry."

"Gone?" I shouted. "What do you mean, gone? Gone where?"

He cleared his throat. "She's passed."

"Heaven help me," George blubbered.

"Dead?" The word came out as a whisper. "You're telling me she's dead?"

He nodded. "I'm sorry."

"She can't be," I cried. "I just brought her in here. We were in bed together, sleeping." I shook my head. He was mistaken. He had the wrong patient in mind. "I'm talking about Abby Northrop. Five-two. Pale skin. Dark hair."

I reached for him, but a hand stopped me. I yanked my arm free. "She came in with a fucking fever," I bellowed. "A fever. You've got the wrong--"

He reached shoulder. "I'm sorry."

A lump rocketed into my throat. I began to shake. Someone touched me. I fell into one of the chairs. I looked up at the doctor.

I swallowed hard. "Is she...she's...dead?"

"Yes, Mister Reeves," he said. "We've lost her. Again, I'm sorry."

I was in an all too familiar place. This time, it was so very much worse. It couldn't be. It simply couldn't. There had to be a misunderstanding.

His mouth moved, but I heard nothing. A dull pain took one limb at a time, until my entire body went numb.

George placed his hand on my shoulder, but I felt nothing. He wept. The light denim of my jeans became dark with tears that dripped from my chin. I couldn't stand. I couldn't reason. I was elsewhere.

Somewhere quiet. Where pain didn't exist. Voices couldn't be heard.

The doctor touched my shoulder again, and then turned away.

I stood over the gurney they'd placed her on. I wanted to take her hospital gown off, and replace it with one of her dresses, and her Converse sneakers.

Her skin was too pale. Much more so than normal.

I took her cold hand in mine. "I'm sorry, Baby," I said, my voice quivering as I spoke. "I tried. I got here as fast as I could. I just…"

My legs turned to rubber.

George pulled me to my feet. As he steadied me, I continued. "I love you. With all my heart," I sobbed. "I just…I love you."

I traced my finger along her ring finger, where I'd failed to place the ring. I'd forever regret not having the courage to follow through with the proposal. Filled with regret, anger, and sorrow, I held her hand in mine.

"Mister Reeves," A voice said. "We need to take her now. I'm sorry."

I raised my right hand to silence him.

Then, I leaned over her, kissed her on the lips, and said my final words.

"Goodnight, Sweetheart. I love you."

I shuffled toward the door, holding onto George's arm for support. We stepped into the hallway and paused. As we both shed another tear for our loss, the doctor pushed the gurney past us.

My vision narrowed until all I could see was the doctor as he pushed Abby away. He reached the double doors at the end of the hallway, paused, and pushed a button on the wall. As he passed through the opening, going completely out of sight, what little faith I had in love vanished right along with him.

GHOST

I lifted my phone from the kitchen island, looked at the screen, and didn't recognize the local phone number. Nonetheless, I answered.

"This is Porter."

"Porter Reeves?"

"Yes," I responded. "This is Porter Reeves."

"Mister Reeves, my name is Martin Wicks," the man said. "I'm Abby Northrop's attorney."

It had been two days since Abby's death. We learned that her cancer returned, and she'd passed away from the bloodborne illness. While her parents were planning her funeral, I was struggling to survive without her. I couldn't fathom living a life without her in it.

"This is Porter," I said.

"Mister Reeves, I called to inform you that Abby has left a current will, and a letter, which is addressed to you. I'll need you to come by, post haste. It was her wish that you make it here before the funeral."

My hand went numb. "She…she knew…she knew she was dying?"

"On the contrary, Mister Reeves. She knew nothing of the sort. She was, however, a very thorough woman. She updated her files with the firm as life-changing events happened in her life. At any rate, there's a letter here for you, and I'd like to go over the will with you. When can I expect you?"

My heart raced at the thought of reading a letter that Abby had left me. Short of her YouTube videos, there were our text messages, some pictures on my phone, and a handful of surfing videos to remember her by.

"Where are you?"

"La Jolla. Right off Miramar Road. Wicks, Frankham, and Beane. I'll text you the address if you'd like."

"Sure."

"See you within the hour?" he asked.

"I'll be there in fifteen minutes."

It seemed strange to see Abby's handwriting on a sheet of paper that she'd written while in good health. Fearing that she'd addressed her death, I folded the sheet of yellow paper and looked at the attorney.

"Can I take this in the other room?"

"Second door on your right is the conference room. You'll be alone," he said. "Take your time."

I walked to the room, pulled the door closed behind me, and turned on the lights. After taking a seat at the end of the table, I unfolded the sheet of paper and took a deep breath.

Porter,

Just so you know, this is the third letter like this I've written to you. The first was the day after I met you. After the rattlesnake hunt. I knew on that day that you were special. I wrote the first letter just in case something happened to me. After battling cancer, I realized we simply never know where life is going to take us. We have much less control over our destiny that we'd like to admit.

The second was the day after we made love. Two days after the first time you kissed me.

As you know, I like to talk, and having the last word is a pretty big deal to me. So, I'm having the last word.

It seems creepy knowing that if you're reading this I'm no longer with you. In writing this, I can't imagine going a day without you. As you're reading this, I suspect you're having a hard time dealing with the fact that I'm gone. Well, I'm having an equally hard time writing this.

Believe me.

I'm truly sorry for whatever grief you're feeling right now, and I wish I could comfort you. Maybe you'll one day find comfort in the message this letter contains.

An advantage of this letter is that I get to say things without you rolling your eyes or getting mad. So, here we go.

I'm in heaven. That's right. Heaven. I'm far from perfect, but I've asked for forgiveness for my sins, and I imagine God's granted me that forgiveness.

I know you don't believe in God, and don't expect this letter will change much about your beliefs. But. I'm going to do my best. I have nothing to base this on but a hunch, and based on that hunch, I'll make a deal with you.

hand shake

You keep on believing what you believe. I love you as I'm writing this, and I'll love you from the heavens above. I can't tell you to never move on with your life, but I can tell you this. Well, I guess I'm asking you.

Ask God for forgiveness. It's simple. Just say, "God, this is Porter. Porter Reeves. Forgive me for my sins." That's it. That'll get you a pass to the pearly gates (maybe they're gold, so don't quote me) Then, when you get to heaven, I'll be waiting. I'll be easy to find. I'll be sitting right at the gate with my legs crossed, and a piece of pecan pie in my hand.

Here's where the hunch comes into play. You and I are connected by the love that we share. Just to prove to you that there is, in fact, a heaven, I'll predict this: one day you will experience something. You will not be able to explain it, but you will know it's from me. I don't know how it works, or any stuff like that, but keep your eyes open for any signs I may send you.

I don't know what we're able to do from up here, but I'll do my best to prove to you that God exists, and that I'm here waiting.

Until we meet again, believe.

I love you.

Abby.

The hair on my neck stood.

I read the letter again, twice.

I stumbled into the attorney's office with the letter clutched in my hand. "Did you read the letter?"

"I did."

"I don't want to talk about it," I said. "Do I have to?"

"You do not."

"Is there anything else?"

"The will. I'll need to go over that with you. She wanted you to have the home. She left some money in a trust for you as well. She left a considerable amount to charity, through various trusts. She also left specific instructions for her funeral. Her parents have a copy of them, and she's asked that you review them as well."

"What are they?"

"They're lengthy," he said. "I'll let you read them."

After reading her requests for the funeral, I laughed. For the first time since the night before she died, I actually laughed.

Out loud.

"Is this everything?" I asked.

He stood. "Yes, Sir."

Instructions in hand, I turned toward the door with a grin on my face.

GHOST

W ith a tear rolling down my cheek, I walked toward the grave site. Abby made me promise not to wipe it away, saying that for once, that she was going to embarrass me. She was sure that my five brothers would see me as a pussy if I cried.

I had news for her. The five of them were crying, too.

She'd left specific instructions for her burial, which included thirty minutes for us to celebrate her life without interruption of the others who she expected might be in attendance. Her casket was to arrive before the funeral procession, and the hearse was to come later, with the masses who were certain to attend the funeral.

She left further instructions for Baker and Andy. As I dragged my feet through the lush green grass, I grinned at what she'd said.

I want Baker and Andy to lead the way in Eleanor, with the empty hearse behind them. I want Andy driving. You can look at the car, and for a minute, as it approaches, squint and think it's me behind the wheel, and you in the passenger seat.

You never let me drive it, Porter.

She'd left further instructions regarding her burial service, stating she wanted it open to anyone who cared to attend. She left letters with her attorney for the news media, and for all the charities that she'd donated money to over the years, advising them of her wishes.

The local news was expecting nothing short of a zoo, but none of us knew what to expect, really. I did know that they had police on the edges of the highway exits when we arrived.

I stood at the gravesite, numb. Abby rested in the casket in front of me, dressed in her favorite dress, and her Converse, just as she'd asked.

I thought of the time we'd spent together. I suspected everyone else was praying. Despite Abby's prediction of sending me a sign, I had yet to see anything. Further proof, in my eyes, that the world took from all of us, and there was no God to protect us from it.

After our thirty minutes of silence passed, I heard Eleanor in the distance.

I glanced to my right.

As instructed, Eleanor led the way, with the empty hearse close behind. Andy did remind me of Abby, and that memory caused me to smile.

After the hearse cleared the hill, cars emerged. One after the other. Two CHP officers on motorcycles zoomed past. Then, two more. It continued until ten had passed. They directed traffic for hours.

In fact, when the graveside service started, there was a sea of people covering the hillside, and standing in the road, for as far as the eyes could see. There wasn't an inch of ground that wasn't occupied by a person, all coming to pay their respects to Uptown Abby.

For that moment, my sorrow turned to pride.

I lifted my chin as the pastor cleared his throat. He then glanced at each of us.

"Abby Northrop wishes to thank all of those in attendance." He peered at the bible he held, raised his head, and continued. "Abby was born on the tenth of November nineteen eighty-seven, in Bridgeport, Connecticut. She moved to San Diego at the age of eighteen to attend college, and soon fell in love with the magic the Pacific Ocean provided her."

"She also fell in love with the people she encountered."

"She lived her life a lover and loved with all her heart. People recognized her love, and they loved her in return."

He waved his hands toward the sea of people who had gathered. "These people stand as proof of that love."

He glanced at the bible, and then looked up. "God gave Abby a gift. She touched all of those she spoke to, and she spoke to many. She took a portion of what was provided to her, and gave the rest, never once allowing a moment to pass that she wasn't grateful for the gifts God bestowed upon her."

'She was a woman of faith. By and through that faith, she was further blessed with many friends, a blessed family, various acquaintances, and one true love, Porter Reeves."

"She did, however, love many."

"Her family asks that in lieu of flowers, donations be provided to cancer research."

"Let us take a moment to pray."

Everyone lowered their heads. After a moment, the pastor raised his head and cleared his throat. One corner of his mouth curled upward.

"She wants you all to realize something." He raised his right hand high in the air and flashed the peace sign. *"It's not that bad."*

Another tear rolled down my cheek, but I didn't dare wipe it.

I love you, Abby.

GHOST

I pulled up to the diner. The new sign stood out against the parapet that had housed the *Devil Dog Diner* sign for years. Now *Abby's Place*, it was only a matter of time before the establishment was going to be crawling with her loyal fans and followers.

Hashtag *it's not that bad* was trending on Twitter and Instagram for two weeks following her funeral. As soon as everyone found out this was her favorite diner, the place would be a mad house.

I parked my Harley at the curb, hoping to get a plate of pancakes before the day started. For the last two weeks, my nights had been spent on the deck, watching old YouTube videos. Despite my open mind and hopeful heart, I had yet to see any sign of Abby's existence beyond earth.

It was nice to think about, though.

An eternal life with her.

I grinned as I pushed the diner's door open.

Lawson waved over his shoulder. "Anywhere you like."

"George still on vacation?" I asked.

"He'll be back Monday," he said.

I took a seat in the booth marked, "If you're not Abby or Porter, please be kind enough to take another seat," and sat down.

As Lawson walked past, I gave a nod. "Short stack," I said.

"Bacon?" he asked.

I smiled. "Please."

I missed Abby dearly. At first, I wondered if I could continue to live, and feared I'd die of nothing short of a broken heart. Although it wasn't easy, and I knew it never would be, it was getting manageable.

I spent my days numb to the world, and to most of those in it. I wasn't bitter, because I knew being so wouldn't please Abby. And, above all things, I wanted to please Abby no differently than if she was still at my side.

After finishing my pancakes, I inched to the back of the booth and glanced around the restaurant. The typical Sunday breakfast crowd was in, which filled the place completely. I peered out the window, and into the street. A tattered Volkswagen Beetle pulled up to the curb and performed an expert parallel parking maneuver.

As I mentally applauded, a dark-haired girl got out of it. She wore a flowered dress. It was one of Abby's staples. Seeing it caused me to smile.

She flipped a backpack over her shoulder, walked to the door, and pushed it open. After scanning the diner, she let out a sigh.

Then, she began to walk in my direction.

I ducked under the partition, not wanting to be caught staring, and certainly not wanting to talk. She probably felt that my booth was empty, as I was slumped out of view.

If nothing else, she'd see the sign on the table when she walked past.

Sure enough, her shadow appeared at my side.

"Oh, shoot," she said. "I thought this was empty."

I shook my head without looking up. "Sorry."

"I'm guessing you're Porter," she said.

I rubbed the outline of the ring that was still occupying my left pocket and offered her a smile. "I am."

I almost choked when I saw what she was wearing on her feet.

Converse Chucks.

My face flashed hot. A lump rose into my throat. I swallowed heavily, but the lump remained. "You can uhhm." I wiped my brow with my forearm. "You can have a seat here."

She leaned forward and glanced at the sign that sat in the center of the table. "But, I'm not Abby."

With a shaking hand, I waved toward the open seat across from me. "Have a seat, she won't mind."

My heart was racing. It was more than likely a coincidence, but I liked thinking it wasn't. The thought of Abby managing to communicate with me excited me. As my skin began to tingle, the woman slid her backpack into the booth, took a seat, and let out a sigh.

"It was a long drive," she said.

"Where'd you come from?"

"Connecticut," she smiled. "It took me two weeks to get here. When I left, I had no idea where I was going. Isn't that crazy? I knew I needed to move, I just didn't know where I was going. I looked at each city I stopped in, and nothing felt like home. It's strange, but I feel like I belong here. It looks like I've found my new home."

My heart raced. "What uhhm. Where about in Connecticut?"

She smiled. "Bridgeport."

Abby was from Bridgeport. Another coincidence, I was sure. At least I was sure for a moment. Then, I began to wonder.

Abby, if this is you. I need to be sure. I want to believe it is, but...

I looked at the women and managed a slight smile. She glanced over each shoulder, and then met my gaze.

"So, Porter, what's this place's best breakfast meal?"

"Pancakes," I said, reaching for my wallet. "You've got to try the pancakes."

She brushed her hair over her ear, and then scratched the bottom of her nose with her finger. "Pancakes are the F-ing best."

Every hair on my body stood on end. My hands shook so violently I had to sit on them. While I stared back at her, in awe of what I'd seen, I recited what Abby had instructed me to.

God,

This is Porter.

I pressed my tongue against the roof of my dry mouth, swallowed heavily, and continued.

Porter Reeves.

Forgive me for my sins.

I stood, steadied my legs with my hands, and tossed a one-hundred-dollar bill on the table. I offered the woman a genuine smile. "Welcome to the SD. That's what we call it, SD." I nodded toward the table. "That'll take care of the meal. Enjoy your breakfast."

"You're not going to stick around?"

"I uhhm. I've got to go see someone."

She flashed me the peace sign. "Keep the shiny side up."

I hadn't even told her I was riding a motorcycle, but somehow, she knew. Claiming coincidence after coincidence was no longer possible.

I nodded. "I'll do my best."

She brushed her hair over her ear and did the nose scratching thing again. "Well, it was nice to meet you. I'm Ally."

I rubbed the hairs on the back of my neck and smiled. I couldn't help it. "Nice to meet you, Ally."

On my way to the door, I asked Lawson to allow Ally to finish her meal at Abby's table. Feeling an odd sense of humility, I walked to my motorcycle, paused, and lowered my head.

Thank you, Baby. I hope you were right about him forgiving me for my sins. I pushed my left hand into my pocked and squeezed the ring. *If he did, and I end up at your side one day, I've got a surprise for you.*

I love you, Baby.

I got on my motorcycle, started it, and strapped on my helmet. I glanced into the restaurant, took one last look at Ally, and then gazed up at the sky.

Thank you, Lord.

EPILOGUE

Kneeling before the gravestone, the man spoke to the deceased as if she could hear his every word. In the past two months he had garnered the faith that she could, in fact, do just that.

"I love you, Baby. It seems strange looking back on things and realizing I lived life without faith. Now, I talk to God every night as I watch the sunset. I'm convinced he hears me. I come here to talk to you, but I think this is where I need to be when we have our talk."

He stood and traced his finger over the words that were etched into the stone, taking time to feel the grain in the void of each letter.

He reached into the left pocket of his tattered jeans and cupped a velvet box in his hand. As his fingers traced the last letter, he stepped away from the headstone and smiled.

"Know that I love you, Baby." He leaned forward, kissed the top of the stone, and then stood. "Know that I'll always love you."

After turning away, he sauntered to his motorcycle, glancing over his shoulder twice before he reached the motorbike. After fastening the strap of his helmet, he straddled the seat.

The motorcycle pulled away from the gravesite. Filled with love, and with promise, the rider maneuvered through the winding roads with expertise. His destination, on that morning, was a pie shop located two hours north of the gravesite.

A reminiscence. One he believed would satisfy his soul.

His thoughts, at that moment, were not of earthly possessions or happenings. His focus was on the heavens above, and of his love, who had joined the departed mere months prior.

Three miles east, a man stumbled to his truck. Stained with the sour smell of the previous night's sins, he entered the vehicle, dropped his keys, and swore the Lord's name in vain when he couldn't find them. A moment later, his hand passed over the fob.

He grinned a drunken smile.

The motorcycle, traveling perpendicular to the truck, gained speed. At slightly under the speed limit, his destination was two hours ahead. Cherishing each passing mile, he subconsciously whistled a tune while he sang the words in his head, recalling the day he kissed the departed for the first time.

A smile formed on his face.

Fumbling for his cigarette lighter, the truck driver moved his eyes away from the road, but only for an instant. In that instant, he traveled through an intersection clearly marked with a red traffic light.

The truck entered the intersection at a blinding rate of speed. Despite the experience of the rider, nothing could be done to avert the collision. The front tire of the motorcycle hit the left front fender of the truck.

The rider was cast from the motorbike, over the hood of the truck, and into the path of a speeding car.

The truck came crashing to a stop against an adjacent light pole. The driver was ejected through the windshield, and onto the truck's hood.

Passersby stopped and rendered aid. The driver of the truck was deceased the moment his vehicle came to an abrupt stop. The rider of the motorcycle lay in the street, hanging onto a sliver of life and a ray of hope.

In moments, the siren of a distant ambulance could be heard.

Generous mortals who assisted the rider peered in the distance and gave their assurances.

"Help," they said. "Is on the way. Hold on."

The attendants cut off the rider's clothes, braced his neck, and placed him on a flat polypropylene board. One searched his clothes for identification. In the left pocket of the blood-stained jeans, the attendant found a velvet box. In it, an engagement ring.

The rider, clinging to life by a thread, lifted his bloody hand. "The ring," he muttered through dry lips. "I need the ring."

Knowing not what to do, the attendant placed the ring in the rider's hand, hoping it could provide the strength he needed to survive. At that instant, he made note of the inscription of the rider's brass bracelet.

"You can make it," the attendant said to himself. "All you must do is *believe*."

He then slid the rider into the ambulance and closed the door.

As the paramedics worked frantically to save the rider's life, the ambulance sped toward the hospital. Moments later, the ambulance came to a stop at the emergency room entrance. The attendant opened the ambulance's rear door. The two paramedics met the attendant's gaze and shook their heads in unison.

"We lost him," one said. "It seemed he just let go."

The attendant opened the rider's clenched hand. Much to his surprise, the ring was gone.

"Where's the ring?" he asked.

The paramedic shrugged. "What ring?"

The attendant looked at the rider's right wrist, only to find it bare. "The bracelet?" he asked.

The paramedic seemed puzzled. "It was there a moment ago, I swear."

The body of the rider was taken away. The ambulance was searched. Neither the bracelet, nor the ring were ever found.

It is believed by many that upon their passing, the departed are delivered to their destination. At the rate of three hundred per hour, souls exit their earthly bodies. Some move on to the heavens above, while others meet an entirely different fate.

On that day, at 9:17, an angel was delivered to the heaven's above. On his right wrist he wore a brass bracelet. Cupped in his right hand, a velvet box bore a symbol of his love.

Waiting cross-legged at the golden gates, holding a piece of pecan pie, was the woman he so dearly loved.

Beyond the gates, beautiful trees lined the horizon. On them, low-hanging fruit clung to the branches, an offering from the heavens. Each piece of fruit gave assurance of one more tomorrow.

And the trees went on forever.

6062

98606576R00154

Made in the USA
Middletown, DE
09 November 2018